LET ME IN
BOOK 1

Heartbreak WARFARE

JESSICA MARIN

Starr,
thank you for
your support!
XOXO,

HEARTBREAK WARFARE

(LET ME IN, BOOK 1)

JESSICA MARIN

Edited by

CISSIE PATTERSON

Cover Design by

NAJLA QAMBER DESIGNS

This book is dedicated to my Grandma Shirley, who introduced me to the world of books. I know she is sitting in heaven, tickled pink by this novel.

And to all the ladies out there....the single working ladies, the full time working mothers, the stay at home mothers and the stay at home wives...
whatever your current life situation is, YOU ARE WORTHY!
You are worthy of all of your dreams, happiness, love and success.
Always make yourself a priority and NEVER STOP DREAMING.

CONTENTS

PROLOGUE

Everyone has days in their lives that will never leave them. Days of happiness, days of experiences, days of sorrows. Today is one of those days for me. A day I thought would never happen to me. When you're writing the story of your life, this day is not in your happily ever after.

Today is the day my marriage officially ended.

Today is the day my husband told me he no longer loves me. Correction – no longer is IN love with me. He says he'll always love me, but that I deserve to be with someone who is IN love with me. He promises there's no one else but after eight months of therapy, he doesn't see his feelings changing and it's unfair to me for him to stay in something that's dead.

I pretend not to hear him as I continue typing on my keyboard, but of course I heard him. I can't look at him. My breath is caught in my throat – words cannot get past the giant lump that has now formed. He knows I heard him – he sees the tears streaming down my cheeks. His words will resonate with me forever. Gone are the happy memories we once ever had. Now when I think of him, this will be that moment.

FUCK YOU my head is screaming as I hear him walking

towards the door. I wish I could say those two words and their significance of how I feel. But the moment is gone. A silence that is filled with anger, defeat, and pain. I will not chase him. I will not beg for him to reconsider. I am done being the only one fighting to save us. If he isn't in love with me anymore, then I shouldn't want him to stay. What I don't understand is where and when did he fall out of love with me?

We just had what seems like our millionth fight. Of course, it was over something stupid – aren't most fights over something stupid? Simple things that could have simple resolutions. Our war with each other has become me wanting his time and him not willing to give it to me anymore. I used to be his number one priority. Now I am more like his mistress and work is his wife. Once upon a time, I WAS his life.

We met while working for the same sports agency firm. I was Assistant Director of Corporate Events and he was the Vice President of Corporate Sponsorship. He was charming, smart, funny, and good-looking. He knew how to use his looks and charm to land sales, especially if he was pitching to the female clientele. Each time he got our company a new corporate sponsor; I threw a lavish event in their honor. We had to work closely together, so we became fast friends. It was hard not to have a little crush on him, but I was professional and enjoyed his friendship, so I assumed that is what we were only ever going to be. I didn't think I was his type in the looks department either. He seemed to always gravitate towards blonde, blue-eyed women. Women who looked exactly like him, the complete opposite of me. Imagine my surprise one night when we were working late and he kissed me. We spent the next three hours kissing instead of working. I was head over heels in love with him. He made me feel like the most beautiful woman on this planet and he always made me feel loved – by the words he would say to me and the looks he bestowed upon me.

We were married two years later and I was in complete bliss, both personally and professionally. After our one-year anniversary, we talked about having a baby. But another year passed, and we still had not conceived. My doctors did more testing and we found out that I had an abnormal uterus. The doctor said it would be "tough" getting pregnant.

I was devastated.

I felt like a complete failure as a woman and as a wife. I started questioning why my husband would want to stay married to me if I couldn't give him a family. He thought I was being ridiculous, and told me it didn't matter to him if we didn't have a baby. That all he needed was me. My intuition didn't believe him, and a woman's intuition is usually right. As the months moved on, I would catch him looking at other people's children with longing in his eyes. I knew my depression was affecting us, and I vowed to try to go back to being that bubbly, positive girl that he married. When I suggested we try using a surrogate, the light immediately came back in his eyes and we started making plans. He was about to accept a new position as Director of Corporate Sales for a Fortune 500 company, so with the extra income coming in, we should be able to afford a surrogate by the following year.

The love for my job was lost once he left the agency for his new position. I had not realized how much I relied on him professionally, as well as personally. I started feeling like maybe I had lost my identity. Sure, I was someone's wife, but I was still ME and needed to do things that made ME happy. With his blessing, I quit my job and started my own event planning business, with a specialty in children's parties. This required me to learn more about social media, including starting my own blog. I loved absorbing all this new information and I was back feeling like I could conquer the world with the best husband by my side supporting me. But as I engrossed myself more into my new business, I failed to notice the newfound changes in my husband.

His new job required that he traveled more, which at first I had no issues with since it gave me the time to devote to growing my business. His travels went from once a month to every week. He was traveling to land the big accounts, and with those big accounts, came big commission checks. Money was always important, but it now was an obsession to him. It became a game – how much money can he make in a short amount of time. All he wanted to do was make more and more. Even when he was home, he was still always on his computer or taking phone calls late at night. His tastes started to become expensive. Our cozy apartment turned into a cold, modern day looking museum from all the remodeling he ordered to be done. He had always been generous with buying me little gifts here and there. Before it would be a new book that I wanted or a gift card to my favorite coffee shop. Now my gifts were lingerie from La Perla and jewelry from Ippolita. The gifts just felt like he was buying my forgiveness for his lack of attention. Maybe some women are fine with that. For me, it was unacceptable, so I demanded we seek couples therapy. At first, he was reluctant to go. He didn't believe that outsiders should know the business of our marriage. But when the fights continued, he finally agreed.

Therapy bored him. He was physically present, but mentally unavailable. Even the easy suggestions of weekly dates seemed difficult for him. I was ecstatic when he suggested we go on a vacation. But in those weeks leading up to our vacation, he was busier than ever and hardly around. Once our vacation arrived, we were walking on eggshells around each other. He felt like a complete stranger to me. Even the sex felt cold and distant. I still never gave up hope though. I knew in my heart that the man I married was still in there, and he wasn't going to give up on me either. I am the same girl he married. Physically, I had not changed much, give or take five pounds or so. I was always his biggest cheerleader. I always put his needs before mine. We were constantly having sex up until he preferred work over me. But he did give up. He gave up on me. He gave up on us.

Why did he give up on ME?

I am trying to concentrate on my daily blog post, but I can barely see through the tears. The keyboard becomes saturated with their wetness, my fingers slipping as I try to type. The post has become more of a journal of my emotions in this moment than an article on a Valentine's Day party. Memories are flooding though my brain like waves during high tide. It's as if my brain wants to wash them right out in order to stop the pain that is throbbing through my heart. The music selection on Pandora Radio is only making things worse, playing every single sad song known to man. It's like she knows what's going on and wants to break me even more.

Pandora, you're a bitch!

I can't take it. Between the music, the memories, and the realization of what's actually happening, I need to find refuge. I run to my room and throw myself on what used to be our bed and cry.

I cry for the girl who thought she got her happily ever after.

I cry for the lost man that use to be my husband.

I cry for the children we will never have.

I cry for the realization that I am now alone.

In my misery of the demise of my marriage, I conveniently don't recall that I just hit publish on a blog post that talks more about my marriage ending than of a child's theme party. I unconsciously just committed career suicide.

Or so I thought.

1

One Year Later

"Oh my, I think I just wet my panties!"

I roll my eyes at my assistant's favorite saying when he sees something he likes, which can range from articles of clothing to a human being. We are sitting in JFK International Airport, waiting for our respective flights. He is people watching while I am trying to write some thank you emails. We just came from speaking at a three-day bloggers workshop, and I am on my way to Las Vegas for another speaking engagement at a women's entrepreneur convention while Robert, my fabulous, fun loving, always cursing, gay assistant and friend, goes back home to Chicago to man the office.

When I accidentally published my emotional blog post over a year ago, never in a million years did I think thousands upon thousands of women would share it with their friends and it would skyrocket me to success. The advice, sympathy, and support I received from strangers was indescribable. It took Robert and I two days to go through all the emails and comments that were left for me. I tried to write everyone back, but ended up just writing a long thank you post. Never underestimate the power of women who band together to support each other when you are down or up.

"Jenna, you need to stop what you are doing and look at this fine specimen of a man!" insists Robert.

"Robert, can you stop talking about wetting your panties so loudly in public?" I chide while continuing to type on my laptop. "Anyone listening can be current or future clients and might not like how you, um, word things." I try to get my point across delicately as I don't want to hurt his feelings, nor do I want him to feel he can't be himself around me.

"If people don't like me for me, then we don't want them for clients anyway."

"Robert..."

"Fine, next time I will whisper it in your ear. Now will you please check this guy out!"

Sighing, I look up to appease him. The object of his lustfulness is talking to the lady at the ticket counter. With his back to me, I notice that he is very tall with curly brown hair peeking out from underneath his baseball cap, and has a very nice butt.

"Tall and a fine backside...right up your alley, Robert!" I go back to typing out my emails, not wanting to waste any more time staring at the stranger.

"That isn't just a butt, Jenna, that is a USDA Grade A Ass!" he laughs at his own joke.

"You are seriously worse than a straight guy checking out women at Hooters," I say, even though the comment was funny.

"Oh lighten up, Jenna. Did you sign away your sense of humor in those divorce papers as well?"

I immediately stiffen at his poor choice of sarcasm, the ink on the papers still a fresh new wound on my heart. Robert knows how devastating my divorce was and still is to me. His first day on the job was the day after that blog post - he was sharply dressed and ready to impress. He didn't anticipate having his boss answering the door in hysterics and looking like a zombie. At that time, I didn't realize I had thousands of emails waiting for me in my inbox, and I dumped it all on him that first day. I had no idea how to deal with it all, ashamed that I'd made my personal life so public. I was an emotional wreck that day; a horrible example of the kind of boss you want to be working for. He left me alone the remainder of that day, but decided I was worth sticking around for. Even today, I can't believe he hasn't quit to look for something, or someone, more stable.

I can tell Robert realizes he has gone too far. His constant chatter has stopped and he is fidgeting in his seat. I ignore him while I finish my emails. He clears his throat, expecting me to look at him or ask if he is okay, but I refuse to acknowledge him.

"Um, Jenna, I am really sorry. That was uncalled for. Please accept my apology?"

I give him a tight smile and nod my head. It is hard for me to stay mad at him because he is right. I have changed since my divorce. When I hired Robert, I was this wide-eyed, excited, energetic new business owner who thought she was the luckiest girl in the world to be her own boss. I was aware of my marriage problems, but to me, life was still good. I still loved my husband and thought we could get through our problems, no matter how bad they got. But that girl left with her ex-husband. That girl has been replaced with an insecure, wounded shell of her former self, who struggles to get out of bed every day, and not be depressed when I realize that I am alone. My heart has a wall of ice around it with cautionary tape. Work is the only thing that keeps me going. I am the only one who pays the bills now and I have people who rely on me in order for them to pay their own bills. I've got to succeed, so I have thrown myself into work. I work twelve-hour days on new party concepts, updating all of our social media outlets with the latest trends in parties, and inspiring other women to keep going, to better themselves and that we ARE worth it. I travel more now that I am in demand to do public speaking engagements. I couldn't have done any of it without Robert and my best friend, Layla. They helped nurse me back to reality and put me in my place when I start getting depressed.

"I am working on trying to lighten up more and have fun. I thought I did a good job while we have been here in NYC."

"Oh yes, I was very proud that you stayed up past midnight," he says with a wink.

After our last seminar, everyone that we were networking with wanted to go out. Not wanting to lose the chance at making new relationships, we went bar hopping and ended up at one of the gay bars, dancing until 4 am. I had so much fun and for a split second, I did feel like my old self. But that vanished as soon as I got back into my hotel room and reality came crashing in. I was about to tell Robert that I will continue to work more on bettering myself when he starts pawing at my arm.

"Jenna, look, he turned around…quick, before he walks away from us," he says with excitement.

The only thing I can see is a strong, chiseled jaw and a very broad chest. His hat is pulled down low over his face. He is wearing a brown leather jacket that is open to reveal a gray t-shirt that clings to his muscled chest, jeans that hug his hips very nicely and sneakers. He seems to be concentrating on whatever his ticket says, and then he turns to make a beeline for the chairs near the entrance of the gate.

"Holy balls, do you KNOW who that is? That is Cal Harrington!" Robert says with glee.

I must have a blank stare on my face, because his expression turns to shock.

"You don't know who Cal Harrington is? The guy who plays Erik in the TV series 'Wrath of The Vikings'?"

"Nope, can't say I know who he is since I don't watch television and when I do, it is all of the Real Housewives series because you live and breathe BravoTV."

"Girl, Cal Harrington is this hot up-and-coming actor who is currently on one of the highest rated TV shows. His character is so hot on that show. You might not recognize him because he wears a long blond wig. He has gorgeous blue eyes and he is mostly bare chested in every episode. And the sex scenes," he sighs. "Let's just say I masturbate to them all the time."

I hear someone laugh and look over my shoulder at a young lady who is listening to our conversation. She quickly looks away and I turn my attention back to Robert.

"Robert, PLEASE lower your voice!" I whisper but he has peaked my curiosity. "So, the sex scenes are man on man?"

"Oh honey, do I wish, but alas, he is banging hot Viking chicks. I just take them out of the equation and insert myself." We continue to watch Cal Harrington as he proceeds to disappear in the crowd.

"OH MY GOODNESS, what if he is on your flight to Las Vegas? I bet you he is. You lucky bitch! If you are sitting next to him, you better kiss him full on the lips, with tongue, and get his autograph for me."

"Highly unlikely since a) I would probably get arrested for kissing him when he shouts that a stranger sexually assaulted him and b) he is probably in first class and I am in coach."

"Jenna, did you not look at your ticket? You ARE in first class." He rolls his eyes at me for not paying attention to where I will be seated on the plane.

I look at my ticket and sure enough, I am in seat 3B, which is first class. I have never sat in first class.

"Robert, you know I can't afford first class! Why would you do this?" I ask, getting angry just thinking about how much a first class ticket from NYC to Las Vegas is going to cost me.

"Have a little faith in me, Jenna. You have a gazillion frequent flyer miles, so I used some of your points to upgrade you. I knew it was going to be a long flight and figured maybe you would use your time on the flight to rest, even though I know you will work the whole time."

Now I am speechless. That is one of the nicest things anyone has done for me. With no rebuttal, I just give him a hug and whisper thank you in his ear for always taking care of me.

"You're welcome. I better get going. My flight back home is going to board soon." He grabs his laptop bag and I stand up to give him a hug.

"Call me when you land," he says, and starts walking away.

"I will – have a safe flight back to Chicago!" I yell after him.

I finish a couple of more emails and put my laptop away. One of my favorite pastimes at an airport is to people watch, so I sit back and entertain myself with the viewings. A few minutes later, the announcement is made that my flight will be boarding, starting with first class. I make my way to the entrance of the gate. I hand the lady at the counter my ticket to scan, trying to act calm, cool and collected, when inside, I am giddy as a kid in a candy shop to be in first class. I get inside the plane and notice there are four rows of first class, with two seats on each side. Someone has boarded the plane ahead of us and I recognize the baseball hat immediately.

It is Cal Harrington...and he is sitting in the seat right next to mine.

2

If Robert only knew I was going to sit next to the object of his lustfulness for a five-hour flight, he really would wet his panties. I am not one of those people that freaks out when in the presence of a celebrity, and since I have never seen any of Cal Harrington's work, I have no emotional feelings sitting next to him. I place my jacket in the overhead bin and sit. I look at him under my lashes while he plays on his phone. I still can't get a good look at his face or see his eyes because of how low his baseball hat is sitting on his head. He is a big man. Even in first class with the bigger seats, he takes up the majority of his seat. I start into my pre-flight ritual of taking all the things I want to use during the flight out of my ridiculously oversized purse, and place everything in the seat pocket in front of me. This includes my laptop, a book, and some magazines. As I struggle to get everything into the now overflowing seat pocket, my purse slips off my lap and spills all of its contents right onto his feet. I gasp and start apologizing profusely for my clumsiness while trying to get everything off of his feet and the floor. He leans down next to me and graciously starts to help. I am suddenly overwhelmed by the most enticing, delicious smell my nose has ever had the pleasure of inhaling. I close my eyes, take another deep breath and smile. The mix of his natural scent with his cologne can make any woman orgasm without even a physical touch. I am basking in his manly aroma when I open up my eyes to see the most incredible blue eyes staring back at me. I immediately turn beat red, realizing that I was just caught inhaling him. I sit back up and wait for him to finish handing back my stuff. As he finally sits upright, I am about to issue another apology when the words are caught in my throat.

He is holding one of my tampons with a charming smile on his face.

Not only am I speechless because he is holding my tampon, but I also finally have a view of his face.

He is one of the most magnificent looking men I have ever seen.

He has chiseled high cheek bones with a straight, strong nose. Full kissable lips cover sparkling white teeth. But it is his eyes that have me mesmerized. They are the color of aquamarine and seem to bear into my soul. His gaze is making me feel raw...almost naked, and I struggle not to squirm in my seat.

"You know, you can do some really evil things with these," he says about my tampon.

He is waving it around in the air as a wand, like he is Harry Potter about to cast a spell. Again, something that should be embarrassing is not holding my attention, because not only am I hypnotized by his eyes, but now his voice. It is strong, masculine and British.

"Hey, are you okay?" he kindly asks.

"Excuse me, but what did you just say?" I ask, snapping out of my trance.

"I asked if you are okay?"

"Oh yes, thank you, but before then?" I ask while trying to get the tampon out of his hand, which is conveniently out of my reach.

"I said you can do evil things with these. I used to pull pranks on my sisters all the time with their tampons." He flashes a smile that I can tell has him fondly recalling those memories.

"That is quite evil of you, and I hope they got you back with something equally humiliating," I say, finally being able to snatch the tampon out of his hand.

He laughs - rich, deep, musical laughter that I immediately want to hear again. I really don't know what to say to him. I mean, what do you say to some hot man who was holding your tampon?

"Right, so, um, thank you for your help." I can't even look at him, so embarrassed that I really want to put this incident behind me.

"You're welcome, and it is Acqua di Gio," he says.

"Excuse me?" I ask, startled that he just said something more to me.

"My cologne – it is called Acqua di Gio by Giorgio Armani. I also noticed that you enjoyed the scent. Just thought you might want to know so you can buy it for your significant other," he responds with grin and a wink.

Oh god, can I be even more embarrassed?

"Yes, well, thank you for that information," I stammer, turning very red again.

He throws his head back and laughs. I stare at him, completely transfixed by his laughter. Why is he laughing at me? How can I get him to laugh again?

Beautiful eyes, handsome face, tall, muscular body, and a scent that makes me want to lick every inch of him. Yup, I am totally not talking to him the rest of this flight.

What the hell is wrong with me? *Get a grip, Jenna!* He is probably used to this adolescent behavior from psychotic fans. I am a grown, professional woman, and can handle sitting next to a gorgeous man.

"My name is Cal, by the way." He holds out his hand for me to shake.

"Jenna, and thanks again for the help." I reluctantly shake his hand back. I knew there is a reason why I didn't want to shake it. His hands are firm, warm and they send sparks tingling over my body. This is absolutely absurd that some hot stranger's touch is making me feel this way. Robert is right – I need to get rid of this pent up sexual tension I have caused myself. I might have to go shopping for the perfect battery-operated boyfriend while in Las Vegas.

"No worries. Are you going to Las Vegas for business or pleasure?"

"Business, although, I do have a couple of days off for some down time. You?"

"Same for me. Relaxation before business begins."

I was just about to ask if he frequents Las Vegas often when the most obnoxious, high-pitched voice rudely interrupts me.

"It is YOU! OHMYGOD, OHMYGOD, OHMYGOD!"

Cal and I look up to see a platinum blond, middle-aged woman with bright pink lipstick, and hair as big as the state of Texas hovering over our seat. Her heavily made up green eyes are bright with excitement at discovering him on the same plane.

"Oh, I just love you! You sure are a good actor - you turn this old woman on every week!" she laughs. "Oh, but I am sorry, I don't mean to say anything disrespectful in front of your girlfriend."

She looks at me when she mentions the word "girlfriend" and I am actually flattered that she thinks I would be. I smile at her, despite feeling mortified for him that she just revealed that he gets her all hot and bothered.

"Thanks, but I am not his girlfriend," I tell her.

"I didn't think so because I just read in a magazine that said he was single, but I didn't want to be rude."

Before I could ask if she believes everything she reads about him, she leans down to my ear and whispers, "if I give you one hundred dollars, would you trade seats with me? I know my seat isn't as fancy as yours since it isn't first class, but please, he is my favorite actor!"

I quickly glance at him to see his reaction, but he looks as if he didn't hear her request, and continues to smile at her. I, on the other hand, cannot believe that this lady has the balls to ask me to trade my beloved first-class seat for her economy seat, and that one hundred dollars would lure me to do so.

"I am sorry, ma'am, but I work hard at my job to be able to afford a first-class seat, so the answer is no, I will not be giving up my seat." She doesn't need to know that I used points to upgrade to first class.

"Well, there is no reason to be rude about it," she huffs.

"I am sorry, but I don't feel that I was being rude about it," I counter back, annoyed that she called me rude.

"You're holding up the line, lady!" an agitated passenger shouts behind her.

"Good gracious, I have never been so insulted! Enjoy your flight, Cal, and I am sorry you are sitting next to such a bitch!" she declares, and stomps off towards her seat.

My mouth falls open in shock. Big head just called me a bitch? I turn to look at Cal, who is biting his sexy lip to keep from laughing. "Oh my god, are all of your fans like that? She calls me a bitch for not giving up my seat for one hundred dollars? That is CRAZY!"

Not being able to contain it any longer, he lets out a deep bellow of laughter. "The expression on your face when she called you a bitch was brilliant," he says, laughing."And no, not all of my fans are as, hmm, how should we describe her...protective of me as she is. I am sorry she called you a bitch."

"No need to apologize for her. I am sorry if I came across that way. I wouldn't want you to lose fans because of how I reacted."

"I don't think I need to worry about losing her as a fan," he laughs. "I am very appreciative of fans like her, even if they can sometimes become overzealous. It is the ones who try to get into your personal business, or talk to you like you are your character in real life that scare me." He looks at me with a devilish grin and says, "let's be honest, for all I know, you could be one of my stalkers."

"Funny, but if I was, I would be the best stalker in the history of stalkers," I say with a laugh. "In all seriousness, I must confess that I have not seen any of your work. I am sorry, I just don't watch TV or get to go to the movies very often."

He stares at me, showing no emotion. I hope I didn't just offend him, but then that would be very egotistical if he did feel that way. *Maybe he doesn't believe me?* I am sure there have been female fans who have said that just to play it cool. How do I convince him that I am telling the truth? *Why do you even care if he believes you or not?*

"I think that is very refreshing to hear," he says, staring straight into my eyes. Blushing, I look down, not being able to hold his gaze any longer. I don't like this feeling of butterflies in my stomach that his gaze is giving me.

The captain of the airplane uses that time to conveniently announce that we will be taking off momentarily, and to expect turbulence for most of our ascent to 35,000 feet. Once we reach 35,000 feet, the air will be calm and the flight attendants will start inflight drink service. I dread this news as I am not the best flyer. I am very uneasy with take-off, but add turbulence to the mix and I am going to be a hot mess.

Wait, why would we have turbulence during take-off? It was beautiful clear blue skies when I arrived at the airport. I look out past him at the window and sure enough, ugly, mean looking gray clouds surround the airport. I must have moaned while grabbing my noise cancellation head phones, because Cal asked if I was okay. "Yeah, I just hate hearing about turbulence. I am not the best flyer, but I shouldn't do anything embarrassing that would make you regret sitting next to me. I keep my turmoil on the inside." *Oh my god, stop rambling, Jenna!*

"I understand about not liking to fly. I find distracting yourself to be the best way to handle it. I can tell you some naughty stories to keep your mind off of the bumpy ride," he says with a wicked smile.

His looks are already causing turbulence inside my body. "Maybe you can tell me the stories for the rest of the flight. For take-off, I just like to put my head phones on, close my eyes and hug myself," I reveal, laughing at how pathetic that sounds.

"That actually sounds really sad. But okay, if you change your mind, you know where I sit," he jokes.

I say thank you and settle into my seat. The plane is just waiting for the control tower to give us the okay for take-off. The cabin is silent, almost like the calm before the storm. We must have received the go ahead, because the jet engines start to roar and we start to move, accelerating faster toward taking off. I start my ritual take-off prayer/chant in my head as I feel the plane lifting off the ground.

Please God Safe Flight.

Please God Safe Flight.

I am not a religious person, but for some reason, saying this over and over inside my head makes me feel better. Soon I start emphasizing the *please* and the *God,* with every bump, shake, and tilt of the plane as it gets worse. Even though I am wearing noise cancellation headphones, I can hear the engines working at top speed, the gasps of the other passengers as the plane turns at an uneven angle. My arms are crossed over my stomach, my hands gripping the arm rails, holding myself down into my seat. My head is permanently settled back into the head rest. My eyes are squeezed shut, and I am pushing my feet as hard as I can into the floor to prevent my body from matching the jerking movements of the plane. I barely hear the first ding signifying we have reached 10,000 feet. Not that it matters, because with the way the plane is jerking all over the place, the flight attendants can't get out of their seats to announce the use of portable electronic devices. You can feel the plane flying with ferocious velocity, the captain trying to get out of this horrible weather to the promise land of clear skies above the dark clouds and swirling air. Suddenly, the plane drops and our bodies are momentarily suspended in the air, our seat belts preventing us from hitting the roof of the plane. We come crashing back into our seats as the plane continues its journey up. My headphones can't cancel out the crying and screaming of other passengers. I feel something rubbing my hand and I quickly open my eyes, look down, and see Cal's hand over mine. I look up at his face to see his jaw muscles clenched, his head motioning down to his open hand for me to take. With that encouragement, I raise up the arm rest, grab his right hand with mine and launch myself onto him. My hand grips his right arm and smothers it into my chest, while I bury my head into his armpit. It doesn't matter that I just threw myself onto a complete stranger. It doesn't seem like I can grip him hard enough to prevent the feeling of falling. His left arm comes around to bring me closer to him, trying to shield me from this nightmare. This would be the perfect time to appreciate feeling his hard body, but the plane takes another dip and I am lost again in my prayer.

Please God safe flight.

Please God stop this turbulence.

Please God I am not ready to die.

Please God, please God...please listen.

I hear him then. Not God, but Cal, softly repeating to me "it's going to be okay." And I start to believe him. I secure my grip on him and focus on his voice, his words. More time passes and I feel the plane evening out, the bumps getting fewer and far between. I stop praying and try to enjoy the feeling of his arms, his chest, and how good it feels to be held by someone. It has been so long since I have been held by a man that I have not realized how much I miss it. I am reflecting on my loneliness when the captain comes on the intercom.

"Folks, I apologize for the scariness of the last five minutes. If anyone has been injured, please press the help button to notify the flight attendants. Flight attendants, please do not leave your seats yet. If there are any injuries, we will be landing at the closest airport away from the storm. I am happy to report that we are out of the storm, but please keep your seat belts fasten for the next five minutes to make sure we don't experience any unexpected rough air."

I keep my eyes closed, waiting to feel another dip in the plane. I am also listening for any call buttons being pushed, signifying the need for help. Five minutes comes and goes and I hear nothing.

"Flight attendants, it is safe to move about the cabin," the captain says, and the whole plane erupts in applause. I open my eyes and feel Cal's left arm still wrapped around me. I am enjoying being held in his arms when I look down to our adjoining hands and suck in my breath. Our hands are conveniently located in my lap, only a few inches from my crotch, and I have completely nestled his arm in between my breasts. I quickly pull out of his arms only to bang my head on his chin. We both say "ouch" at the same time and look at each other - him rubbing his chin, while I rub my head. We can't contain the burst of laughter that bubbles out of both of us.

"Holy fucking shit, that was scary!"

"Oh my god, I thought we were going to die!"

We continue laughing, letting the therapy of laughter ease the tension out of our bodies.

3

I am not one to indulge on flights for work, but a cocktail is definitely in order after what seemed like a near death experience. The flight attendants start their inflight beverage services, and we are more than happy to receive the free champagne. Personally, I feel that the whole flight deserves some champagne and not just first class. The attendant brings us our drinks and without realizing what I am doing, I gulp my drink down.

"Well, I was going to toast to us being alive, but now I see you have started the fun without me," Cal jokes as he notices my empty glass.

"Sorry," I say, as I grimace from the taste of the not so great quality champagne. "I just needed something quick to calm my nerves and let's not jinx ourselves, the flight isn't over yet."

"This is true. Let's get you another drink." He attempts to get the flight attendant's attention, but I stop him before he can hit the help button.

"No, that is all right. I usually don't drink on flights, and I have a bottle of water in my bag that will be just fine." I grab the water from my bag underneath the seat in front of me. He holds out his drink to me and toasts "to a quiet, calm, and easy remaining flight." We clink our drinks together - his champagne to my water bottle - and drink, our eyes locked together as we enjoy the cool liquid going down our dry throats. His eyes move to my lips as a drop of water escapes from the tip of the water bottle and runs down my chin. Blushing, I wipe the back of my hand against my mouth and chin, breaking the intense gaze he has captured over me. Drinking water just turned VERY sensual as thoughts of him licking the water off me enter my mind. I need to start doing some work to get my mind off of what this man would be like in bed. I reach down to retrieve my laptop to start working on some more theme party ideas for my blog.

"Please don't tell me you are going to ignore me for the rest of the flight after our groping session," he teases while nodding toward my laptop. Of course, I don't want to work, but I am afraid that I will make a fool out of myself if I keep talking to him.

"I wasn't necessarily going to ignore you, I was just going to try to do some work in between our conversations," I respond back with a grin.

"Good answer, but what exactly do you do for a living that makes working right now so important?"

"I own an event planning business, my specialty being children's theme parties. I create the parties, and then showcase them on my blog. We also sell the products that we use on our website." I pull up a design board of saved pictures from our recent photo shoot of a country fair birthday party to show him. "My assistant and I will create a party, design it with products from the vendors we use, then set it up for a photo shoot. We will then upload the photos and create a blog post on that party. Sometimes clients want the type of parties we already feature on the blog or we have a meeting with them, and custom design a party to match their children's interests or hobbies."

"I had no idea that children's parties can get so detailed. Very impressive. This makes you enough money for it to be your full-time job?" he pins me with a skeptical look, one eyebrow arched higher than the other.

"Yes, Dad, I make enough money to support myself and pay an assistant," I joke, noting that he sounds just like my father did when I first told him my business idea. "People who have lots of money want to have fabulous and unique parties. We understand that the average person is on a budget and might not be able to afford to hire an event planner, so we also give advice on our blog on how you can do the party yourself on a budget."

"What made you get into this kind of business? Do you have children of your own?"

"No, no kids and I just fell out of love doing only corporate business meetings and parties. I will still do those parties when hired, but to me, there is nothing better than seeing the pure joy on a child's face when they see their birthday party for the very first time. I like to create that imaginary world for them." There is no need to tell him that creating these parties for other people's children fills the void and ache that I feel for not having my own. He is probably so far removed from having kids, let alone a serious relationship.

"No kids and I don't see a ring on your finger?" It isn't a statement, but more of a question. It is a simple answer really, but one that stills makes me swallow down the lump in my throat.

"I am divorced," I say quietly, not giving any more detail.

"Divorce is painful and I am sorry you went through that, but I must admit I am a bit relieved to know that I don't have to feel guilty flirting with you."

"Yes, but do I need to feel guilty flirting with YOU?" I smile with a questioning look.

"If what you have been doing is flirting, then you need a better teacher," he responds back with a devilish smirk.

Shocked, I just stare at him with an incredulous look on my face, not believing that he actually insulted me. But now that I think of it, he is probably right. I have become cold, and probably so dull and boring compared to other women who sit next to him. Am I trying too hard to be calm, and play it cool around him while he is making my insides turn into jelly? He makes me want to behave like a high school girl, twirling their hair while talking to their crush. If high school girls even do that anymore. I am just an uncool, divorced, fuddy-duddy who has cobwebs on her vagina from the lack of sex.

He throws back his head and laughs. "You are so brilliantly fun to mess with!" He rubs his hands together as if he has more insults up his sleeve. I relax since he is joking with me, and I start to laugh with him.

And that is how the rest of the flight goes - filled with questions about each other, laughing and flirting. I feel like I am on a first date, the giddiness of getting to know someone new for the very first time should feel foreign, but comes easily with him. I learn that besides being single, he has two sisters, is from Broadstairs, England and lives in London when he is not shooting his TV series or a film. He got into acting because a scouting agent approached him while he was on break from school, and asked if he was interested in becoming an actor.

"I truly believe that fate played a role that day because the agent not only chose me, but also my two best mates, and we were the only ones out of our group of school friends who were on break together hired to be in a commercial. All these years later and all three of us are still acting. It just feels like it was meant to be."

"That is pretty amazing that all three of you got chosen and are still acting," I agree, wondering who his friends were, but didn't want to ask.

"My friend Sean is the one who has the biggest career out of all of us. You might have heard of him if you at least go to the movies - Sean Lindsay?"

My mouth drops open. Of course, I even know who Sean

Lindsay is. He is a huge movie star, especially with romantic comedies. Rumor is that he even might be the next James Bond.

"Yes, I know of him. Who is your other friend?"

"Cora Gregory."

Cora Gregory is every male species object of wet dreams. One look at her, and men probably blow a load in their pants. She is gorgeous, with green cat-like eyes and long, black hair. In photos, she either has resting bitch face or is making love to the camera with those hypnotizing eyes that make men bend to her will.

"Wow, Cora Gregory, huh? She's beautiful. Why are you not dating her?" The question slips out of my mouth before I could keep my curiosity at bay.

"Everyone asks me that because we attend events together, but to be quite honest, she's more like family to me. I just don't have those feelings for her."

My face must have shown my utter disbelief at his statement because he smiles and laughs. "Why does everyone think that is bullshit coming out of my mouth? I am well aware of her beauty. I wouldn't be a man if I didn't notice it, but even to this day, I only see her as one of my sisters. I have known her since she was a lanky, skinny young girl who had a horrible home life. Sean and I decided we were going to protect her at school from all of the wankers and mean girls. That's all it has ever been for me."

I silently ponder what he just said. As we sit in compatible silence for once, the captain choses this time to announce that we will be making our descent into Las Vegas and for the flight attendants to prepare for landing. Cal and I smile at each other as I pack up my carry-on bag with my items, being very careful to make sure it doesn't fall on his feet again. As I place the bag underneath the seat in front of me and wait for us to land, I realize that this has been one of the best flights I have ever been on, despite the turbulence from take-off. Not because I am sitting next to a man who is physically gorgeous, but because I am sitting next to a human being who cared enough about my well-being, and was curious as to the type of person I am. He engaged with me the whole flight, and genuinely listened to everything I said. I would expect actors to not even give the time of day to the stranger sitting next to them on a flight.

"Are you okay? Do you need to hold on to me for landing?" he asks with concern as the plane is about to touch down.

"I actually like landing!" I say with a laugh.

"Really? That is the most dangerous part!"

"I know, silly isn't it? But to me, landing signifies that we have arrived, and that makes me happy."

"Well, I get scared at landings and you owe me some emotional support, so hold my hand." He grabs my hand and holds it on his tight thigh.

"I find it VERY hard to believe that you are scared of landing." I laugh back at him.

"Men can be as sensitive as women, just in different departments," he says, holding my eye contact.

I blush and look away, telling myself that he is just being nice and not to read into anything.

"Thank you for helping me," I say softly, not wanting to say anything more but hoping he can see my sincerity and gratitude through my eyes.

"The pleasure has been all mine," he says, as the plane touches down with a small bump.

I smile at him and pat his hand, breaking the contact. We reach for our phones, turning them on while the flight attendants welcome us to Las Vegas and ask that we stay seated until we safely stop at the gate. I scroll through my text messages from Robert and Layla, trying to stay focused and busy, while realizing that I will probably never see him again. A reality that is surprisingly disappointing.

We reach the gate and as soon as the plane parks, the clicks of seatbelts unbuckling fill the air. I suddenly feel shy, like I have no idea how to say goodbye to him. I decide to stand up and stretch my legs instead. Since we are in first class, we really don't have a long wait to depart the plane. I turn and notice he has decided to stand as well.

"Thank you again, and I truly hope you have a wonderful time here."

"Thank you, I hope you do too. When does your conference start?" he asks.

"It officially starts Wednesday morning, but I have some prep work I have to do before then," I say, as I move out onto the aisle to depart.

"CAL! CAL! Can you please wait so I can get a picture with you?" We turn to look down the aisle to see Big Head frantically trying to make her way past people to get to the front. He gives her thumbs up and we continue to walk out of the airplane.

"Mr. Harrington, would you mind stepping aside and taking some photos with our flight crew real quick?" one of the flight attendants asks him as well.

"I don't mind at all," he says, smiling at them. I feel that this is the perfect opportunity to just walk away and stop feeling so awkward about saying goodbye.

"Best of luck, Cal Harrington!" I wave and without waiting for a response back, I turn and walk up the jetway.

4

The sounds of the ringing are faint at first, but increase through the jetway, the noise intensifing to the point of hammering in the eardrums. The vibration gets the heart racing faster and faster. The mysterious noise coming from the terminal can only be identified at the end of the jetway.

Slot machines. Rows upon rows of them. A pastime for passengers to use while they wait.

Welcome to Las Vegas! A place where you find yourself amongst the most opulent and the seediest. I watch in wonder as I walk past the slot machines to catch the tram to baggage claim. I have never been much of a gambler, and don't understand how one can get addicted to something that majority of the time will take your money with no return on investment. I have occasionally indulged, but never spent more than twenty dollars. My enjoyment in Las Vegas comes from the shows and the themed hotels along the Strip, which has become a mini Times Square. Even though this is a business trip, I hope for some play and relaxation time. With the convention starting on Wednesday, I plan on using my two and a half extra days to catch up on work, relax, and take the sights in. Thinking about nice sights, my thoughts wander to the fine specimen that is Cal Harrington. I take my time getting to the tram, trying to look casual as I take one more look around, hoping for a glimpse of him. Realizing I am just wasting my time, I get on the crowded tram.

How did I not know about him? I know he is an up and coming actor, but I have never seen a more beautiful looking human in my life. Despite my lack of television consumption, I am surprised I have not seen him on the cover of the magazines that are in the newsstand right outside my apartment building. I would have definitely picked up any of those magazines to read about him. *How is a man like that single?* Those full sensual lips, I wonder what they would even feel like.

Ugh, stop it Jenna! I need to just stop my thoughts in their tracks. Rid my mind of him, as he is not reality, but complete fantasy. And we all know that most fantasies do not come true. With that mental pep talk, I start checking my emails while the tram takes us to baggage claim. As the tram slows to our destination, I flag the emails that need an immediate response when I get to the hotel. I join the exiting crowd, and look for my flight's designated area. Since our luggage has not arrived yet, I decide to call Robert.

"Hola, mi amore," he answers.

"You jinxed me."

"How?"

"I sat next to Cal Harrington on the plane," I whisper, looking around to make sure no one is standing too close to hear my conversation.

"In your dreams!" he laughs.

"No seriously, I actually did. And you are right, he is completely gorgeous. I know you really appreciated his back view, but it doesn't even come close to the breathtaking front view."

"WHAT?! First off, OF COURSE his front view is going to be better than the back view because that's where his big, lovely cock is and secondly, I cannot believe that I put out there in the universe that you might be sitting next to him and you actually did! Did you get his phone number? I swear, I am a fucking psychic. I deserve a raise for your five-hour pleasurable flight. Did you join the mile-high club at least? I so hate you right now."

I laugh at his utter ridiculousness. "No, I did not join the mile-high club or get his phone number. Why would he even give someone like me his phone number? And your raise all depends on if we surpass our revenue quota this year."

"Yeah, yeah, yeah, get back to the part of Cal Harrington. What did you all talk about?"

"You know, like the basic stuff. Where we are from, our careers, umm…" I pause to think of what else we talked about.

"BOOORRRIIINNGGG. You are lucky he didn't fall asleep on you."

"Ah yes, because as you like to remind me, I am so boring."

"Just keeping it real, Jens, just keeping it real," he laughs.

"Conveniently, the conveyor belt for baggage has started to move, so on that note, I am done talking to you. I hope you have a wonderful day of stormy weather and itchy balls!" I hang up on him as he continues laughing at me.

I roll my eyes with a smile on my face at our conversation. I think it was a wise decision that I came alone to Las Vegas. Sin City would have been too much temptation for my dear Robert, who doesn't like to miss a party where he can't be the center of attention. I have zero interest in personal attention or partying. Maybe I have become boring, but I have worked too hard building my career up. One night of making bad decisions can ruin it all, and I am not willing to gamble it all away.

The movement of people around me grabbing their luggage brings me out of my thoughts, and I immediately recognize my large red suitcase rounding the corner towards me. I put my cell phone back into my purse and lean down to retrieve the handle.

"That looks heavy, let me get it for you."

I look up just as Cal is grabbing my bag for me. I can't help the overly bright smile that is now plastered on my face.

"Thank you so much for doing that. Where is your luggage?" I look around for his bag but don't see anything with him.

"It is already in the car. They were kind enough to pull it from the plane first while I was signing autographs. I saw you as I was walking out, so I handed it to my driver first before coming back over to help."

"That was really nice of you to stop, thank you. You mentioned you have a driver? Did you fail your American Driver License's test that you can't drive yourself around?" Why I even attempt to try to sound witty and flirty with him is beyond me. Why would he rent a car when he is a celebrity and gets drivers? He is so good looking that it makes me feel uncomfortable to the point that I feel like I sound like a complete idiot when talking to him.

"I am proud to inform you that I did not fail my American Driver's License test, but the hotel sent a car for me, so why attempt to drive? And since I have never been to Las Vegas before, and am worried about getting lost or worse, being kidnapped, I was hoping you would accompany me to keep me safe and we can give you a ride to your hotel?" he smoothly jokes with me.

No words come out of my mouth as I just stare at him and blink. *He wants me to ride in his car with him?*

"I am sorry, I should have asked if you were waiting for someone instead of assuming you would just come with a complete stranger whom you just met."

"No, I am sorry, I am not waiting for anyone, and that is really nice of you to offer me a ride, but I wouldn't want to inconvenience you and the driver by having to go to separate hotels."

"It's not an inconvenience at all since I'm not the one driving. Where are you staying?"

"I'm staying at the MGM Grand," I confirm by checking my hotel reservation on my phone.

"Brilliant, because so am I." He flashes me a wicked smile. "C'mon, let's go."

He grabs my bag and starts walking to the exit. I quicken my pace to try to keep up with his long legs. I stop in my tracks as I stare dumbfounded as he greets the driver of a Rolls Royce Phantom. I watch as the driver puts my luggage into the trunk and they both wait for me to get into the car.

"I am so surprised that the hotel provided you with such a junker of a car," I sarcastically say while getting in the car and observing the interior of this extraordinary vehicle.

"Right? This is such an embarrassment to be driving around Las Vegas in," we laugh and admire the car. I thought my ex-husband's car was going to be the nicest car I'd ever entered, but I was mistaken. The driver tells us to help ourselves to the beverages available in the center console and eases into traffic towards our hotel.

"So, is this your everyday norm, being driven around in cars worth more than most people make in a year?"

"Being driven around by someone else is definitely not normal for me. I do appreciate the art form of a well-made car though," he sheepishly admits. "I am fortunate that my family, especially my sisters, make sure to keep me very well grounded, and not let the aspect of my career alter my ego too much."

"So, would you say cars are a weakness of yours?"

"Cars and good-looking woman," he locks those gorgeous blue eyes with mine and I can't look away. *What am I doing here with this man?* He is pure fire - lures you in with his confidence, and can leave scars from burning you with his charm. I am uncomfortably hot in places that have not been alive in a very long time.

"I am sure you have zero problems meeting women," I say, fidgeting in my seat under his gaze.

He shrugs his shoulders at that, and glances out the window before answering.

"Yes, this industry brings a lot of beautiful women in my path, but beauty on the outside does not mean beauty on the inside. I like strong women, and am not attracted to anyone who wants to ride my coattails."

"You are young, you have plenty of time to find that person. Don't rush it."

"True, but I like being in relationships. I am fascinated with exploring as much as I can about that person, emotionally and physically."

I swallow at the thought of being physically explored by him and refuse to let my thoughts continue down that path.

"What are you looking forward to the most during your time in Las Vegas?" I ask, hoping the change of topic, and not directly looking him in the eye, will also help cool me down.

"I am excited about the writing in this movie script, so getting the ball rolling on filming. I got to Las Vegas early because I like to get myself mentally prepared for my role, and have some time to myself first. This is also my first major film with Sean, so that's always fun to make movies with your friends. What about you?"

"I am new to the whole public speaking gig, and not too sure if I am even good at. It isn't what I love to do," I say with a laugh. "Honestly though, I really just hope that I can inspire someone to stop being afraid, and go forth with their dreams. If one person out of everyone at the conference starts their journey, then I would deem the trip a success."

I look back into his eyes, anticipating some sort of sarcastic response to my sincere answer.

"Was my answer too cheesy for you?" I ask with an uncomfortable giggle as he continues to stare at me.

"Your answer was pretty amazing to me," he answers seriously, holding my gaze. The honk of a horn breaks our hold, and we realize we are already pulling into the entrance of the hotel. Figures that there would be no traffic when you are having a nice conversation with a handsome man.

I gather my purse, and step out of the door the driver has

opened for me. Cal reaches into the trunk to take my suitcase out. He notices my strange look when he shuts the trunk with his suitcase still inside of it.

"Apparently, I am staying on a side of the hotel that has a private entrance that I have to be driven too," he says with an irritated look towards the driver.

"I completely understand, high roller!" I joke. "Seriously though, thank you again for the ride, and I sincerely hope the movie is a big success."

"Thank you, and good luck with your conference," he smiles and nods his head at me as I let a hotel employee grab my bag to escort me to the front desk. I turn around, and force myself to not look back.

5

After waiting in line for thirty minutes to get my key, I finally head to my room. I arrive to find a very large spacious suite with a separate living and dining room from the bedroom and a workstation. I immediately jot down a note to remind myself to thank the organizer of the conference for upgrading me to a suite. I start to unpack my clothes into the closet and drawers, wanting to get comfortable since I will be here for almost a week. I put some clothes that I wore during the conference in New York in the dry-cleaning bag to send out for cleaning. The thought of giving dry cleaning services my underwear to wash horrifies me. Shopping for new underwear for the week is a must. Once all the unpacking is done, I put away my suitcase in the closet, and glance at my watch. With the time change, it's only just past lunch and I groan at the thought that I have a full day's work ahead of me. What I wouldn't give for a nap. I look longingly at the bed, debating whether or not to take a two hour nap. If I want to try to go to the Grand Canyon tomorrow for some sightseeing, I need to skip the nap. With my decision made, I grab my laptop, order room service for lunch and start working.

Five hours later, and I am feeling confident enough to stop working for the day. I managed to finish sending all of my thank you emails to people from the conference in New York, got up to date with my incoming emails, finished the final touches on my speech, and worked on a couple of blog posts to schedule for the week pending Robert's proofreading approval. Feeling accomplished, it is time to get out of this room, grab dinner, and walk up and down the Strip for some people watching, then back for a decent night's sleep. I change into a long maxi dress with a jean jacket and some comfortable wedges. Foregoing a shower until the morning, I put my long brown hair in a messy ponytail, touch up my makeup, put on fresh deodorant, a spritz of perfume, and finally my hoop earrings. Satisfied with my appearance, I head downstairs to find somewhere to eat.

The hotel is packed with people walking around, getting ready for the nighttime activities. With my tummy rumbling, I decide to stick to one of the restaurants in the hotel. I walk to the concierge desk and ask for recommendations. Being that this is one of the largest hotels in the world, the options seem endless. I walk away from the desk, overwhelmed by too many choices, and the amount of people in my path. *Maybe I should just walk to another hotel?* But my hunger pains are starting to affect me. I take out my phone from my purse, and decide to look at the hotel app to see what the closest food option is to my current location and that'll be the winner. At this point, I don't even care if it's fast food.

"So, we meet again."

I look up from my phone to see the megawatt smile of Cal Harrington. He is wearing a long sleeve button down light blue shirt, navy dress slacks with a brown belt and brown dress shoes. His curly hair is on full display and he has shaved. He looks so delicious that I unconsciously lick my lips.

"Fancy seeing you in this neck of the hotel. What are you doing here?" I ask, pleasantly surprised that I am seeing him again.

"I wanted to get a tour of the whole hotel and check out the sights," he says, as he looks me up and down, giving me a look of appreciation. I immediately blush, and mentally give myself a high five for deciding to try to look cute in my solo excursion for food.

"Where are you off to?" he asks, and that is when I notice a hotel employee standing next to him, listening to our conversation, but looking around to make sure other guests do not bother Cal.

"I'm trying to find dinner." I hold up my phone to show him the hotel app. "Is this your new bodyguard?" I nod to the hotel employee.

"No, not today, and as for dinner, Randall is taking me to one of the hotel restaurants that has amazing French cuisine. I think you need to join me."

It takes me a moment to fully comprehend that he just asked me to dinner. *Can I even eat in front of him? Is he the type of guy who SAYS they like a woman with an appetite when in reality, he would be horrified if he sees me eat anything else besides a salad?*

"No need to hesitate in your answer. I KNOW you want to eat dinner with me!" he says with a confident smirk. "Randall, please lead the way." He grabs my arm, and turns me in the direction of the restaurant while laughing at my stupefied expression at his cockiness.

"Making assumptions are we?" I raise my eyebrow at him, hoping I sound flirty and not obvious to the fact that he's right.

He shrugs at my question. "I've enjoyed our conversations thus far, and selfishly, I would like to continue getting to know you. You're a very intriguing woman, Jenna." His compliments flow easily from that mesmerizing mouth. "And let's be honest, no one likes to eat alone."

We arrive at the entrance of the restaurant and as I look around, I realize that I might be underdressed. The restaurant's decor is decadent with inspiration from an 1800s' French Chateaux. My denim jean jacket sticks out like a sore thumb amongst the finely dressed patrons.

"Cal," I whisper, while we wait for Randall to finish talking to the maître d'. "I think I need to decline your invite. I'm not suitably dressed for this place."

"You look perfect. All will be fine." As if on cue, the maître d' tells us our table is ready, and Cal places his hand on the small of my back with a slight push forward. We are seated at a private table in the back of the restaurant. Menus are handed to us, and we're left alone until our waiter arrives. I feel like all eyes are on us and as I start to look around the restaurant, my suspicions are confirmed. *What am I doing here with a Hollywood actor?*

"Jenna, look at me," Cal demands, noticing my uneasiness. I finally pull my gaze away from the crowd and look him in the eyes. "Don't worry about anyone else, and stop looking at them. Just concentrate on you and me and what you want for dinner, ok?" he says softly with a smile and looks back down at his menu. I follow suit and try to focus on my food options. When I finally do focus, I groan inwardly. The style of food matches the decor - rich and upscale. I have never been a "foodie". I am perfectly content with bar food and this style of food is way out of my food palette league. I am notorious for eating a bowl of cereal for dinner most nights. I search for even a small side salad, but apparently this place is too good to even serve that. I turn the menu over, hoping there is more on the back, but I am out of luck. At that moment, the waiter comes by to take our drink order, and tells us what their specials are for evening. Cal orders us a bottle of wine and appetizers that sound absolutely foreign to me. The waiter leaves, and I am feeling hopeless about having a tasty meal tonight.

Snap out of it, Jenna. Be open-minded! Try something new!

I finally settle on an item that I can understand two out of the three ingredients in it, and pray it will be able to satisfy me until I can be alone in my hotel room where I can secretly order room service and no one but myself will know how gluttonous I plan on being.

"Everything okay over there? By the expressions that have been crossing your face for the last two minutes, it seems you are having an internal battle with yourself." So engrossed was I in trying to decide what to eat, I didn't notice he was watching me.

"Everything looks great!" I lie a little too enthusiastically. He laughs at me while the waiter arrives with our first appetizer and pours us a glass of wine. The appetizer looks like slimy red meat on top of French bread. I take a big gulp of wine, grimacing at the bitterness of it. The thought of having to eat this appetizer makes me throw up a little in my mouth. I take a sip of water to clear my mouth as the waiter asks for our dinner order. With a "bon appetite" he leaves us to go to the kitchen.

"Let's have a toast." Cal raises his wine glass to me, "cheers to making new friends!" I smile and touch my glass with his, making sure to take a smaller sip than last time. The words of his toast are sweet, but I have no doubt this will probably be the last time we see each other once my conference starts.

"So what did you do today?" I ask, hoping to distract him enough that he won't notice me not eating the appetizer that he serves on a small plate to me.

"I found that I still had a lot of adrenaline from the flight, so I went to work out, took a dip in the pool, had a nap, showered and lounged around. It has been a relaxing day. What about you?" he asks before taking a bite of the questionable looking meat.

I watch his face closely, waiting for a look of disgust or disdain, but his expression remains blank while he chews. "I actually worked all day." I immediately laugh at his incredulous look at my admission. "So much to do, so little time. Besides, I really want to try to have some down time tomorrow and Tuesday. When the conference begins, I will be pretty busy," I admit.

"What does one do at conferences like this that keeps you so busy?" He sits back in his chair and crosses his arms across his chest, drawing my attention to his bulging biceps.

I clear my throat and bring my attention back to his face.

"Well, I am the opening speaker for the conference, which I have never done before and am pretty nervous about. After the speech, there will be workshops, seminars, q&a's, and we'll get together with anyone who wants thirty minutes of free private coaching to help start their business, help with an obstacle they are going through or just answer general questions."

"And all of that will take place in 3 days?"

"Yes, everything will happen starting Wednesday morning and will go all the way to early evening on Friday. The organizer of this conference likes to start on a Wednesday, and end on a Friday in fun destinations for people to have personal time. It is actually quite smart of her to do so, as it increases her attendance. Case in point, my best friend Layla will be arriving on Friday night for some girl time, even though she actually has business to attend here as well, and then we leave on Sunday."

"What is the typical time frame for the other similar conferences you have attended?" he asks, seeming genuinely interested and not just trying to make small talk.

"Majority of the other conferences have started on a Sunday and end on a Wednesday."

"Very interesting," he says. "So, when are you going to try the appetizer?" He smiles at me with a dangerous glint to his eyes.

"You asked me questions, so I answered them. It's rude to talk with food in your mouth, you know?" I smirk at him. "So...um, what IS this?" I ask while stabbing the red slime with my fork.

He leans forward with his elbows on the table, the lighting illuminating his chiseled facial features as he leans closer to me. "It's ham in a tomato sauce on top of bread."

"Ah," is all that comes out my mouth, not wanting to tell him that I'm not a fan of ham. The ham doesn't even look like it's cooked. With Cal intently watching me, I pick it up, salute him with my food, and take a large bite. My taste buds immediately send my brain warning signals that slime is not welcomed in this mouth, and all I want to do is spit it out in my napkin. I refuse to show my agony, and I grip the napkin in my lap tightly while I slowly chew the slime, hoping that if my teeth grind it into small pieces, I will be able to swallow it. Cal has a look of pure, smug satisfaction while he fills my wine glass up. I eye the glass, knowing I am going to need it to push the contents down my throat. He rests his chin in his hand and waits for my next move. He is completely enjoying my reaction. Not able to take it anymore, I grab my wine glass and down it, choking on the food as it barely makes its way down my throat. He throws his head back and laughs while I wipe my mouth with my napkin. I can't hide the sour look on my face any longer.

"I have never been more entertained by watching someone eat as I was in that moment," he says after he stops laughing.

"That stuff is awful," the thought of it making me shudder. "You are never allowed to order food for me again."

"Is this your first time eating French cuisine?"

"Does a French bakery count? What about french fries?" I joke, knowing full well that french fries are not even considered to be French.

"You need to go to France one day, Jenna. It's such a beautiful country, and the food is delicious."

"So I have been told, and I would love to. I want to see all of Europe. I have been to Italy and Greece ,and loved both of those countries. I can't even imagine what the rest of Europe is like."

"When you were in Italy, did you notice certain types of meats they offered on their menus in restaurants?" he asks with a twinkle in his eye.

"If you are referring to the meat known as horse that they serve, then yes, I stayed far, far away from eating that there," I confirm with all seriousness.

He continues to laugh as the waiter arrives with our main entrees. The look of shock must have crossed my face, because the waiter immediately asks me if everything is okay.

"Fine, thank you," I say in another fake, ridiculously high voice.

The food is anything but fine. Not only is the portion size of my main entree smaller than my hand, but it looks like a small shrimp fetus in an embryo. There is no way in hell I am eating this. I look up at Cal, who is equaling eyeing my food with a questionable look.

"Cal, I will be more than happy to pay for my food, but I am NOT eating this. Sorry to not be able to entertain you further."

He takes a bite of his steak, closes his eyes in happiness and just smiles while chewing with his mouth closed. Some woman might find his reaction rude, but I can't help but smile at him.

"Tell you what, Jenna. After I finish this succulent, juicy, melt in your mouth, steak, I will take you to the pub for some french fries and ice cream."

"Do not tease a girl with french fries, Cal. You might get hurt if you don't deliver," I warn, as french fries sound divine right now.

"I always make sure I deliver with the upmost satisfaction," he says with another wicked smile. I drink the rest of my wine, trying to ignore the butterflies he gives me when he looks at me that way.

He finishes his meal, and the waiter comes to clear our plates. We decline dessert and Cal refuses to let me pay. We get up to leave and I immediately feel those stares on us as we walk through the restaurant. Cal grabs my elbow to guide me out of the restaurant that I do not plan on ever going to again. At some point, Randall returns during our walk to ask if we need assistance getting anywhere. He escorts us to the pub and talks to the hostess. The pub is packed with people watching soccer and rugby. She escorts us to a booth that is surrounded with TV's, much to Cal's delight.

"Rugby and Guinness, Jenna! This is my kind of place." He rubs his hands together like an adorable little boy does when seeing birthday presents.

"This place seems like a lot of fun," I agree, excited to have some bar food, and happy to hear that he prefers this type of atmosphere over fancy restaurants. We order some drinks and food and settle into our booth. Cal asks me if I know about rugby and I admit I don't. He proceeds to explain the rules to me, but I am too distracted by him to retain anything he tells me. A few minutes later, the waiter comes back with our order ,and I dive right into my cider and french fries. So happy am I that I let out a small moan of sheer bliss.

"If I would have known earlier that cider and fries were going to make you this happy, we would have come here first," he says, as he plops a french fry in his mouth.

"We didn't know our experience with the French restaurant was going to be so interesting." I shrug as if it was no big deal that I didn't like any of the food.

"My dinner was quite delicious."

"Glad to hear someone's was." I take a sip of my drink while he laughs. The crowd in the bar starts booing at one of the TVs and I immediately ask Cal what happened.

"There's an infringement," Cal says while looking at the TV.

"What's an infringement?" I ask, confused as I take another bite of a fry.

"Didn't you pay any attention to me when I was explaining the rules?"

"Nope. Your good looks were distracting me," I boldly tell him, realizing that I am getting tipsy if I just said that out loud.

"Ah, well, thank you. Happy to hear that you think so." The look he's giving me makes me shift in my seat. I take another sip of my drink. *No more drinks, Jenna, or you might be saying and doing things you don't need to be doing.*

Two more drinks later, and I am almost to the point of being drunk. We finally decide to leave the pub after Cal's favorite team wins. Randall magically appears again to escort us through the hotel. The hotel seems to be even busier than earlier. Cal offers me his arm to hold, as we weave our way through the crowd.

"The night is still young. Should we go for that ice cream I promised you earlier?"

"I can't eat or drink anything else." I place my hand on my protruding stomach, noting that I must work out tomorrow since I ate almost two baskets of fries by myself.

"What about we go back to my place and watch a movie?" he asks.

I can't help but laugh out loud at his question. "Sorry pal, but I am NOT having sex with someone I just met!" I say so loudly that Randall looks over at me with a smirk, the most emotion I have seen out of him all evening.

Cal chuckles and even his chuckle is sexy. "I had zero expectations of that tonight. I was being serious as I have a movie room in my suite."

Zero expectations? Does that mean he isn't attracted to me to even want sex?

"I am extremely attracted to you, Jenna. I just don't assume that every beautiful woman is going to have sex with me," he laughs at my horrified expression that I said what I was thinking out loud.

"Well, maybe just a short movie as I want to get up early and go to the Grand Canyon tomorrow." I ignore the warning bells going off in my head that I should not be going to his suite at all.

"You're going to the Grand Canyon tomorrow? I have been wanting to go as well," he says, as we walk further away from the main casino, past the public movie theater. I don't answer him as I am trying to figure out where Randall is taking us. We come to a private door where he slides his key card in, and we proceed to walk through beautiful long marble hallways. We walk up to a wrought iron guarded gate, where Randall greets the guard, slides his key card and opens the door for us. The sound of water falling greets us and I gasp as I take in the beauty of the main courtyard of what looks like a huge Tuscan style mansion, with balconies facing the center water fountain in the courtyard. Lush green trees and vivid flowers are everywhere, giving you the deception of feeling like you are in Italy. I glance up to see the stars, only to see the illusion of being outdoors is just that, and that we are actually in an atrium. I never even knew a place like this existed on the property which, as I glance at Cal, now makes complete sense as this is a place for people of his caliber. We enter another decadent looking hallway where Randall stops in front of a beautifully intricate wood door.

"Welcome back to your villa, sir." He bows to Cal and turns to me. "Miss, when you are ready to go back to your room, please let the butler know and he will get you a car to take you to the main entrance of the hotel." We say thank you and Cal hands him a tip by way of a handshake. He puts his key card in and opens the door. We are immediately greeted by the butler.

"Good evening sir, ma'am. My name is Steven, and I will be taking care of you this evening. Would you like a late-night snack and cocktail?" I vaguely hear Cal talk to him about watching a movie as I move past them in complete awe of this place. This Tuscan styled "villa" has twenty-five foot arched ceilings with sparkling chandeliers, gorgeous drapery, and terra cotta lined floors covered with beautiful rugs.

"Would you like a tour?" Cal asks me with a smile. I nod my head, and he proceeds to show me the living room that contains a baby grand piano, the dining room with a large circular table that can seat eight, the fully stocked bar, the kitchen, the workout room, two large bedrooms, and then the master bedroom that is bigger than my apartment back home. Lastly, we arrive at the movie room.

"Wow, this place..." I shake my head as I take a seat on one of the reclining chairs.

"It is beautiful," he agrees, as he hands me some water to drink.

"Thank you." Taking a sip, I look around at the surroundings of the room, suddenly feeling awkward at being alone with him.

"What type of genre do you like to watch in movies?" He picks up an iPad and starts to scroll through movie titles.

"I like everything except scary movies." I sincerely hope that my revelation doesn't give him any ideas to torture me by watching one.

"Define scary in your opinion?" That mischievous smile is back, and I know he is up to no good.

"People or alien objects killing the good guys with lots of goriness. I don't want to see any of that." I shiver in pure disgust as I get horrible nightmares from those type of movies. I understand that those movies are far from real, but my brain just can't handle the morbidness.

"I will be a gentleman tonight, and not put anything on that will distress you," he says with some mockery. "How about suspense?"

"Sounds good." I take off my shoes and proceed to move back into the chair. I debate whether or not I should recline the chair. If I recline, then the chances of me falling asleep are high. I purposely do not reveal to Cal that my friends make fun of me for always being the first person to fall asleep when we watch a movie at home.

"I am going to go change. Get comfortable and I will be right back." While he leaves, I grab a blanket and stare at my surroundings.

This is not a good idea, Jenna! You are going to fall asleep and be helpless. You don't know this guy! It doesn't matter that he is a Hollywood actor. Even famous people can do bad things.

"Sorry for the delay." He comes back five minutes later, wearing a white tee shirt and sweat pants, which does not diminish his sexiness whatsoever. He dims the lights to a lower setting and starts the movie. I lean my head back to get more comfortable. "You know you can recline your seat, right?"

"Yes, but I'm really afraid that if I recline this seat, you'll have an overnight guest and I really do not want that to happen."

"It's fine if you fall asleep here. I promise I won't compromise your virtue while you're sleeping." He wiggles his eyebrows up and down that prompts me to laugh.

"Good to know my virtue is safe with you," I laugh and we turn our attention to the movie.

"I think I left my phone in the other room. Keep the movie running and I will be right back." He gets up and leaves.

And that is the last time I remember seeing him as I drift off to sleep.

6

A delicious aroma permeates the air and awakens my senses. A smile forms on my face as I inhale the smell of coffee being brewed and food being cooked. I open my eyes, and realize I am still in Cal's movie room, a blanket protecting me from the coldness of the air conditioning. I quickly peek inside the blanket, and breathe a sigh of relief to see all of my clothes are still on. Last thing I remember from last night was Cal going to get his phone and that was it. How I didn't hear him come back in or put a blanket on me shows what a deep sleep I was in. I pull off the blanket, stand up, and fold it to put back on the couch.

"Good morning!"

"Ah!" I gasp, and turn around, startled to see him standing in the doorway. He is leaning on the door frame, wearing his pajamas from the previous night with a big grin on his face at my reaction. "You scared me!"

"I'm sorry, I didn't mean to," he laughs, pushing off the door frame and coming towards me. I take a step back and fall onto the couch as he approaches me.

"Thanks for letting me crash here last night. I'm so sorry that I fell asleep." I stand up, feeling awkward that I fell asleep before we could even watch the movie.

"It wasn't a problem. You're quite entertaining asleep as well as awake."

I narrow my eyes at his devilish grin. "What does that mean?" I ask, as embarrassment starts to creep in. Moaning, farting, snoring...the list is endless of things my ex-husband has told me occur in my nightly unconsciousness and I'll be horrified if I did any of those in front of Cal.

"Did you know you talk in your sleep?"

"I have been told that," I confirm. He remains silent with a childish grin still on his face.

"So are you going to tell me what I said?"

"Hmm, I think not. Maybe I'll give you clues throughout the day. By the way, breakfast is ready, I hope you're hungry." He heads back toward the door.

My stomach rumbles as if answering him. "Where's the restroom?" I ask. He points toward its location, and I head briskly in that direction, my bladder screaming at me for release. I relieve my bladder and stifle a scream at my raccoon eyes in the mirror while washing my hands. No wonder he was laughing at me this morning. *Why can't I wake up with my make-up still looking perfect from the night before?* While wiping away my mascara, I notice the toiletries on the sink include mouthwash. I take a quick swig, spit it out, and wipe my mouth. I make my way toward the dining room, where I am greeted by the butler, who asks me what I would like to drink.

"Coffee and water would be lovely," I say, as I look around at all the food options available. Eggs, waffles, fruit, bagels, and danishes are all lined up, ready to be devoured.

"I didn't know what you like to eat or if you even eat breakfast, so I ordered multiple items. Please dig in." Cal hands me a plate and proceeds to pile food on his plate.

"I love breakfast, but I actually was going to just grab something light and quick as I need to get on the road if I don't want to be at the Grand Canyon past dark." I look at my watch to see it is already 7:30 in the morning. I wanted to be on the road already.

"We can go right after we eat." Cal shovels a mouthful of eggs into his mouth.

"We?" I raise my eyebrows at him in surprise. I recall him saying he has always wanted to go to the Grand Canyon, but we never discussed him accompanying me.

"I don't have anything going on today, and figured it would be okay to tag along with you. Do you mind?" He sips his coffee while waiting for my response.

"No, of course I don't mind," I say, annoyed with how quickly my pulse starts racing at the thought of another day spent with him.

"I was hoping you'd say that. Why don't you sit down to eat, and then a car can take you back to the main entrance so you can get ready?" He nods to Steven, who nods in agreement and leaves to go make arrangements for my transportation.

"Thanks," I softly say and put some eggs and fruit on my plate. I sit down and stare at my plate while I eat, the feeling of confusion overwhelming me. It has been a long time since someone has taken care of details for me. It's almost unnerving. *Why does he want to go with me?* He must not like being alone. I take a quick peek at him, and notice he's just sitting there, reading a newspaper, looking like a supermodel. As if sensing being watched, he looks up and smiles at me.

"Anything interesting going on in the world today?" I motion toward his newspaper.

"Nope, looks like we are all doomed." He puts it down and smiles.

I chuckle and put my napkin down. "Well, then I better get ready to go to the Grand Canyon with a stranger who can push me off the cliff and no one will know," I joke, standing up to get ready to leave.

He laughs and escorts me to do the door. "Is an hour enough time for you to get ready?" I nod and Steven greets us at the door.

"Steven will escort you to the car. I'll pick you up at the main entrance where you're being dropped off. See you soon." He hugs me tight, kisses my forehead and goes back into his room. I follow Steven to the car in a dazed state. *He just kissed me on the forehead!*

The car brings me to the front entrance of the hotel and I briskly walk to the elevators. Once I get into my suite, I shower, lotion up, blow dry my hair, put on some jeans, a cute top, and sneakers. I keep my make-up light since we might be walking around and sweating. The thought of not knowing what we are doing makes me pause. I have never not had anything planned out and not having a car rented or an itinerary to the Grand Canyon makes me nervous. With five minutes left to spare, I spritz on some perfume, stuff two granola bars, and some water into my purse and head for the elevators. I immediately see the same driver as I had before and walk towards him. He opens the door for me, and inside is Cal, hair still wet, smelling divine and looking incredible. He is in dark blue jeans, a black v neck t-shirt that tightens against his chest and aviator sunglasses. There's probably nothing that this man does not look good in.

"Are you ready for our grand adventure today?" he asks with excitement.

"I'm ready!" I enthusiastically answer back. "But...where are we going?" I ask, wondering if he has made any arrangements in the hour that I was gone.

"To the Grand Canyon." Cal looks at me as if I'm crazy.

I roll my eyes at his smart-ass response. "Duh, but how are we getting there? Is this car driving us all the way there?"

"Oh no, that would take too long. We're taking a helicopter there, where a tour guide will show us around."

I can't help but just stare and blink at him "A helicopter?" My palms start to feel itchy and wet at the thought of being in any transportation that requires being in the air. "How do we know this is a reputable company? Did you read reviews on them? Check to see how many crashes they've had?"

He presses his lips together to suppress his smile. "No, I personally didn't look up any reviews on this company, but I trusted that since the hotel books them for their clients on a regular basis, that they would come highly recommended."

I nod and bite my lip, not wanting to sound even more ridiculous than I already do. I hate to show my fear of flying, but it's an emotion that I've been trying to overcome with no success. *Let it go, Jenna. This is a once in a lifetime experience. Just trust that everything will be okay.*

"What is the name of the company? I will just quickly look them up online." I open Safari on my phone to search for reviews, clearly not able to let go of my fear.

"Jenna," he covers my phone with his hand, "even if I knew the name of the company, I wouldn't tell you. We're not going to crash. Positive thoughts, everything will be fine. We're going to have an amazing time!" His reassurance makes me feel only slightly better. I look out the window, and am thankful to see clear skies. Before I can think of any more excuses, we have arrived at the terminal for the helicopter.

"We're here already? How did we get here so fast?" I nervously giggle, trying to hide my mounting anxiety. I have never been in a helicopter before, and the thought of anything with a propeller scares me more than getting on any jet plane. Our driver opens my car door and I reluctantly get out of the car. I look towards the helicopter, its sleek design shining in the sunshine, and quietly say a little prayer to keep us safe. The pilot is outside of the helicopter, waiting to greet us. Cal grabs my hand and practically drags me with him, his excitement overpowering my weariness.

"Good morning, Mr. Harrington, Ms. Pruitt. My name is Captain Michael Bowen, and it's my pleasure to be taking you to the Grand Canyon today. Let's quickly go over some safety features before we get into the helicopter." I listen intently to our captain, making mental notes of everything he shows us inside the helicopter. With his safety speech ending much to quickly for my liking, he opens the helicopter door. With both men being chivalrous, I climb in first with Cal trailing in behind me. We put our seat belts on, then add our headphones so we can hear the pilot. I take a deep breath as I watch the pilot get into his seat to get ready. I start my silent prayers to keep us safe and close my eyes when I hear the engine turn on and the rotor start to spin. I feel a warm, strong hand squeeze mine and I open my eyes to look at Cal.

"Whatever is meant to be, will be, Jenna. Live in the moment. This is going to be incredible." He kisses my forehead and tries to pull me as close to him as the seat belts will allow. I mouth "thank you" to him and squeeze his hand, hoping he can sense my appreciation. He is absolutely right - I do need to live in the moment and enjoy it. *Keep your eyes open the whole time, Jenna. You can do it!*

The pilot lifts the helicopter off the ground, and I immediately plant my head into Cal's arm from the unsteadiness of take-off. *You are such a chicken shit, Jenna!* I feel us slowly spinning 180 degrees and push forward to our destination. I peek my eyes out when Cal tells me we are flying over the Las Vegas Strip. He points out our hotel, and it is amazing to see how massive all the hotels are from above. Residential houses start to appear, but soon the desert changes to ridges and Lake Mead is in our sights. The glittering teal of the water is so stunning that I grab my phone to take pictures. We veer right, and head over to the structural masterpiece of the Hoover Dam, the pilot giving us some background information on the architectural aspect of it as we fly over. We make our way over parts of the Mojave Desert, one side of the helicopter giving us glimpses of Lake Mead, the other side showing us the vastness of the desert. I snap more pictures, trying to stop my mind from telling my eyes to look below at the glass windows underneath my feet, not wanting to put more mental images of crashing inside my head.

Every little tiny dip makes me want to bury my head back into Cal's strong arms, but the anticipation of being in the Canyon soon makes me keep my big girl panties on. The pilot announces that we are approaching the edge of the rim, and I gasp at the sheer beauty as we enter into the Grand Canyon. The colors of the landscaping and the magnitude of the size seem never-ending. We are silent as we continue snapping photos of the mesmerizing views. We follow the twists and turns of the Colorado River as we enter into the canyon and descend below the rim. As we make our way lower into the canyon, the pilot informs us that we will be landing on the river's edge at the bottom of the canyon. I look at Cal with questioning eyes as to why we would be landing, but all he does is raise his eyebrows and smiles. A ramp with a boat docked at it comes to view as we arrive for landing. We touch down, and the pilot informs us to wait until the rotor stops for us to exit.

"Are we about to get on that boat?" I point towards it.

"I figured a tour from the sky just wasn't enough," he shrugs with a sexy smile as an attendant opens our door. Cal grabs my purse for me and we head to the boat. We are greeted by our tour guide who helps us on. We sit back and relax as we cruise up and down the Colorado River, taking photos of the rock layers that were created from the consistent erosion of the river, revealing millions of years of the Earth's history. Forty-five minutes later, we arrive back to the dock and depart the boat. As we make our way back up to the helicopter, I notice a table dressed with a tablecloth and chairs for two people.

"I hope you enjoyed the boat ride, Mr. Harrington and Ms. Pruitt. Lunch is ready for you. We will have thirty minutes of private time until the public tours start to arrive," our pilot gestures for us to sit down. He pours us some champagne and leaves us to eat our lunch.

"A toast to the Grand Canyon!" Cal clinks his glass to mine and we take a sip of the bubbly.

"I can't believe we're here doing this," I say, still in disbelief over the experience of it so far.

"I remember looking at photos of the Grand Canyon as a young lad in school, but photos don't even do it justice."

"What were you like as a boy in school?" I ask, before taking a bite of my sandwich, trying to envision what he may have looked like.

"I was awkward and fat," he laughs, shaking his head at his memories. "I was popular because when people would make fun of me, I would start making fun of myself with them. Self-deprecation. One day, my sister dragged me to her boyfriend's rugby game and I fell in love with the sport. It was the first time I felt a part of something. The weight quickly came off and I have to work very hard to keep it off."

"I have a hard time believing that," I say, glancing at his body that seems to have zero body fat.

"Life is too short to deprive yourself of pizza and Guinness," he laughs. "I am very regimented before and during a movie, but I always give myself cheat days. Sometimes one day a week, sometimes weeks on end. What were you like in school?"

"I was a nerd, but not part of any one clique. I tried to befriend everybody, but of course, that is never possible in high school. I played softball for one year, but did not like my coach. Yearbook and student government were my true passion during those four years."

"And here I was picturing you as a hot cheerleader," he bestows his devilish smile upon me.

"Sorry to disillusion your fantasy," the idea of me being a cheerleader laughable.

"No need to be sorry as reality is proving to be far better than fantasy." He holds my gaze and I cannot look away. An overwhelming urge to kiss him suddenly takes over me. Our pilot interrupts my thoughts to remind us it is time to go. We take a couple more photos and load up into the helicopter for take-off. Cal holds my hand again as we slowly lift off, and head up the Colorado River, moving into the South Rim of the Canyon. The views of the Grand Canyon are completely indescribable. The pilot takes the helicopter north, and then west as we head back to Las Vegas, passing the Valley of Fire and Lake Mead on our way. The ridges of the Canyon start to slowly fade away as the outskirts of Las Vegas come into view and finally the Strip, where we do one more fly by before we land. The landing pad for our helicopter comes into view, and our pilot steadily makes a safe landing.

We take off our headphones and unbuckle our seat belts as we wait for the rotor to stop spinning to exit. I turn to Cal, not knowing how I can ever pay him back for the unbelievable experience that I wouldn't have treated myself to.

"Today was one of the most memorable days I have had in a really long time. Thank you for such a special day." I lean in to hug him and kiss his cheek, but he turns his head, and my lips land on his mouth. He holds me in place so that I cannot pull away, his sensual lips demanding that I stay. His mouth is more than what I imagined - warm, firm lips that taste so good that I want more. I put my hands in his hair and bring him closer. He caresses his tongue against my lips, and I open them with a low moan escaping. He deepens the kiss and our whole environment fades away, so lost am I in the moment, in him. A knock on the window startles us apart as we look at the pilot, who sheepishly gives us a smile. "Sorry," I mutter to the pilot as he helps me out of the helicopter. We thank him and head to the waiting car to take us back to our hotel. As soon as the driver closes the door after us, Cal grabs me and continues to devour my lips, each thrust of his tongue increasing my appetite for him. We stay this way for the whole car ride until the driver's honk of the horn makes us break away. I try to catch my breath, my chest moving up and down in rapid movements.

"Have dinner with me tonight," he commands, as he kisses up the side of my neck.

"Okay," I agree, shivering from the heat of his kisses.

"I promise you I will make it worth your while - no French food." He touches his forehead to mine as I smile at his joke.

The car pulls into the main entrance of our hotel and stops for the valet to open my door.

"I'll see you at 7:30 p.m." Cal kisses my hand and I depart the car. As I walk into the hotel, I immediately go shopping for clothes, especially some upgraded underwear.

7

I finish my shopping excursion with an hour to spare. I race back up to my room, take a quick shower, and decide on what new undergarments and dress I am going to wear tonight. Cal gave no indication of where we are going, so I am clueless as to what the dress code is. I decide to play it safe with a black dress that has a V neckline that teases a hint of cleavage - sexy, but still classy. I pair it with strappy heels, gold jewelry, and a magenta cardigan to keep me warm. I apply dramatic eye make-up, but keep my lips more natural. Satisfied with my hair, I look at my watch to see it is time to go. I grab my purse and head toward the elevator.

While in the elevator, I realize Cal didn't clarify where he or anyone else would be picking me up. I exit the elevator, not knowing which way I should even be going. I decide to head to the main lobby toward the front entrance. Relief spreads over me as I see Steven waiting for me at the concierge desk.

"Good evening, Ms. Pruitt. Mr. Harrington had to answer an unexpected call. He asks me to escort you to the restaurant where he will be joining you shortly." He gestures to me to follow him and we head toward our destination. I can't help but chuckle to myself, recalling Cal's comment of no French food, as we approach a high-end Japanese restaurant. Steven nods to the hostess, who escorts us to a table already picked out. Steven asks if I need anything else and departs when I decline. I look through the menu while I wait, my stomach ready to be filled with food.

"I am so sorry to keep you waiting." Cal comes up from behind me, and brushes his lips against my cheek, sending shivers up my spine. I can't help but admire my new view as he walks past me to his seat, noting how his dress pants mold perfectly to his backside. Tonight he is wearing a crisp white dress shirt tucked into navy pinstriped slacks while carrying a matching blazer. He hangs the blazer on the back of his chair, sits down and rolls up his sleeves, showcasing his strong forearms.

"You look ravishing," he says, so engrossed was I in checking him out that I failed to notice he was doing the same to me.

"As do you,"I say, my compliment back earning me a raised brow with a sexy smirk.

"I trust that you have found something suitable to your liking on this menu?" he teases, as he peruses his own menu.

"Yes," I laugh. "I don't think I'll be wasting any food tonight."

"Good, because I want you to be fully satisfied," the underlying sexual innuendo making me blush and smile, breaking our heated eye contact. The waiter arrives to take our drink and food order, and I can't prevent my mind from wondering what is in store for me tonight.

"Was everything okay with the phone call you received?" My curiosity peaking as to what kept him, even though it is none of my business.

"Yes, it was my assistant, Valerie, wanting to go over my schedule for the next couple of days before she arrives. I try to be as organized as possible, but she keeps me in check. I honestly don't know what I would do without her."

"How long has she been your assistant?" I casually ask before taking a sip of my wine. I wonder what she looks like and if he is attracted to her. *Why do you even care, Jenna?*

"About four years now. We were both in acting class together and I was getting opportunities, while her career kind of stalled. I was having a hard time keeping up with the administration aspect, so she offered to help me and has been with me ever since."

"That is great that you have someone you can trust, especially in your industry."

He nods. "You would be horrified by the behavior of some people, and what they get away with in Hollywood."

"I feel that way about people who are NOT in Hollywood," we laugh before inspecting the food the waiter just delivered. With Cal watching me, I take a bite of my food and give him a thumbs up of approval. He laughs and dives right into his. We taste test each other's food, order more wine, and recap the incredible day we had at the Grand Canyon. It takes such little effort to make conversation with each other that before we know it, the restaurant is clearing out.

"Are you ready for dessert?" The overhead light catching the gleam in his eyes.

"No, thank you," I say to the waiter who hands Cal the check.

He watches the waiter walk away and leans in close "I wasn't talking about the edible kind of dessert." Before I can even react, he quickly signs the check, stands up, grabs his coat and holds out his hand to me. I gaze up at him, match the heat of his look with my own and place my hand in his. His kisses earlier reignited a fire that I thought was burned out and like an addict, I crave more.

We walk in silence back to his room, the anticipation of what's to come moving us briskly through the hotel. After what seems like forever, we finally make it to his villa. He opens the door, walks us in, spins me around, and pushes me against the door to devour my lips. He was wrong about not having edible dessert, as his lips are the most decadent of desserts I've ever had. I run my hands up his chest and into his hair, directing his lips to the side of my neck, his kisses clouding my thinking. I hear a noise and realize that Steven is in the vicinity.

"Cal, your butler," I whisper, nudging him to step back and make Steven go away.

"Go to my bedroom." He kisses my lips and walks away to go talk with Steven. I stumble the whole way, my knees weak from his touch. I get in his room and am unsure what to do with myself. *Should I take my clothes off and get into bed? Should I just sit down on the bed and patiently wait for him? What am I even doing here?* I have never been with a man that I barely know, and as I think about what I am about to do, uneasiness creeps in. I decide to stand at the window and gaze at the pool. With the water mesmerizing my senses, I never hear Cal come in. I only feel him against me as he snakes his arm around my waist to bring me closer. As he starts to kiss my neck, I realize I have no willpower to stop him, and instead, I turn my head to the side to give him easier access. My body starts to move against his erection as I push my backside into him, hearing him moan at the pressure. I turn around, and he immediately claims my lips, demanding that I open them to welcome his tongue.

"I want more of you," he whispers, as he peels off my cardigan to kiss my shoulders, making his way back to my neck, and then down my chest. He pushes aside my dress straps, making the dress cascade down my legs. I am left standing in my bra, thong, and heels as he continues his descent down my body, leaving trails of scalding kisses on my skin. He gets on his knees, his mouth perfectly aligned with my entrance. He starts kissing my panties, the feel of his breath against the fabric making me whimper. He nips at the fabric and brings my panties down my legs with his teeth. I gasp, as he kisses his way up my calves, my knees, and thighs. Using his head, he nudges my legs wider apart, kissing so close, yet so far away, from my core. My breathing is rapid, harsh exhales come out every time his tongue comes in contact with a part of my thigh. Suddenly, he stops and I look down to see why.

"Watch me, Jenna." He places his hands on my ass, his eyes never wavering from mine. I moan while watching him and feeling the touch of his lips on me. He makes a path of hot destruction, touching everywhere but where I need him to touch. With my body vibrating with desire, I wind my hands in his hair and pull.

"Please Cal." He smiles at my begging and with a low growl, he starts slowly licking me. He alternates between licking and sucking, sending shockwaves through me like a defibrillator does to the heart. Watching his long, firm tongue touch me only heightens the sensations, and I can barely keep my eyes open. Sensing that my knees are about to buckle, he pushes me back against the bed and continues his assault on me. I release my grip on his hair and fist the sheets in my hands, my head rocking back and forth from the buildup. My hips start to gyrate against his mouth as he licks harder and faster. I wrap my legs around his head, and squeeze him deeper until I scream out my orgasm.

As my body goes limp from the explosion of my release, I struggle to regain my breath. Never have I experienced such an intense orgasm from oral sex. I wonder if it's because it has been a while or just his talented skills. I open my eyes to find him standing over me with a satisfied smile on his face.

"That was unbelievable." I watch as he undresses, his muscle definition a work of art. He leaves his boxers on, but it does nothing to hide his enormous erection. He gets beside me in bed and pulls me to his side.

"Get some sleep, Jenna, because that was just a preview," he whispers, before he kisses me deeply and holds me close. I usually prefer to have my own space when sleeping, but with the warmth of his body, and his strong arms around me, I drift into a deep sleep.

8

It takes me a while to get out of bed, my body tired, but relaxed. A smile drifts to my face at the memory of Cal waking me up with his mouth. At first I thought it was a dream, but then as it became more sensual, the tingling sensations made me realize I wasn't dreaming. After making me come again, I was wide awake and ready to reciprocate, but he refused and told me to sleep. I have never been with a man who so generously gives oral sex twice in one night with no expectations of a return. *Is something wrong with his penis?* I couldn't tell since he kept his boxers on. Hopefully, I will get another opportunity to find out. Just then the object of my thoughts walks in, dressed in a short sleeve button down shirt with khaki chino pants, clean shaven, and his hair curling from air drying with no product in it. For someone who has barely slept, he looks refreshed, energized, and hot.

"Good morning, beautiful. I was hoping you would be awake before I left." He sits down on the side of the bed and kisses me full on the lips.

"Where are you going?" I ask, trying to hide the disappointment I feel at not spending the day with him.

"There was a re-cast and the director wants me to come in and read some lines with the new actor they hired." He brings down the sheet that I have over my body to play with my nipple. "I should hopefully be back before dinner. I think you should stay here, relax by the pool, and when I get back, we can go get a bite and maybe a show?"

His caresses cloud my ability to think. "I, uh, don't have a swimsuit here," and I smack his hand away so I can concentrate. He laughs and retaliates by playing with the other nipple.

"My pool is private - I think you should just go naked," he whispers, as he leans down and takes my nipple in his mouth. He alternates between sucking and lashing with his tongue, the combination making me moan out loud. He leaves my nipple, makes a kissing trail across my breast to the other nipple, which he then takes inside his mouth for some attention. I arch my back, and place my hands in his hair to try to bring him closer. My legs open and I try to maneuver him in between them for me to wrap around, but he doesn't move and instead, releases my nipple.

"Think of me today, Jenna, and know that I absolutely plan on continuing where we are leaving off tonight." He gives me one last kiss and stands up to head out the door.

"You're blue balling me right now?" I look at him incredulously, my voice a higher octane than normal due to the frustrated state he is leaving me in.

He laughs at my choice of words, "I think I'm the one left in that state," and winces while looking down at the big bulge straining against his pants. I have some small satisfaction at seeing he is suffering too. *Serves him right since he started it.*

"Wait," so distracted am I by the sight of him that I place my hand on my forehead to recall my thoughts, "I need to grab some items from my room. How can I get back in?"

"Steven has an extra key for you to come and go as you please from now on." He glances down as his phone beeps. "I'm sorry, but I must go. Breakfast is waiting for you, and I look forward to seeing you later," and with that, he heads out of the bedroom and shuts the door.

I fall back against the pillow and let out a slow exhale. While I would love to lay around all day and go skinny dipping in his pool, the thought of only Steven and myself being around makes me slightly uncomfortable. Sunbathing was not part of my original plan, but it does sound tempting. Trying to decide what store I would shop in for a suit, I get out of bed, get dressed and head to the dining room.

"Good Morning, Ms. Pruitt, what would you like for breakfast today?" Steven gestures to the array of food that can feed ten people. I make my selection and he brings me water and coffee. I unfold the napkin from the silverware and as I place it on my lap, I am suddenly very conscious about being in my clothes from the previous evening. *I can only imagine what Steven thinks of me.* I pick at my food with my fork, my appetite decreasing with every thought of the picture I am presenting of myself. *Does he think I am a whore? Why do I care? I haven't done anything wrong. I am a strong, independent woman!* Wanting to distance myself, I tell Steven I will be back later and leave the table, my food barely touched. I go to collect my purse and notice the extra key laying by it. I hesitate about taking it, but wanting to see Cal wins out and I stuff it in my purse.

"Ms. Pruitt, a car is waiting to take you back to the main lobby," Steven says, as he races to open the door for me before I get to it.

"I am sorry, Steven, but I prefer to walk. Can you cancel it?" I ask, as I have no desire to do the walk a shame through the main lobby for the second time. He insists on walking me back to my room and I decline, bidding him a good day and make my way through the Atrium to the door that leads into the main part of the hotel. By the time I get to the elevators that lead to my room, my feet are screaming at me for declining the car, while my head decides to beat the pride right out of my heart. Layla and Robert would be my biggest cheerleaders for what I have been up to these last couple of days. Why all of a sudden do I feel so guilty? I never judge Layla on her many escapades, so why am I judging myself? I try to think about the root of what is really making me feel this way when I feel my phone vibrate and look down to see three missed calls and five text messages from Robert. I let myself into my room, start up my laptop to talk business, and call him back.

"Hi, what's wrong?" I nervously grip the phone, waiting for bad news as to why he would call and text me so much.

"What's wrong is that I haven't heard from you in almost two days! I was about to call the cops! Where have you been?" I grimace at his tone of voice. It is never fun to be on the receiving end of an angry Robert Jordan.

"I'm sorry, Robert, for worrying you. I didn't realize I missed your calls and texts. I've been, uh, distracted." I am so not ready to have this conversation with him yet.

"Distracted? By what or should I ask, whom? You owe me details and it better be juicy and scandalous," he huffs into the phone.

"Oh, you know, distracted by Las Vegas." I roll my eyes at my pathetic answer as I try to stall to think of some other story to tell him, but I can't because I hate to lie and when I try to tell an innocent one, I always get called out. Nothing good every comes from lying, even from the small little ones.

"No Jenna, I don't KNOW what it is like to be distracted by Las Vegas, because SOMEONE didn't fucking take me with her! Furthermore, not only was I frazzled with not hearing from you, but I was also not prepared to have to deal with the wrath of Pamela, who has called me a gazillion times asking why you didn't call her when you landed!" His reference to my mother makes me giggle as I wouldn't want to be left to deal with her either. "You owe me two whole days of spa treatments for dealing with that shit storm."

"Again, I apologize, Robert, and will make sure to book you

two spa days. Will you forgive me?" I use my soothing tone of voice on him while jotting down a note for some spa days for both of us.

"I will forgive you once you tell me the real reason why you haven't been glued to your phone or laptop to miss my very important calls. You are NEVER distracted." He is right, unfortunately.

"Well, I went to the Grand Canyon and that took up most of my day ,and then came back and went out to dinner." I purposely sound as vague as I possibly can.

"Who were you with?" he asks, suspicion lacing his voice.

"People."

"How many people?"

"Three." I quickly count the pilot, the tour guide and Cal as my three-other people.

"People from the conference or new people?"

"New people...?" I drift off, unsure how to answer it. Knowing that my uncertainty of an answer will further convince him that I am lying, I am going to have to give him something more in order to stop the line of questioning. "Okay, fine. One new person. Are you happy now?"

"HA! I KNEW IT!" he exclaims excitedly "Who is he and you better be slapping some skin with him."

"No skin slapping and why are you assuming it is a he? What if it is a she?" I challenge him on being presumptuous.

"Oh please, you're as straight as an arrow and wouldn't touch another girl in a sexual way if you two were the last species on earth," he laughs.

"That is not true, I think women are beautiful and if I was horny enough, I would so have sex with a woman...if we were the last two species on earth." I shake my head as I just confirmed his statement. I need to change this subject fast. "Enough of this, I just gave you the truth. Forgive me and let's move on."

He continues to laugh and starts to tsk me. "Oh Jenna, you are not forgiven, because you tried to lie to me and have still left out the pertinent details, like his looks and his penis size. I will let this information slide for today since it is imperative we talk business, but tomorrow is a new day and if you want my forgiveness, then you need to give up some dirt." I accept his reprieve and immediately switch gears to business in order to avoid any conversation about Cal.

I spend the rest of my day doing work by answering emails, writing articles and content for our blog, and preparing for the first day of the conference by ironing my clothes and hanging them up, along with picking out my jewelry and shoes. I set my alarm on my phone to make sure I am up early tomorrow to not be rushed, and have plenty of time in the morning to get myself ready both mentally and physically. Feeling good with all the tasks I completed, I decide to get a workout in and head down to the hotel gym. It's packed with good looking women and muscular, handsome men. I hop on the elliptical machine, stick my headphones in my ear, and ignore everyone for an hour. Once that hour was up, it's time to head upstairs to my room to get ready for the evening. I get in the shower and scrub my body well, making sure I smell good in all the right places. Once done, I wrap my hair and body in towels and start to pick out my attire for the evening. With Cal mentioning dinner and a show, I decide upon a royal blue wrap dress whose fabric clings so tightly to my body that I question whether I can even wear undergarments. I try the dress on and the doubt that I had earlier reappears. It isn't that I am unhappy with how I look, but I start to question why I am putting in so much effort to make sure I look sexy enough for a man I just met to want to sleep with me? And why do I feel guilty for wanting to sleep with him already? Then the realization hits me. It is because even after my first make out session with my ex-husband, I wouldn't sleep with him right away. But yet, here I am, ready to sleep with Cal. I thought our sexual chemistry was the best I had, but there is no comparison as to the feelings I am experiencing with Cal. I worked and was friends with my ex, so of course I wanted our relationship to be more than just sex, as there was more to lose. With Cal, I never expect to hear or see from him again. I have never known that feeling of addiction, but the only drug I am addicted to right now is Cal Harrington's mouth. He has awakened feelings that have been buried since my ex walked out the door. I need to feel again and if having sex with Cal evokes those feelings, then I'm ready and willing. With this acceptance, I squash any residual guilt and continue to get ready.

Thirty minutes later, I leave and make my way to Cal's. Pulling out the key he gave me, I let myself into the VIP door and walk through the Atrium to his villa. I hesitate before using the key on his door, not knowing if I should knock or not. I decide to knock first and then let myself in. I faintly hear music playing, so I follow the tune into the movie room only to find it empty, credits rolling on the screen from the movie that was just playing. I go back to the living room and look out the window at the pool. Not finding Cal outside, I turn to head to the master bedroom and jump at the site of him standing in the hallway, watching me.

"That's the second time you've done that to me!" I exclaim, my heart racing from the scare. It continues to beat faster at the site of Cal, wet from a shower and only wrapped in a towel. He stalks toward me, his eyes raking over me from head to toe. My breath catches as my eyes roam from his chest that has a small amount of hair on it, down his defined six pack, to the v's at his side that disappear under his towel. I watch a single drop of water slide down his stomach into the towel and I gulp, wishing I could have licked that off of him. I look back up at his face, hypnotized by the desire in his eyes.

"This dress," he admires, and places his index finger on my sternum and caresses down towards the skin between my breasts.

"You're all wet," I choke out, his finger sending mini shock waves with each touch.

"And you will be too later." He traces his finger back up my chest, lifts my chin with it and sears me with a kiss. He pulls away, gives me a wicked smile and turns to walk away. "I will be right back. Make yourself at home." I just stand there and blink while I watch his muscular back retreat to his bedroom to get dressed. I shake my head, not knowing how I am going to survive dinner if he keeps looking at me that way. I decide a drink is in order to help calm my nerves. I pour myself a vodka tonic with a lime and settle on the couch, playing on my phone while I wait. He doesn't keep me waiting long as he appears five minutes later, looking gorgeous in a long sleeve royal blue shirt, black dress pants with black shoes.

"Let's be cheesy and wear matching outfits!" He claps his hand together, like it's a grand scheme in a master plan. I laugh at him, thoroughly enjoying seeing his goofy side. He goes to the bar, pours himself a scotch on the rocks, and sits down on the couch with me. "Do you believe in magic, Jenna? Because that it what we are toasting to tonight." He clinks his glass to mine and takes a sip.

"Magic?" I raise my eyebrows at him in question.

"We are going to have a magical dinner, then go see the greatest illusionist in the world. And after that, we are going to make some magic of our own," the corniness of his joke makes me shake my head with laughter. He checks his watch and puts down his drink. "We must get going if we are going to eat before the show." He stands up and holds his hand out to me. I accept it and he immediately pulls me up into his chest and claims my lips. His lips demand I open for him, which I obey immediately and become completely lost in the kiss. I grip the back of his shirt tighter, trying to get as close as I can for more. He slowly pulls his lips away, but keeps his forehead touching mine, his eyes closed as he tries to gain his composure back. I can't help but stare at him and watch his process as I stand there, panting, not looking composed whatsoever.

"Let's go!" he smiles, and with that, we head to dinner.

9

True to his word, dinner is pretty magical. Cal made reservations at the steakhouse in the hotel. We are escorted to a table well hidden in the back of the restaurant, which makes me feel more at ease, my uncomfortableness coming from all the eyes who are staring at us when we arrive. We are seated and immediately order drinks and food. As we go through the details of our day, I do not lose sight of the fact that our worlds are so completely different.

"Do you get nervous with your job?" I ask after he describes how his table read went with the new actor. I don't think I could handle the pressure of being an actress. Always being watched, always being scrutinized, always having to look a certain way. How can that not mess with your psyche?

"When I first started out, auditioning was pretty daunting. Now I would say that the sex scenes make me nervous," he laughs at my surprised expression. "The actual sex scene is so far removed from being intimate due to the amount of people that are around watching you. You are being told how to pretend to have sex. Then you worry about if your breath smells, if you are covered in the right places, if you are being respectful to the actress or even if you are looking like you have sexual chemistry with this person. There is nothing natural about it at all."

"How do you not get turned on by the kissing and um, dry humping?" I blush a little at the visual of how I might have looked trying to dry hump Cal this morning.

"Absolutely we get turned on!" He leans in and puts his forearms on the table "While the scenes make me nervous, I would be completely lying if I didn't say they weren't fun. So many actors complain about how horrible those scenes are - that is complete bullshit. They say that so they don't get in trouble with their partners. If they truly wanted to be respectful to their partners, they would do movies without sex scenes or ask for script changes for the scene to be just kissing with the scene fading out, alluding that they are going to have sex." His honesty is refreshing as I would never have thought that the actor could even ask for the scene to be re-written.

"Are you nervous for tomorrow?" He changes the subject as our waiter brings our food.

"A little," I pause. "Normally I get more nervous the day of. I'm confident with the content of my speech, it's just making sure my delivery is effective and meaningful."

"I'm sure you are going to be brilliant. Maybe I'll come and watch you," he smiles, as he chews his food.

"Perfect idea as I wouldn't be nervous knowing all eyes will be on you instead of me." I cannot even imagine the chaos he would cause amongst the hundreds of women who will be there. "Seriously, you would be a huge distraction, so it's probably best if you don't show up."

"I don't even know if I can, anyway. I have an appointment with wardrobe and I'm not sure what time that is yet." He takes out his phone and starts to text. "Honestly, though, I really would like to see you speak."

"Usually the conference records the keynote speakers. Maybe I can get a copy of it, if you really want to see it, but don't expect me to watch it with you." I shake my head at the thought, knowing I would be truly embarrassed at watching myself, especially with Cal.

"I don't like watching myself either. I made the mistake of doing it once and will never do it again." He finishes his text and puts his phone away.

"You mean to tell me you don't watch your own TV shows or movies?" I ask skeptically, not really believing what I'm hearing. How can actors not watch their own work to see where they need improvement?

He shakes his head. "No, I don't. This is how I see it - I work hard on my craft, I take care of my body, I show up early on set, I make sure I know all of my lines. I don't waste people's time. I am respectful to everyone who deserves my respect. I know I'm good looking, but I take pride in my work ethic and it shows. And that's why I'm being offered parts. There's no need to watch my work if I know at the end of the day, I've given it my all." His confidence is such a turn on that I have to cross my legs to help squash the pulsing in between them.

We finish our dinner and get up to leave to go to the show. Cal grabs my hand and leads the way out of the restaurant. We get stopped twice on our way to the show for autographs and photos, which I volunteer to take for his fans. The women freak out and give me dirty looks while the men act less extreme. Despite some of the outrageous things they say to him, he is genuine with each and every person, always thanking them for their support.

We make it to the show right as the lights dim and are escorted to a private table off to the side, away from the other tables. I have been entertained by illusionists before, but I do think it is a little ridiculous when they try to convince people that they can make the Statue of Liberty disappear. The illusionist starts to create a story, and soon we get sucked into his world of magic for an hour and a half. We give him a standing ovation at the conclusion of the show and wait until everyone else leaves before we make our departure.

"What did you think of the show?" Cal asks as we walk toward the exit.

"I thought it was actually really good. I liked the storytelling aspect of it."

"I agree. The show flowed very well with no slow points. Is there anywhere else you want to go?" Cal stops and looks at me.

"I think I'm ready for bed," I say, stifling a yawn. I have to be up very early and don't want to go to bed too late, especially if Cal plans to join me. I just need to be honest with myself - I am beyond turned on by this man, and I am ready to continue where we left off this morning.

"Well then, let's get you tucked in," he says wickedly, grabbing my hand and leading us to his place. We briskly walk through the casino to the VIP door, no words needing to be spoken as the anticipation of tonight making my heart race. We say good evening to the security guard while we go through to the hallway to the atrium. We continue walking down the corridor that leads to his door, the only sound being my heels clicking against the floor. We arrive at his door where he pulls out his key card and lets us in. All the lights are turned on and soft music is playing. I send Cal a quizzical look and he just shrugs his shoulders. "Steven must still be here." As if on cue, Steven enters the hallway.

"Good evening, Mr. Harrington, Ms. Pruitt. I hope your evening is going well so far. Would you like me to order any food or make you a drink?" he asks, looking between Cal and me.

"I would like a vodka tonic with a lime, please." I ask for a drink to help calm my unexpected nervousness about tonight.

"I can make Jenna's drink from the bar, Steven. Why don't you go home as we are all set for the evening?" Cal gives him a tip, shakes his hand and escorts him to the door. He locks the door behind Steven, turns around and stares at me. "Do you really need that drink?" he asks, as his smoldering eyes bore into me.

I shake my head no as he slowly walks toward me, like a lion about to pounce on his prey. There is no turning back on tonight, and I suddenly feel confident with my decision. He stands in front of me, and places his hands on each side of my face, tilting my head up toward him. My gaze drops down to those inviting lips. I briefly look back up at him as he descends upon me, his kiss soft and hesitant. He pulls back to look into my eyes, his nose briefly touching mine before he goes in for another kiss. With parted lips, he starts to tease my upper lip first, catching it when he closes his mouth. He repeats this pattern with my bottom lip, sending tingling sensations down my body. I dart my tongue through his parted lips and he moans softly, meeting my tongue with his own. As we deepen the kiss, he wraps one arm around my torso, his other arm wrapped around my ass, and crushes me to him. I cling to him as he demands I keep up with the lashing his tongue is giving me. We slowly break apart to catch our breaths and he lifts me up, my legs immediately wrapping around him as he carries me into the bedroom.

The room is dark with only the dim lights from his private pool reflecting in. He kicks the door shut as I continue to kiss along his neck, making a brief appearance at his lips as I make my way to the other side of his neck. He stops right before the bed and I slowly slide off him, enjoying the feel of his hard erection against me. I start to unbutton his shirt, taking my time to reveal his hard chest. Once I reach the bottom of his shirt, I place my hands underneath it and caress my way upward, his muscles rippling underneath my touch. I grasp the edges of each side, spread his shirt wide, and take it down over his sculpted arms until it is a laying on the floor. Fascinated by the sight of him, I start a path of kisses on his sternum and make my way to his right nipple. He hisses and tugs my hair with his hands as I graze his nipple with my teeth and suck on it. I alternate between licking and sucking, his noises all the encouragement I need to continue. I eventually kiss my way up and down his six-pack and give his left nipple the attention it deserves. He places his hands in my hair, holding my head as close as it can to his nipple. When I start to suck on it, he moves his hands to my waist to try to untie the knot of my wrap dress.

"Take this damn thing off," he growls out his frustration after numerous unsuccessful attempts at untying the knot. I leave his nipple and stare intently into his eyes as I untie the knot, unwrap the dress from my body and throw it to the floor. His mouth parts slightly as his eyes roam down my black satin bra, black thong with a matching black garter belt hooked to black stockings.

"You are so beautiful." He places his hands on top of my shoulders and rubs down, bringing the straps of my bra with him. I shiver from the touch of his warm hands as he leans down, and starts to leave a trail of hot kisses down my neck to my collarbone. I move my head to the side so he can get better access as I grab blindly for his belt buckle. I manage to unbuckle his belt, unhook his pants and slide them off his hips. I slip my hands into his boxers, wrap my hands around his cock, and squeeze slightly. He groans against my neck as I stroke my hands up and down his length. He is round and thick and for a moment, I realize that sex with Cal might hurt if he is really as big as he feels. My thoughts dissipate as his hot, wet mouth latches onto my nipple, making me gasp. His tongue assaults it, sending sparks straight down to my core. I remove my hands from his cock, grab a hold of his head and bring him closer as I arch my back and moan in pleasure. He wraps his arms around me, lifts me onto the bed and lays down on top of me, his mouth continuing its deadly attack. I wrap my legs around him and start to rub up against him, the friction against him making the need for him to be inside me stronger. His hands caress my stomach until they reach the top of the garter belt, where his fingers slip underneath into my panties.

"You are so wet," he whispers, as he makes his way to my other nipple while his fingers continue to rub up and down against me. I can't help but grind against his hand, squeezing it with my thighs to try to bring his fingers deeper inside me. My moans becoming louder as my desire for him only intensifies.

"Cal," I rasp, as he kisses down my stomach, grabs the top of my garter belt and thong, and slides it down my legs. He kisses up my thighs while he pulls my shoes off and takes the stockings off. Once I am free, he spreads my legs, blows on my clit as a small warning before he flicks his tongue against it. I moan louder and tangle my hands in his hair, positioning him so his tongue can go deeper. There is no way I will last long, my body already starting to spasm from the shock waves his tongue is creating.

"Please Cal," I beg. "Please….I need you inside me." I must have him inside me now before I explode against his mouth. With one final suck, he lifts his body off of me and tells me to move to the headboard. I scoot backwards as he makes his way around the bed, opens the drawer to the nightstand and takes out a condom. I watch with hooded eyes as he removes the condom from the wrapper, pinches the top and wraps it slowly over his glistening tip, down his magnificent shaft. My eyes make their way up his body to his face to find him watching me. We stare at each other as he gets back on the bed, sits on his knees and brings me closer by moving my ass up on top of his thighs. With my legs spread apart, he grabs his cock and positions it as he rubs his tip up and down my bud, and then down to my opening. I shake my head from side to side and dig my nails in his forearms, not knowing how much more I can take the teasing of having him so close to being inside of me.

"Cal," I pant, "please…" With that last plea, he slowly enters me, inching his way deeper. Despite my wetness, my body tenses at the shock from having someone so big inside me.

"Fuck, you are so tight." He clenches his teeth while slowly pulling back out. "Are you okay?" he whispers, as I wince from the pain that has now replaced the pleasure.

"For some reason, it hurts. I don't know if it's because it's been a long time or the position we're in." I am glad it's somewhat dark in here so he can't see the flush of embarrassment that's crept up my face from revealing that it's been a long time since I've had sex.

He moves over me, keeping the majority of his weight on his elbows as he slips his hands underneath my head and kisses me. I soon become engulfed with desire again as his kisses attack my senses, and I can't keep my body from moving against his. He suddenly thrusts back into me and I gasp loudly, this time at the unexpected pleasure. He starts to move in and out, and my hands immediately grab his ass to help move against him, the up and down motion creating a delicious friction against me. My body starts to vibrate from the buildup that is happening inside me. He thrusts faster, his moans becoming louder and more frequent. My hands grip him tighter, bringing his pelvis closer against me. Feeling as if I am about to come, I scream out my orgasm, clinging to every last thrust as he soon screams out his own release. It feels like my body leapt off a cliff and I am a light as a feather, slowly floating back down to the ground. When I come back to myself, I wrap my arms around him, relishing in the deliciousness of him still being inside of me. He lifts his head up and gives me a slow, sensual kiss that starts the tingle back up in my toes.

"You are amazing," he says, as he stares into my eyes. I immediately feel overwhelmed with unwanted emotion, so I remain silent and just smile at him. He leans down to kiss me again and while doing so, slowly pulls out of me. I groan at the loss against his mouth, not liking the feeling of emptiness. As I watch him get up to go to the restroom, I quickly come to the realization that he has completely ruined me for sex with any other man.

10

The sound of bells wakes me up from the deep slumber I was in. I pick up my phone from the nightstand and turn off the alarm. Six o'clock, unfortunately, came way too soon. With Cal taking me two more times, we barely got any sleep. I try to stand up, but immediately have to sit back down again, my legs wobbly from the overexertion.

"What was that dreadful noise?" I look over my shoulder to see Cal laying on his stomach, his handsome face turned toward me with his eyes still close.

"Sorry, my alarm clock. I have to go get ready." I sigh and push my hair behind my ears.

"You didn't bring your stuff here, did you?" he asks with his eyes still closed.

"No, I didn't. Go back to sleep. I'm sorry I woke you." I kiss him on the check and rise off the bed.

He rolls over onto his back and finally opens his eyes. "I am sorry I don't have breakfast ready for you this morning, as I didn't realize what time you would need to leave. Do you want me to order you a car?"

"No, I can walk. Thank you for the offer." I am about to walk away from the bed when he suddenly lunges for my wrists and pulls me back onto the bed. He pushes me down, leans over, and pins me to the bed with both of my wrists in his hands.

"I really do not like you walking by yourself in the hotel in that hot dress of yours. I will get you a car," he demands, his blue eyes and hard body making it hard for me to concentrate.

"Are you forgetting that I still would have to walk from the front entrance through the lobby and casino to get to my room?" I tease.

He narrows his eyes at me, knowing I am right. "I still don't like it. What about an escort?" I shake my head no. "Maybe I will just have you followed without your knowledge."

My mouth drops open at his shit-eating grin.

"Listen, I know you need to go, but I have zero doubts that you're going to be brilliant today. Good luck, and we'll celebrate you tonight." He kisses me hard before releasing me.

I lay there for a few seconds, trying to blink back my sanity and calm my pulse that he sets a flutter. Feeling more myself, I get off the bed and head toward the door. "Have fun trying on clothes today." I smirk at him, secretly wishing I could watch him as I KNOW what a sight that would be. The man would look good in a potato sack.

As I make my way out of the Atrium toward the main hotel, I do look over my shoulder to see if I'm being followed per Cal's threat. Shaking my head at myself when I don't see anyone, I continue on my way, learning that 6:30 a.m. is a great time to walk back to your room as barely anyone is in the casino and the lobby is a ghost town. Not worrying that anyone is noticing my disheveled clothing, I smile as memories from last night start to occupy my mind. I order room service for breakfast when I arrive at my room. Once the call has been placed, I undress and get in the shower. The scalding water awakens my senses, and I wince in delicious pleasure as I rub the wash cloth over my sore nipples, down my stomach and over the sensitive areas between my legs.

Cal wanting to see me again tonight only boosts my self-confidence and I do a little congratulatory dance for finally having sex since my divorce. I finish my shower, get into the big, fluffy white robe that the hotel provides, and wrap my hair in a towel. I grab my phone to check the time only to see I have a missed call from Robert. I quickly check my email to see if there were any outstanding emails before calling him back.

"Sorry I missed your call, I was in the shower," I say when he picks up.

"Did you have company?" he asks while I hear him typing on his keyboard.

"Just me, myself and I," I confirm, as I put him on speaker phone so I can apply lotion to my face and body.

"Yuck, that is a visual I do not want to have. Anyhoo, how are we feeling about today?"

I stick my tongue out at the phone before answering. "Feeling great, ready to get the morning over with." We go over the rest of my schedule for the conference and for the following week before ending the call.

"That's all I have on the agenda this morning to talk about. Good luck today, go woman power, and I hate you for not taking me with you as I know today is going to be epic."

"Love you too, Robert. I'll call you later." I hang up the phone just as a knock sounds on my door, indicating room service has arrived. My stomach starts to rumble as my nose gets a whiff of the delicious scents coming from the cart being wheeled in. I sign off on the check, shut the door after the delivery man, and start to read the newspaper that got delivered while I eat.

One hour later, I am fully dressed, with hair and make-up done. I place my laptop in my bag, grab my phone and key card, and leave my room to go to the conference center to check out the layout of the room, and to test the audio-visual equipment for my speech. I am grateful that the walk to the conference center is less than ten minutes, since I am wearing six inch black peep toe

Christian Louboutin heels. I know by the end of the speech, my feet will be on fire, but I'm well aware how short I am without the heels, plus they make me feel more confident wearing them. I need all the confidence I can get, as this will be the largest crowd I've ever spoken in front of.

One of the organizers greets me at the front of the ballroom and shows me where they prefer I enter and exit. I hand over my USB drive that contains my entrance music, my speech and power point presentation to the audio visual director. We go through everything, making sure all equipment is working and ready to go. With rehearsal done, I'm escorted to one of the waiting rooms. Since I'm there before the doors open, I take advantage of the silence, and go through the copy of my speech one last time. I start to hear murmurs of voices in the hallway that soon escalates to hundreds of voices waiting to get into the ballroom. Fifteen minutes later, an assistant comes to escort me. I walk with her to the side doors of the ballroom, over four hundred people inside waiting for me to inspire and motivate them with new practices that they can use in their businesses. As I hear the MC say my name and my music cues, I take a deep breath, say a little prayer, and smile as the doors open for me to enter, all eyes watching me with anticipation.

"You were amazing," one of the organizers whispers in my ear as the doors behind me shut to block out the thundering applause and the standing ovation I so graciously received. I nailed my speech, letting my emotions of my journey flow, showing them my appreciation and sincerity that I wouldn't be here without them. I then dove right into analytics of my business, and how they can apply some of my general methods to their own. It was by far one of my most successful speeches, and as I look around at the strangers congratulating me, I get a little whimsical of the fact that I'm here all by myself. *Maybe I should have brought Robert.* A doubt I can never reveal to him. I take a little comfort in knowing that I'll have Cal to celebrate with tonight. I look at the photos on my phone that the assistant took for me while I made my speech and text them to Robert for him to post on our social media pages.

"How did it go?" he immediately calls as soon as he received the texts.

"I fucking rocked it!" I scream, thankful that no one else was in the waiting room at that moment. "Robert, it was truly amazing. They were up dancing at the music you picked out, nodding their heads in agreement with things I was teaching them, lots of them were even taking notes. Most of them even laughed at my jokes!"

"Now that in itself is amazing since you aren't even that funny!" he laughs. "Seriously, I am so proud of you and can't wait to watch the replay!"

"I have to go, I only get an hour break and I have got to get out of these shoes. I'll call you later." I hang up with Robert and grab my bag. I normally would have brought a pair of flip flops to wear between sessions, but with so many people around, I didn't feel that would be professional. I quickly make my way to my room, mentally reminding myself to grab a protein bar just in case I am not a fan of the food they are providing for lunch. I open the door, go to the bedroom, and open the closet doors to find it completely empty. *Where is all of my stuff?* I start to panic, and pull open the dresser drawers to find those empty as well. I go back into the living room, and look around in complete disbelief that my things are gone. *How can this happen in such a reputable hotel?* I pick up the phone to report my items stolen, when it suddenly dawns on me that Cal might have had something to do with this and had my belongings taken to his villa. Hoping this is the case, but still mad as hell at the idea of him not talking to me about it, I hang up the phone and leave as fast as my heels will let me.

I storm towards his place and let myself in once I arrival. I hear noises coming from the media room and I stop in the doorway to see Cal playing a video game.

"Did you move my belongings out of my room?" My voice is surprisingly calm.

"Hey, you're back early! How'd it go?" he pays attention to his video game while asking me.

"Cal, answer my question! Did you move my stuff out of my room?"

My tone of voice catches his attention and he pauses the game to look at me.

"Yes, I did. Everything is in the master bedroom. What's wrong?"

I ignore his question and run toward the bedroom. Sure enough, my clothes are hanging in the walk-in closet, my undergarments and pajamas in the drawers, toiletries in the bathroom with my jewelry case. I open the case to make sure all of my jewelry is accounted for and sigh with relief to see that it is. I walk back into the bedroom, where Cal is leaning against the door frame with his arms crossed.

"What's the problem, Jenna?" he raises his eyebrow at me.

"The problem is that you didn't ASK me if I was okay with complete strangers having their hands on my personal items. Which I'm not! Strange people touching my jewelry, my underwear." I shudder at the thought of dirty, grimy hands on all of my belongings.

"First off, they were wearing gloves when packing your items and secondly, we talked about moving your stuff here and since you have been busy, I thought it would be helpful to have it done for you. I never intended to upset you, but I told you I didn't like you walking through the hotel by yourself, going back and forth between my place and yours. This was an easier solution."

"I think this solution was easier for YOU so I can be at your beck and call whenever you want to fuck," I angrily say without thinking clearly.

He moves off the door frame swiftly and with two long strides, is in front of me, gripping my biceps roughly. "Don't do that. Don't degrade yourself or what we have been doing. We are two consensual adults enjoying each other's company. Am I wrong?" He intently stares into my eyes, daring me to argue back.

Of course he is right, which irritates me even more. I shake off his arms and turn my back to him to look at the pool. The issues have nothing to do with him, but my guilt for sleeping with someone I just met, and loosing that feeling of control. I haven't had anyone take care of me since my ex-husband and I have a love/hate relationship with it. Love it because there is nothing sexier when a man can take control without direction and take care of his woman. Hate it because when my husband stopped taking care of me, it left me feeling completely worthless, and I never want to feel that way again. These are my issues, not Cal's, and my reaction was unfair to his good intentions. I count to ten, take a deep breath and turn back to look at him.

"Can we start over, please?" I ask.

He gives me a questionable look and nods.

"Cal, did you move my clothes from my room without asking me?"

"Yes," he answers with narrowed eyes, wondering if this is a trick question.

"Thank you so much for thinking of my well-being and organizing the move. If there is any instance of something similar to this happening again within the next couple of days, please feel free to ask me what I think first." I move toward him, get on my tippy toes, and kiss his cheek.

"Is that it?" he asks skeptically, not believing that I am going to drop the conversation.

"That's it, unless you feel we need to talk about it more."

"The only thing I think we need to talk about is how fucking hot you look when you get angry." His eyes rake over me and stop to appreciate my legs in this short dress. "I need those legs with your heels still on wrapped around me, NOW!" He lifts me up, and I have no choice but to obey his command. He kisses me hard and plunges his tongue into my mouth. I kiss back with equal demand, our emotions from our argument pouring into our kisses.

"Wait," I eventually break our kiss as he settles me onto the bed. "I don't know if I have time for this. I am supposed to be on a panel session in ten minutes." The travel time between rooms ate up most of my lunch break.

"We will be done in five minutes." He takes off my thong and drops it to the floor. He unbuttons his jeans and releases his massive erection. My mouth goes dry, and my hunger for food dissipates as all I want right now is him inside of me. He slips on the condom, moves my hips closer to the edge of the bed, and plunges into me. I gasp at the slight pain of not being wet enough to accommodate him. He slowly starts moving in and out while fingering me. The combination of his rough hands on me with the slow thrusting builds my desire.

"Harder," I pant, as I place my hands on his ass to bring him deeper. He removes his fingers from me and places both hands on my hips, bringing me back and forth against his cock. I replace his fingers with my own and continue to rub, my fingers matching the faster pace of his thrusts. I watch him watch our bodies come together, and I completely come undone at the sight of him throwing his head back and yelling out his release. He collapses on top of me, and I wrap my arms around him, not carrying that he is crushing my dress. When our heartbeats start to slow down to their normal pace, he lifts himself up to his forearms and moves my hair off my face.

"If this is what make-up sex with you is going to feel like, then we are going to argue all the time." I giggle at him, not knowing what we would even argue about after this. He pulls out of me, gets up, and brings his pants up to his hips.

"See, five minutes." He points at his watch and winks down at me. He grabs my hand to help me get up and hands me my thong. I make my way to the bathroom to freshen up, choosing to ignore the wrinkled state of my dress since I don't have the time to iron. I give him a quick kiss goodbye, grab my purse and a protein bar to eat on the way, and run back to the conference center.

11

Five hours later, and I am finally done with day one of the conference. I come back to Cal's place only to find it empty, a note left on the bed saying he got called in for wardrobe. I sit down, take my shoes off, and lay back against the bed. As I stare at the ceiling, I remember that I am supposed to call Robert back. With a groan, I sit up, take my phone out of my purse, dial his number, and lay right back down.

He picks up, but all I hear is music and loud voices.

"Helloooo…?"

"JEN-NA!!" I pull the phone away from my ear as Layla and Robert scream into it over the background noise.

"What are you guys doing?" I ask before I yawn.

"It's Malley night! We're hanging with the hottest bartender in Chicago, drinking whiskey, and eating artery clogging food." Malley is our nickname for O'Malley's, our favorite neighborhood Irish bar that we congregate at every Wednesday to hang out and catch up. "What are YOU doing?" Robert asks.

"I just got back from the conference. I'm exhausted!" A nap might be in my future as I can barely keep my eyes open.

"Hanging with mysterious, new men can be exhausting," Robert smartly says.

"What mysterious new man?" I hear Layla ask in the background.

"Did you ever think I might be exhausted because I was up early preparing for one of the biggest crowds I've ever spoken in front of and had to be on my A game all day long?" I leave out the part of all the sex I have had.

"Ooooh, you haven't told Layla yet?" Robert laughs and Layla immediately takes the phone away from him.

"What's he talking about, Jenna? I'm about to get REAL jealous if Robert knows something that I don't." I hear Robert's evil laughter in the background.

"Sorry, Layla, I've been pre-occupied and he's making a big deal out of nothing," I reassure her.

"Preoccupied with what? The conference?"

"She's been preoccupied with cock!" Robert yells in the background.

"Have you really? Why haven't you sent us any dick pics? I'm so disappointed in you." Layla slurs.

"When have I ever participated in sending dick pics? NEVER! That is yours and Robert's pastime." It's shocking to me how many times a day these two send pictures of men's penises back and forth between each other. That's just not my thing to do.

I hear lots of rowdy laughter and shake my head. "You guys are trashed."

"We don't have Mother Goose Pruitt here to reign us in. Seriously, am I going to meet him this weekend?"

"Possibly..." Cal and I haven't really discussed what is going to happen once our friends arrive, so I don't want to promise her anything.

"Ha, Robert, I get to meet him and you don't!"

"That's just fucked up. Layla, get both of them drunk, and

when Jenna passes out, YOU take the dick pic and send it to me!" They both laugh hysterically at the naughty idea.

"Alright children, I am getting off the phone. I love you both and will talk with you tomorrow. Please be safe and don't get any STDs tonight." I smile as I hang up on their laughter. I'm forever thankful for the close friendship that formed between the two of them. I don't think they realize that while they were picking up the pieces of my shattered heart, they also were in need of each other.

I plug my charger into my phone and set my alarm for tomorrow morning. I open my laptop to catch up on my emails, but soon the words start to blur and I fall asleep.

"Wake up, Sleeping Beauty."

I moan at the sound of his husky voice and reach for him, my arms wrapping around his strong torso. I inhale his shirt and smile at his intoxicating scent. I open my eyes and look up at him. His eyes look like dark sapphires in the dimly lit room. I suddenly realize how much I have missed the small moments of intimacy shared between two people. I squeeze him tighter, trying to ignore the sadness that invades me as I realize the temporariness of the situation.

"What time is it?" I ask, wanting to distract myself from my current thoughts.

"Almost 9 p.m." He kisses me on the forehead and hugs me tighter.

"What? I can't believe I have been asleep for that long!" I give him an incredulous look, almost not believing that it's that late.

"You had a big day today and not a lot of sleep last night. I think we should order in, play a game of pool, and continue the exploration of our bodies in every room here." He pulls back the covers, grabs my leg and wraps it around his hip so I can feel his growing erection.

"Hmm, that sounds heavenly." I bring his head down to kiss his lips as I am delighted that he does not want to go out tonight.

"I will go get the menu. Be right back." He leaves the room and I decide to get up to use the restroom to freshen up. After I finish, I walk back into the bedroom to find him sitting on the edge of the bed with a menu. He motions for me to sit on his lap, and we review the menu together. With our decision made on salad and pizza, he picks up the phone to call room service. While on the phone, he starts to unzip the back of my dress that I fell asleep in. I give him a mischievous smile over my shoulder as he kisses my back in between placing our order. He hangs up and rubs his hands over my back and shoulders, proceeding to give me a massage. I can't help containing the moans of pleasure as he works on the knots in between my shoulder blades.

"It'll take about forty-five minutes until our food arrives. It's time to shower." He gently lifts me off his lap and takes me into the bathroom. He sets me down, turns on the water, and starts to undress me. I lift his shirt off above his head, and my hands are drawn to his rock hard abs. I move my hands over them and up to his nipples, which I rub with my thumb pads. As soon as we are both naked, he grabs hold of my hands and leads me into the shower. The shower is very large, with multiple shower heads and a bench. I sigh contently as the hot water covers my body and relaxes me. Cal grabs a wash cloth, pours body gel into it, and kneels in front of me. He starts with my left foot, lathering his way up my shin, going around to my calf, making his way up my knee and thigh. I place my hands on his shoulders to steady myself, his touch making me weak. He reaches behind my thigh and washes up over my backside, gently cleaning between my butt cheeks. Needing more of his touch, I bring his head towards my breast where he takes my nipple in his mouth. I cry out in pleasure as he sucks hard, his hands still busy washing over me and heading towards my right leg. He washes down my leg as his mouth continues to wreak havoc on my nipple. When he finishes with my leg, his mouth makes his way to my other nipple, while he washes the breast he just devoured. After he is done, he washes down my stomach and makes his way between my legs. As he gently washes my most sensitive area, I whimper out his name, my senses on complete overload from his hands and mouth. He gets back on his feet and starts to trail kisses up my body, his hand replacing the wash cloth and rubbing back and forth over my clit. He slowly stands up, his lips finally making it up to mine, and I throw my arms around his neck, crushing him to me. He plunges his tongue inside my mouth and my insides turn to liquid lava. I can't get enough of him, each thrust of his tongue making me hotter.

"Sit on the bench," he commands and as soon as I do, he kneels down, grabs my hips and brings them to the edge. He lifts one of my legs up over his shoulder and heads toward my core. His mouth continues where his hands left off, and I am withering in desire. My hands look for something to hold as my body begins to shake with anticipation. Not being able to take any more of his tongue's attack on my clit, I arch my back against his mouth and scream out my release. I have to physically force his head away from me in order to catch my breath and calm down, my sex too sensitive for his continuous touch.

"I want more of you," he says seductively, kissing the inside of my thigh, up my rib cage and back to my mouth. I halt our kissing to find the washcloth and pour more body gel on it. I lather it up and look him in the eyes.

"It's my turn now." I give him a flirtatious smile and continue kissing him as I start to wash his back. I move the washcloth over his right shoulder, down and back up his arm. I move it in between our bodies to wash his chest, switching the cloth to my other hand as I wash his left shoulder and arm. We continue to kiss, and then his mouth moves across to my ears and down my neck. I bring the washcloth back to his chest, where I wash over his nipples and with my free hand, lightly pinch the other one I am not washing. He nips at my neck and groans. I alternate sides and then trail my hands down to his erection where I wrap the washcloth around it and squeeze. He groans and thrusts against my hands. I move the cloth over his balls and cup gently.

"Stand up," I insist and when he obeys, I drop the wash cloth, grab his cock with both hands and look up at him as I take him in my mouth. He tangles his hands in my hair as I take him deeper. I slowly lick up his shaft, twirling my tongue around his tip, and start to suck. When I taste his pre-cum, I move him in and out of my mouth faster.

"Fuck Jenna," he hisses, as his hips start to thrust faster. I look up at him to see his head thrown back, mouth open as he is on the verge of climax. I rub his shaft faster while licking and sucking harder, enjoying the power of knowing I am making him feel this way.

"I am going to come," he warns, and I take him as far as I can to the back of my throat. When his body starts jerking with his release, I grab his ass and squeeze while sucking and swallowing as he finishes in my mouth. As soon as he is done, I release him and he leans against the shower wall to catch his breath. I stand up, grab the shampoo, and start washing my hair. I rinse my hair and when I open my eyes, Cal is watching me, his eyes raking over my body, and I see he is getting hard again. I squirt some shampoo in my hands and lather his head with soap.

"We probably should finish up and get out, as the food should be here soon," I say, kissing him one more time before I put conditioner in my hair. We finish washing ourselves and get out of the shower to get dressed. He throws on a white t-shirt and some pajama pants and looks just as sexy in those as he does a suit. I rummage through my pajamas and realize that while I bought new sexy undergarments, I did nothing to improve my pajamas.

Hearing a knock on our door, I settle on a tank top and pajama pants. I get dressed and join Cal in the dining room for dinner.

"You're really bad at this game," I tease, two hours later as we play air hockey, and I am winning, 6-0. After we stuffed our faces with pizza and beer, we attempted to play a round of pool, but the game ended quicker than expected with Cal taking me from behind as he claims watching me bend over with a pool stick was too much of a distraction for him. You would think we would be tired, but sex has only fueled our endorphins, so I challenged him to a game of air hockey. I scored six goals quickly as he seems distracted again.

"Do you miss your ex-husband?" he casually asks. So shocked am I by his question, I let my defense down and he scores his first goal. "Looks like it will not be a shut out for you now."

"Did you intentionally ask that question to try to score?" I narrow my eyes at him.

"Actually, no, but I am glad it worked."

"Why would you ask me that?"

"I am just trying to understand how someone like you is still available," he says with a shrug.

"What do you mean, someone like me?" I ask defensively, not really knowing if I want to continue on with this conversation.

"A beautiful, sexy, independent woman who is intelligent, self-sufficient, caring and witty."

"You have only known me for four days. This might all be a facade," I joke.

"I doubt that."

"I have my idiosyncrasy. I can be cold and aloof sometimes. When you wrong me, I tend to not forgive so easily." I look down and play around with the mallet. "I am trying to work on myself though. To answer your original question if I miss my ex-husband, no, I actually don't. I don't miss being ignored, nor do I miss walking on eggshells. Only thing I miss is sharing my life with someone." I look back up at him with a sad smile. No one tells you how lonely divorce can be. You get used to sharing your life with someone, whether that life together is good or bad and when that ends, the silence is deafening. At first you don't feel it because you are angry and hurt, and you keep telling yourself that you made the right decision. When those emotions finally calm down, silence fills the void. I work as late as I can, trying to avoid feeling destitute.

He walks around to my side of the table, pulls me close, and forces me to look into his eyes by lifting up my chin. "Jenna, you were disappointed by someone you loved very much. It's understandable to be guarded. Just don't let it prevent you from ever finding happiness again." He kisses me softly on the lips. I close my eyes and relish the feel of having strong arms around me, making me feel protected.

"Let's go to bed." He takes my hand and leads me to the bedroom. Sex this time is more tender and loving. He holds me close in his arms afterwards and while he falls asleep, I can't help but hope I will one day soon feel this way again.

12

The next two days fly by, my mind occupied by business during the day, while my body is occupied by Cal at night. After today's closing ceremonies, I say goodbye to all the wonderful new contacts I made at the conference and go back to Cal's place, hoping to get a couple of hours with him before Layla arrives. I have no idea if we're going our separate ways tonight and if we are, I would like to be packed up and moved back into my old room before her arrival. Despite multiple sessions of sex into the early hours of this morning, he seemed to be distant at breakfast. I wasn't interested in asking, not really wanting to believe our time together is almost up. I knew this was only going to last for the week, and I have enjoyed every single minute of it. *Maybe it is better if it ends today.* Layla deserves my full attention anyway as we have not had a girl's weekend in a very long time.

I open the door and deep, masculine laughter greets me. With my curiosity peaked at the unfamiliar sound, I follow it to the media room. I look in to find Cal engaged in a game of pool with the infamous Sean Lindsay, international mega-star and known womanizer. Famous for his piercing green eyes and making women drop their panties with his wicked smile, he has found much success being the guy you fall in love with in rom-com movies.

"Well, who do we have here?" Sean sees me first and flashes me one of his famous smiles.

"Jenna, you're back. Come meet my best mate, Sean." As Cal comes towards me, I realize that despite Sean's good looks, he pales in comparison to Cal. Both men ooze sex appeal, but Cal is more primal. He kisses me hard on the lips, his mood much better than it was this morning. I shake myself out of the trance his kiss puts me in while he pulls me with him to meet Sean.

"Sean, this is Jenna, and before you get any ideas, do not flirt with her as she is off limits to you." Sean laughs and takes my hand into his stronghold.

"So very nice to meet you, Jenna. I can now see why it has been so hard to get him on the phone all this week as I, too, would ignore the whole world if you were gracing me with your presence." He leans in to kiss my hand, but Cal intercepts and removes my hand from Sean's grasp with a menacing look. I can't help but laugh watching the two of them.

"Since we usually aren't together during the hours of 9 a.m. - 5 p.m., he has no excuse to not call you back." I give Cal a teasing smile, busting him on his lack of calling his friend back. I can relate though as I, too, have been lax with calling Layla back.

"That's it - we must keep you. I need a partner in crime to call out Cal's bullshit."

"You are out of luck as she refuses to give me her phone number," Cal says with a pointed look in my direction.

"Technically, you haven't even asked for it," I remind him and that is the truth. While I am very hesitant to give it to him in order to keep things casual, he has not needed to have my number ,as our schedules have been in sync with each other this week.

"Wait, how do you get a hold of each then?" Sean asks, skepticism lacing his voice.

"Easy, he moved my belongings in here without my permission, so I had no choice but to come back," Sean throws his head back and laughs while Cal looks quite proud of himself. I am happy I can now laugh at this without getting mad at the memory of him not asking me.

"Yes, but you chose to keep your belongings here, which I am so happy you did." Cal wraps his arms around me and hugs me.

"Great, now I know I'll be sleeping with my noise cancellation headphones on." I blush at Sean's implication and decide to study my heels instead of looking at him.

"Even the best headsets won't muffle out the loudness of how hard I make her come." My mouth drops open in shock at Cal, and I hit him in the chest. They both laugh and he hugs me tighter. I bury my face in my hands, my mind reeling from embarrassment.

"I can't believe you just announced that!" I whine into his chest, which rumbles harder with laughter. "Is there nothing that you guys don't share with each other?"

"We haven't shared women yet, but that can be negotiated if you are up for it, Jenna?" Sean winks at me, and I immediately shake my head no. "That was just a test on your part. Cal would never share you and has never shared in the past." Relief spreads through me at this revelation. Some people might find that sexy, but it would make me uncomfortable knowing they'd shared a woman at the same time.

"What kind of mischief shall we get into tonight?" Sean wiggles his eyebrows up and down while looking between Cal and me for an answer.

"My best friend, Layla, arrives at 8 p.m. I'll meet her in the lobby and take her back to my old room. If you guys are wanting a night out to yourself, she and I can just go to dinner and do our own thing."

"You will absolutely NOT be going out without us," Cal demands. "I think ordering in and hanging out here sounds just fine, right Sean?"

"Um...well, we are in Vegas..." Sean rubs the back of his neck, looking slightly uneasy.

"We can go out tomorrow night. Let's have a good time here tonight. We have everything at our disposal here. Besides, we have to be up early for training."

"Why don't we wait to see what Layla wants to do before deciding?" I suggest, as I know she is going to want to go out.

"Sean and Layla can always go out. You and I are staying here." Cal gives me a heated look that makes my insides quiver. I would love nothing more than to stay here with him, but I also cannot ditch my best friend.

"Jenna, I think Cal is missing his balls and they might be in your hands." Sean laughs while Cal gives him a look of disgust.

"My balls are right where they need to be and are ready to resume kicking your ass in this game of pool. Jenna, you're in charge of making us some drinks, please." They head back towards the pool table and I head to the bar.

Two hours later, I am waiting for Layla in the lobby, slightly buzzed and trying to contain the ridiculous smile that won't stop forming on my face. I've never had so much fun watching two people play pool as I did with Cal and Sean. They reminisced with funny stories about their time together in boarding school, and laughed about some of the pranks they have pulled on set. Every time I heard Cal's deep, sexy laugh, my panties seemed to get wetter and wetter. He must have sensed how my body was reacting to him, because he wouldn't stop teasing me any chance he got. When Sean would be concentrating on making his pool shot, Cal would stare at me with hooded eyes, stroking the pool stick slowly up and down. If he needed to walk by me, he would caress my thigh. I was getting so turned on that I kept getting up to make more drinks for myself, downing them to try to keep my mind from not thinking of what he feels like inside me. I was getting so uncomfortable, that before I left to get Layla, I had to change my underwear and pants. When I came out with my new outfit, his eyes lit up, and that damn mouth of his gave me a slow, devilish smile. This man has completely overloaded my senses. It's a good thing this is about to end, because he'd completely consume me if I let him.

And I most certainly would.

"JENNA!" My name brings me out of my trance, and I turn to see Layla moving towards me, rolling her luggage behind her. We hug each other tight and squeal like little girls at the excitement of being together. We do a little dance together, chanting 'girls trip' and laugh at our silliness, not caring about the stares we are getting.

"Damn girl…you are glowing." She stops laughing and stares at me.

"Of course I am, I am in Vegas with my bestie!"

"No…you look different." She gets closer to me, looks me up and down, and then sniffs me.

"What are you doing?" I lean back from her, trying to regain my personal space back.

"That is an interesting concoction of perfume you've got going on, Jenna. Mixture of your usual Tory Burch perfume, mixed with some alcohol and SEX!" She practically screams it out at me and places her hands on her hips with an accusatory stare.

"Not possible since I showered since my last sex session," I laugh when I see her mouth drop open in surprise. I sniff my shirt and it smells just like Cal. His cologne must have rubbed off onto me when we were hugging. "C'mon, let's talk about this in the room." I lace my arm through hers and guide her to the elevators.

"I cannot believe Robert knew all about this and I didn't," she pouts.

"He doesn't know anything - he was hoping what he was

guessing was true. Only thing I ever confirmed was that I met new people." Layla gets extremely jealous if Robert knows something about me that she doesn't. Robert works with me, so I can't help if he learns something before she does.

"Nice room," Layla says as we enter the room. She rolls her suitcase through the living room and into the bedroom. "I love how the bedroom is separate. Is that a pull out couch? Because you are going to need a place to sleep if I bring a hot piece of ass home."

"Ha, yeah...um, about that..."

"Jenna, I am not following that stupid rule you had on our last girls' trip of no men. This is Vegas, where all the good looking people come out to play!" She goes into the bathroom before I respond, but comes right back out.

"Where are your things, Jenna?" Her eyes narrowed, she walks to the closet, opens the door, and then looks backs at me with her hands on her hips and a questionable stare once she finds it empty.

"You get to bring whoever you want here this weekend, as I won't be sleeping here with you. Yeah for you!" My words come out quickly as I hold my breath, waiting for the explosion of her temper as I know she is going to be upset.

"So basically, you are ditching your sister from another mister for a penis?"

"Let's not play victim as we both know if the roles were reversed, you would do the exact same thing. In fact, you HAVE done it!"

"It's not a true girls' trip if one of us can't hear the other one shacking up." So delusional is her definition of a true girls' trip that I start to laugh.

"I am pretty confident that most girls' trips do not involve friends bringing random strangers back to their rooms for sex. The last time I heard you with someone, I had nightmares for days due to the animal noises that were coming out of your room." I met up with her in Miami last year, and it was one of the worst girls' trips we have ever had. I was on my own the whole weekend as she chose to stay in bed with a guy she met at a party. Hence why I had to make up a rule of no more bringing men back to our rooms if we were ever going to go on another trip together.

"I need to meet your mystery man first before I decide how to feel about this. When am I meeting him?"

"He and his friend are waiting for us now back at their place."

"He has a friend?" Her eyes light up at the thought of a prospect for her. She walks back into the bathroom to freshen up, and I follow.

"Listen, I need you to be cool though when you meet them," I tell her as I watch her apply some lipstick. Last time Layla met a celebrity, it was two soap opera stars in a bar in Nashville and she went completely crazy, talking to them as if they were in character.

"Why are you telling me to be cool? I am the mother-fucking queen of cool!" I roll my eyes at her as she waves her arm in the air and snaps her fingers.

"I don't want you to flip out if you know them."

She drops her lipstick in her bag and turns to me. "Jenna, if this man turns out to be your ex-husband, I am locking you in this room and beating some sense into you."

"Trust me when I say that this man is definitely NOT my ex-husband." After this week, I realize my sex life with my ex-husband was nowhere near the level of intensity as it is with Cal. No second thoughts on ever wanting to go back to that! "I only said that you might know them because they are both actors." Layla watches more television than I do, so she might recognize Cal. I know she will recognize Sean Lindsay since we saw his last movie together, and I completely expect her to throw herself at him.

"Seriously? You are banging an actor?" She looks at me in total disbelief.

"Seriously, I am having sex with a human being whose occupation happens to be an actor." I always try to point out to Layla and Robert that celebrities are regular human beings too...just more popular than the average person. It's almost as if the whole planet is in high school and the celebrities are the cool clique that everyone knows of, just are not friends with.

"Enough with the suspense already! Who is the mystery man? If you don't want me to embarrass you, it's best if you tell me upfront." I consider this as I don't think I want a repeat performance of the behavior she displayed with the soap opera hunks.

"You're right, I don't want you to embarrass me or yourself." I take a deep breath. "The mystery man is Cal Harrington."

She tilts her head to the side with a puzzled look on her face, "Cal Harrington?" It seems that her brain only needed the words to come out of her own mouth, because her facial expression changes to recognition, and then shock. "The hot Viking guy?"

"Yes."

"Shut UP!" she yells excitedly. "Wait a minute, is this the guy Robert said you met on the plane? I was half listening to him when he told me that story."

"Yes, we sat next to each other on the plane. We had a scary incident with turbulence, and you know how I am not good with that!"

"Did you throw yourself at him while the plane was rocking back and forth?"

"No, I didn't throw myself at him. The turbulence was BAD - the worst I have ever been through. He saw my distress and offered me to hold on to him. It was really quite nice of him."

"Then what happened?"

"He offered me a ride to the hotel, and we went our separate ways, but saw each other again later on that evening in the lobby where he asked me to dinner."

"Then what happened?" The look in her eyes was starting to get far away and dreamy.

"And here we are, five days later," I say with a bright smile, hoping to move on with the conversation.

"You have spent every single day with him? You little hussy!" She jumps up and down in excitement.

"I didn't sleep with him on the first night! It was the third night," I reveal, my cheeks feeling hot with embarrassment.

"Way to put out. I totally would have given it to him the first night." Layla has always been more sexually confident than I have. She never has worried about what people think of her when it pertains to her active sex life. She's always said that it isn't fair for men to have casual sex with whoever they want, but women get labeled horrible names if they do. She is right, it is completely unfair, but Layla has always been better at emotionally turning her feelings off and sex is just that to her - sex. Sex has always been something intimate for me and until this week, I have never had casual sex.

"Proud bestie here. Our little Jenna is no longer a one night stand virgin." She wipes away at an imaginary tear.

"Technically, I still am because it hasn't been a one night stand," I correct her, because for some reason, I don't want to label this a one night stand.

"You know what I mean!" She huffs. "I cannot wait to meet him, and I will try my best not to stare at his crotch to try to determine his dick size." She imitates a dog sticking out his tongue, huffing, and I burst out laughing.

"I have a feeling you are going to be preoccupied by his friend." I tease, wondering if I should keep him a mystery.

"Who's his friend?"

"Sean Lindsay."

She stares at me, speechless, which is a rare occasion for Layla.

"Do not even mess with me."

"I am dead serious," I say, with the best serious face I can muster since it's really hard not to laugh at the hysterical expression on her face.

She grabs her more than a handful of breasts and starts to rub them. "Well, ladies, it's time for you to come out and play with the new boys tonight!" With that, she goes into her suitcase to find a more revealing outfit for our evening.

13

"I think there is something seriously wrong with this dress," I tug at the sleeves of the copper sequin dress that Layla picked out for me. After the men left for their training session this morning, we went to our spa appointment and decided that we needed some retail therapy after deciding that our outfits for tonight are unsatisfactory.

"I will show you mine if you show me yours. Open up!" Layla knocks on the dressing room door, and I unlock it for her. My mouth drops open at the vision that enters.

"Well, hello, boobs! Your nipples are barely being covered!" She is wearing a sky blue long sleeve dress, with a very deep v neckline that showcases her voluptuous breasts. The dress then flares out past her hips and down to her ankles. She looks angelic, in a very naughty, sexy way. "You look beautiful," I tell her sincerely, wishing she would believe me, knowing that she won't. Strangers have always come up to her, telling her they think she is beautiful, but because of her curvaceous size, she dismisses every compliment thrown her way. Only the people in her inner circle know her lack of self-confidence as to the outside world, she wears the mask of a strong, confident woman.

"If this dress doesn't hypnotize Sean into fucking me, then he most certainly bats for the other team," she laughs while pushing her boobs up. After the initial shock of being in Sean's presence wore off last night, Layla tried her hardest to get him in her clutches. But we all fell asleep watching a movie after indulging in too much delicious food and flowing cocktails.

"Cal thinks Sean has found someone, but for some reason, won't go into details with him about her." Cal told me this morning after I wondered out loud if Layla and Sean hooked up since she slept in his bed with him. I don't want her to get disappointed if she gets zero response from him sexually.

"That would explain how he didn't even get hard from me trying to give him a hand job then. Enough about Sean, what is wrong with your dress?" She makes me turn around to see why the dress keep falling off my back. "Silly, you don't have it zippered all the way up." She zippers it up, which stops right at the small of my back and looks at me in the mirror. "Damn, you look hot, Jenna."

The color of the dress brings out my eyes and the golden highlights in my brown hair. While the dress is short and shows a lot of my legs, it is the back of the dress that is the most revealing part.

"I don't know about this dress. It is super short, and I can't even wear a bra. Doesn't it look a little 1980's-ish?"

"80's clothing are coming back in style, but this doesn't have the shoulder pads. It does come with a built-in bra, so bounce up and down to see if your boobs pass the dance test." I obey, and we laugh at how ridiculous I look. "You didn't poke yourself or me in the eyes, so you pass! This is THE dress, Jenna. Your legs look killer in it and one look at the back and Cal is going to want to fuck you from behind."

He already did this morning. I blush at the memory and avert my eyes from her stare.

"I don't know how you two made it out of bed this morning

with the way he was looking at you. Please tell me you plan on keeping in touch with that fine specimen of a man?" She unzips the dress for me so I can get back into my regular clothes.

"I have no idea what I'm doing," I sigh. "We haven't even exchanged phone numbers, and I think it's best we don't."

"Why not?" She looks at me as if I'm completely crazy.

"What's the point, really? He's an actor who's working on his career, is never in one place at the same time, and gets to kiss beautiful women for a living. I don't want to compete with that." I expect her to argue, and am pleasantly surprised when she doesn't. I thought long and hard about this after another mind blowing orgasm he gave me and couldn't quite figure out how we would keep up a long distance relationship, which is something I don't even want, not to mention if he would even want. I have been doing so well these last couple of months on working at making myself stronger, both mentally and physically, that getting into a relationship with someone like Cal and it not working would completely ruin all of my hard work.

"Will you at least start dating again, because happiness looks really awesome on you." She squeezes my shoulders and looks at me with hope. She's always looking out for me.

"I will if you will." I give her a pointed look, and she rolls her eyes at me. She always deflects from her own single-hood, claiming she is happy being a 'man-eater' instead of having someone who loves her again in her life.

"C'mon, it is time to find the perfect shoes to go with our dresses." We get dressed, pay for our purchases and continue shopping.

Six hours later, we are back in the villa getting ready for our big night out. We stop at Layla's room to get her things so we can get ready together, and do each other's hair and make-up.

"Remember that guy in Fort Lauderdale who tried to hit on you by saying he was a baseball player, only for you to call him out because you actually knew of the player he was impersonating?" We start to laugh hysterically at the memory of the guy's shocked expression when I called out his lie.

"What about the guy in Cancun who came all over himself from the hand job you gave him on the dance floor at Señor Frogs? He had to walk around with that wet patch on his khaki pants for the rest of the night," I recall, which throws us into another bout of laughter.

"Stop making me laugh or I will pee all over this floor." Layla stops curling my hair to bend over to help prevent from peeing.

I giggle as we hear a knock at the door. Sean enters with another bottle of champagne to refill our empty glasses with.

"Ladies, how much longer do we think we are going to be, as you look magnificent just as you are," he asks, as he pours our drinks, his charm flowing as quickly as the champagne into the flutes.

"Why do you keep trying to get us drunk before dinner? You know I am a guarantee, baby!" Layla winks at him and takes a sip out of her refilled glass. Sean laughs and shakes his head.

"We should only be about twenty more minutes." I look at my watch to see we have forty minutes before our dinner reservation, which means we can probably add another ten minutes to our getting ready time.

"Good, because Cal is getting impatient to see you after hearing all of this laughter and something about hand jobs." He gives us a wink and exits the bathroom.

Twenty-five minutes later, we are ready to go. I'm about to walk out of the room with Layla, but remember that I forget to put my new earrings on. I tell her I'll meet her in the living room, and I go back into the bathroom to find them. I put them in my ears and turn to look in the mirror where I see Cal watching me from the doorway.

"Hey!" I jump and turn around to face him. "You're lucky you are so sexy, otherwise this scaring me thing would be creepy." Tonight, he looks dangerously sexy dressed in a tight charcoal grey sweater, with black pants that do nothing to hide his muscular thighs. The darkness of his clothes combined with a day's worth of hair growth on his face makes his eyes look like the blue of the hottest part of a flame.

He doesn't say a word as he makes his way towards me, his gaze starting at my peep toe ankle boots, up my legs, past the dress, and in the mirror to see the revealing cut out showing off my back. When his eyes do reach mine, they are so heated with desire that I immediately clinch my thighs together from the need that is building. He pulls me into his arms, places his hands on my exposed back, and slides them down. He cups my ass and pulls me into him so I can feel how hard he is.

"Can you feel what you do to me?" My breath catches, and I watch his lips slowly descend upon mine. His kiss starts slow, tantalizing. I tease his lips with the tip of my tongue, and am rewarded with entry into his mouth. I can't help the moan that slips out as I start to rub myself against him. He keeps one hand on my ass and moves the other hand up my spine and into my hair, holding my head so he can thrust his tongue deeper. So lost am I in his kiss that I don't feel my legs moving backwards as he pushes me toward the counter. He hoists me up, and I immediately wrap my arms and legs around him, bringing him as close as I can get to him. The hand that was previously on my ass snakes up my thigh and pushes my thong aside to tease my clit with his fingers. I lightly bite down on his lips when he pinches my bud. He growls and kisses me harder, while inserting one of his fingers into me. As he starts to pump his finger in and out of me, I vaguely hear Layla's voice trying to interrupt us.

"All right you two, ENOUGH! We have to get going. You can finish this in the bathroom at the club." Cal breaks our kiss to look over his shoulder at Layla. I hide my face in his chest, mortified that my best friend just caught us, but needing something to muffle my gasp as he pushes his finger higher into me, not caring that she is there.

"Just to warn you, Layla, that Jenna will not be out late tonight." He slowly removes his finger from me and puts my thong back into place. I whimper into his sweater as he swipes my clit with his thumb one last time. I try to catch my breath and peak up at him. His stare is so intense that I have to bite my lip to keep back the moan that wants to slip out, my body wishing he was back inside of me.

"Well, calm your dick down and let's get going then. Two minutes and if you're not out, I will send Sean in here to carry you out." With that threat, she leaves so we can get ourselves together.

"If you don't stop biting your lip like that, we are not going anywhere." I quickly release my lips and smirk at him. He gives me one last hard kiss before helping me off the counter. I smooth down my dress while he washes his hands and splashes his face with cold water. While he dries off, I reapply my lipstick and grab my purse. Once we're ready, he grabs my hand and we leave to join Sean and Layla.

By the time we finish dinner and get into the club, the dance floor is packed with people moving to the music of the famous resident deejay. We are escorted to the VIP booth upstairs where the waitress swoops in on our table with alcohol provided by Layla's company. With Layla's permission, Sean invites a couple of other people from the movie set, so our booth gets very crowded, most notably with more good looking men. I am sandwiched between Cal and Sean, people watching, and sipping my drink while Cal talks with his stunt double, who looks nothing like him. When he introduced us, I couldn't help but keep looking between the two with a puzzled expression on my face.

"It isn't about the face, but the body," Cal educates me and was right that their body types were almost identical. Sean's stunt double looks more like him than Cal's did. Both men good looking in their own way.

As I look out into the crowd to find Layla, I start to notice all the women who slowly walk by our table, hoping to catch the eye of the famous Hollywood actors they are now recognizing. The men sitting at the edge of our booth start to take notice and decide to stand up to talk with the ladies, while Cal and Sean are oblivious to the stares. Some of these women are drop dead gorgeous, and my mind wonders to how many one stands Cal has had if all the women he encounters look like this. *Stop thinking, as it doesn't even matter, Jenna.*

The music changes to some dance songs I recognize, and I stand up to look for Layla, who has been talking with the manager of the club for quite some time now.

"Where are you going?" Cal tugs on my hand, pulling me into his lap.

"I am going to find Layla to dance with me," I say in his ear in order to hear me over the loud music.

"I don't want you going on that dance floor without me." He leans in and kisses me.

"Why?" I try to focus on what I am asking, but his kisses along my neck are distracting me.

"Because you are beautiful and men are going to be all over you."

"I highly doubt that with the caliber of women who are in this club tonight. You just haven't noticed yet."

"I don't need to notice when I have the sexiest one of them all." He captures my mouth before I can answer. He cups my face with one of his hands and starts penetrating my mouth with his tongue. We make out like teenagers, not caring who is watching us. I finally break our kiss when I hear whistles from his friends, and I meet Cal's gaze with my own, my mind trying to come out of the fog that his kisses put me in.

"Keep looking at me that way, Jenna, and I will take up Layla's suggestion of fucking you in the club's bathroom." His hand starts rubbing up and down my back, his touch and the thought of him inside me causing me to shiver.

"Jenna, they are playing my jam! Get your ass over here and let's go dance!" Layla arrives back at the table and holds her hand out for me. I grab Cal's face with both of my hands and kiss him one last time before I get up to join her. As I take her hand to lead me away, I look over my shoulder at Cal to see him staring intently at me, not listening to a word Sean is trying to tell him. I give him my best sexiest smile before I turn back to follow Layla down to the dance floor.

With the dance floor packed, we take a spot at the edge of the floor and start to dance. I look up to where our booth is to see Cal, Sean, and their stunt doubles standing up and scanning the crowd. Layla and I wave, and I see Cal's face soften slightly from his intense glare at trying to find me in the crowd. As we continue to dance and enjoy our old school dance music, we don't notice at first that we are being forced into the middle of the dance floor. When the deejay plays a tune from Britney and Will.i.am, the crowd goes wild and more people enter the dance floor. Layla and I are now pushed up against each other and as I look around, I suddenly notice that we are surrounded my men, staring at us like vultures circling their prey. I look back up to our booth to signal for help, but see no signs of Cal or Sean watching us anymore.

"Looks like we are surrounded," I yell into Layla's ear as she has yet to notice since she's so engrossed in the music. I start to feel a hand on my hip, and I remove it while glaring at the man behind me. He holds up his hands and mouth's 'sorry' and dances away.

"Let's find another place to dance."

"Where?" We look around as people are dancing right at the edge of the booths now.

"I don't know, but you have some major creepers behind you,"

I say, not liking the looks the men are giving Layla as they watch her boobs bounce up and down while she dances.

"I see reinforcements coming in behind you, so we're good." As soon as she says this, I am grabbed from behind by my waist and slammed into a hard chest. I don't need to look behind me to know that it is Cal. Sean walks around me and gets behind Layla, while their stunt doubles flank us on either side to make our own little box. We all start singing to the lyrics and swaying together to the music. I push my ass into Cal's crouch and purposely start to dance seductively against him. Surprisingly, he's able to keep up with my dance moves, which turns me on even more. I start to slide my hands down his thighs and wrap them around his hamstrings, pulling him closer to me. His one arm stays wrapped around my waist, while his other hand wraps around my hair and pulls, bringing my head back against his chest so his lips can claim mine.

I turn around in his arms to deepen the kiss, my body demanding that I bring him closer. I slide my hands in his back pockets and squeeze his delectable ass. Our dancing slows to swaying, and eventually our bodies stop moving as our tongues continue to tango with each other. His hands have resumed their earlier position of being in the back of dress, alternating between rubbing and squeezing my backside. I slide my hands in between our bodies to rub his hard erection in his pants.

"We're leaving NOW!" he commands in my ear. I nod and turn back around to Layla, who gives me a thumbs up, indicating she knows where we are going and is good with it.

"Don't worry, I've got her," Sean yells, and I mouth a thank you to him as I hug her goodbye.

"See you in the morning," I say in her ear and she kisses me on the cheek. "Please be safe and don't do anything too crazy." She salutes me as Cal takes my hand and starts leading me off the dance floor.

We head straight for the valet and take one of the hotel cars back. We sit close together in the car, making an appearance to be just looking out the window at traffic. What the driver can't see in his rear-view mirror is where are hands are, caressing and stroking each other, making promises of more to come. Fifteen minutes later, we are back inside the villa. No words are said as Cal leads me to his room, shuts the door and locks it.

Our clothes can't come off fast enough, our hands and lips crashing into each other until we are completely naked. Our hunger for each other is so insatiable that no foreplay is necessary as he lays me down on the bed and as soon as I wrap my legs around him, he is inside me. Each thrust taking me higher into my own stratosphere. I look into his eyes as I come undone, my orgasm so intense that I feel like I am exploding. As I wrap my arms around him to hold him tighter, I slowly drift back into my body, never wanting this feeling to end.

14

The night seems to stay young, time moving slowly so we can spend it talking, laughing, touching. We finally close our eyes as the sky turns pink, the promise of sunshine imminent. My alarm goes off in the late morning, and Cal orders lunch in while I pack. We take one last shower together, staying in there so long that our lunch gets cold from being untouched. Once we get out, we eat in compatible silence, making small talk here and there. I leave him at the table once I am done to finish getting ready. Layla and Sean slept in my old room in order to give Cal and I privacy, so I text her to let her know Cal will be escorting us to the airport, and we'll pick her up at the front of the hotel. I zip up my suitcase, take one last look around and leave the room. I enter the living room and come up short by the presence of a young woman sitting at the table, shuffling through some papers. She looks up and smiles at me.

"Hi, you must be Jenna. I am Valerie, Cal's assistant." She stands up to walk around the table to shake my hand. She is beautiful, with her blonde hair curled past her shoulders, brown eyes that are accentuated by perfectly applied makeup, and a friendly smile. "Cal has told me so many lovely things about you that I am sorry we won't be getting a chance to hang out together."

"He has said some wonderful things about you as well." I shake her hand back, trying to squash the tiny hint of jealousy I feel towards her.

Cal and Sean enter the room, and Sean engulfs me in a hug. "I truly hope to see you again, Jenna. Thanks to you and Layla for the fun times." He slaps Cal on the back and walks to his bedroom.

Cal tells Valerie he'll be back, grabs my hand, and takes my luggage with his other. I wave goodbye to her and we depart.

We get into the awaiting car and pick up Layla at the front of the hotel. Our short car ride to the airport is filled with her enthusiastic chatter, telling us how her, Sean and the rest of the guys ended up the pub, where Sean taught the whole bar how to sing Irish folk songs. "I had so much fun last night! Good thing I wasn't left alone, who knows what kind of trouble I could have gotten into." She gives me a look, and I blush.

"Thank you for letting me intrude on your girls' weekend." Cal squeezes my hand as he talks to Layla.

"You can intrude any time if it always makes her look this damn happy." They both laugh as my face gets red from the attention.

"Layla, do you mind if I have a couple of minutes alone with Jenna?" Cal asks, as we pull up to the curb for departures. She looks at her watch, nods her head, and exits the vehicle.

I turn to Cal, swallowing the lump that has now formed in my throat. "Thank you so much for an incredible week."

"This doesn't have to be the end, Jenna. Stop being stubborn and give me your phone number."

"Cal..."

"Friends have each other's phone numbers. Why can't we?"

I bite my lip, trying to grasp for any excuse, but have none. How can you just be friends with someone after the type of week we had? I can't be a casual friend with Cal. I don't want to be just friends. I want more, and the reality of that is unrealistic. When I give someone my phone number, I expect them to call. I don't want to feel the disappointment of knowing he has it and doesn't call. I don't need the emotions that come with empty promises.

"You are going to be busy with the movie, traveling to different countries, and I am busy with my career. I think it would be best if we just leave things as is."

"Best for whom?" He pushes a strand of my hair behind my ears and kisses me softly on the cheek.

"Best for me," I whisper, as he claims my lips in a hungry kiss. He has the ability to make everything around me cease to exist as I kiss him back, matching each thrust of his tongue with my own. Our kiss is about to take its usual heated turn, but the knock on the window from Layla pulls us out of our inferno.

"Email," I say, trying to catching my breath. "I'll give you my personal email. Let's start with that."

"I'll take whatever you're willing to give me." I pull a piece of paper out of my purse and write down my email address for him. He, in turn, hands me a card with his cell phone. "Please call me when the emails start to not be enough for you."

He opens the doors, steps out, and reaches for my hand to help me. He gives Layla a hug goodbye before turning and pulling me into his arms. I squeeze him tightly before I pull back and look into his eyes, willing my brain to memorize every single detail of his handsome face.

"Stop looking at me as if this is a final goodbye, Jenna, because it's far from it. Don't give up on me." He kisses me one last time before releasing me. "You'll have an email by the time you land. I'll see you later." He winks at me, waves at Layla and gets back in the car. I walk with Layla into the airport, my brain telling my heart to ignore the hope he has ignited in it.

As we settle into our cruising altitude of 39,000 feet back to Chicago, I can't seem to keep quiet my sigh of contentment as I relax into my seat and reflect on what an amazing week it has been. Professionally, attending this conference will help launch my brand on a wider national level. I've already been invited to speak at three more conferences, and one of the local Chicago news stations called Robert, requesting a meeting to discuss a possible monthly segment on themed party ideas. This could really catapult my business in the local area with higher-end clients. So energized am I by the new possibilities, I grab my notepad from the seat pocket, and start writing down party ideas I think viewers would be interested in.

"I need you to stop what you are doing and talk to me about this weekend, sister to sister." I turn to look at Layla, expecting her to have her usual shit-eating grin on her face, but am surprised by her serious expression.

"Okay…what's going on?" I put my pen down to give her my undivided attention.

"I want to know what's going on in that brain of yours. You haven't said a word about what you're feelings regarding Cal."

I shrug, momentarily lost for words regarding my emotions. "Honestly, I don't know what to feel about it. I feel it needs to be left as it is - two grown adults, who are attracted to each other, chose to act on it and that's it."

"Bullshit, Jenna. Don't hide what you're feeling from me!" Anger sparks in her beautiful blue eyes, and I can't help but smile at how lucky I am to have her as my best friend. I look around to make sure none of the other passengers are looking at us before responding to her.

"Okay, fine, I'll tell you everything, but you can't interrupt me and must wait to speak until I'm done. Deal?" She nods in agreement right away, her eyes now beaming with anticipation.

"You, out of everyone, know how my divorce wrecked me. I thought I found the perfect person for me. Turns out, he wasn't. I have come to terms with that, and am trying to work on how it has changed me - how the bitterness and skepticism are now more present in my thoughts on life. Trust me when I say, it definitely isn't how I used to feel. It's not that I want to be alone - I just don't want to feel broken again."

"But this week, I met someone who made me come back alive. He completely consumed me, and I didn't want to fight it. I wanted him to overwhelm me because it felt so... amazing! He made me feel special. He made me feel beautiful. He made me feel worthy! He made the outside world disappear when he looked at me. And the realism of it all scares me. How does a person I just meet evict these kind of emotions out of me? Is it real or am I feeling this way because I am lonely?" I shake my head with a sad smile.

"While most of the time it was easy to forget who Cal is, the fact remains that he's an actor, going up the roller coaster ride of his career. We live in different countries. He travels all the time. His life, and whom he is with, will always be public scrutiny. We couldn't be more polar opposites with our own life trajectories. I don't know why he chose me to spend this week with." I hold up my hand to shush her interrupting reasons as to why he did. "But I have zero regrets about this week. If anything, I believe he was meant to help me feel again. And I will forever be grateful for that."

"But Jenna, what if you two continue corresponding, and he wants more?"

"I can't think about the what ifs, Layla. I can't start to worry about whether he emails me or not. Because if I do, it'll distract me. If I'm being honest with myself, based on how he made me feel, it would probably derail me. He's a distraction that I can't handle, so I won't let myself whimsically daydream of a fictitious life with Cal Harrington. He's a complete fantasy. I need to live in the present and the present is me and my career."

She studies me and slowly nods her head. "I completely understand and probably would be thinking the same way." I nod my head, not telling her that I regret giving him my email address. "Will you at least start dating again now?"

"Like I said before, I will if you will." I smile with questioning eyes at her.

"I don't know if I am ready," she whispers, her watery eyes giving away her fears from her past experience with love.

"We don't have to actively try, we can just be more open to it." I give her hand a squeeze of encouragement.

"Yeah...I like that idea." She slowly smiles as she thinks about it and squeezes my hand back with affirmation.

"I love you for loving me. Thank you for being such an amazing friend." I lean over and hug her with all the strength I have.

"Right back at you. Now let's get working together on creating some fabulous party ideas for you!" I laugh at her enthusiasm and we start brainstorming.

Five hours later, I unlock the door to my apartment and breathe a sigh of relief to be home. I leave my luggage by the door and sit for a moment on my couch. I have a spectacular view of Lake Michigan, courtesy of my Nana, who left me this amazing piece of real estate when she passed. She bought this place in 1976, which is located in a high rise overlooking Lake Michigan. She was astute enough to pay it off and now if I wanted to sell it, I would make at least ten times the amount she paid for it or more. I can never see myself selling it. Not only because of the sentimental value that it was hers, but also because it's the perfect fit for me and where I need to be in the city.

I was exhausted when we landed, but now I sit with adrenaline pumping, my body still on Las Vegas time. The internal debate with myself starts on whether or not I should check my personal email, as I think about Cal and what he's doing right now. This is exactly why I didn't want to keep in contact with him. I should be going to sleep, not missing him and his touch as much as I do.

With a frustrated groan at my lack of willpower, I give in and check my email. To my surprise, I find three emails from him.

To: Jenna Pruitt
From: Cal Harrington
Subject: I miss you

Your delicious scent is everywhere...in the car, in my room, on my sheets. This is torture. Please write me when you arrive home.

Cal

To: Jenna Pruitt
From: Cal Harrington
Subject: Where are you?

I just stalked your flight and it says you've landed. This is why email is stupid, and you should just call me to let me know you are okay.

Cal

To: Jenna Pruitt
From: Cal Harrington
Subject: Call Me.....

You know you want too. :)

I can't help the giggle that escapes me from him last email. Of course I want too, but I can't. *Should I even bother emailing him back? It would be very rude of me not too.* I ignore the warning signals my head is sending to my heart and email him.

To: Cal Harrington
From: Jenna Pruitt
Subject: Call Me...Maybe?

Sorry for the delay in response. I am safe and sound, tucked in bed, wearing nothing, and thinking of you.
Sweet, wet dreams Cal...
Jenna

I smile an evil smile as I hit send and get up to go get ready for bed, my heart beating with excitement at the anticipation of his response. Already I am falling down the rabbit hole of distraction.

15

It took longer than I expected to get back into my work routine, and I place all the blame on the email affair I am having with Cal. Our emails to each other have started to get more frequent and longer. His movie started filming, so he explains to me in detail what his daily activities are like and what's coming up for him. He includes pictures of himself on set or just lounging in his room, which only intensifies my want for him. He always ends his emails asking what I am doing, how my day was, what Chicago is like, and why I haven't picked up the phone yet. As soon as I told Robert about what happened in Las Vegas, he is on the pro-Cal band wagon and even helps takes photos of the city when we are around town to send in my emails. He thinks I'm crazy for not calling him, but I still stand firm with my decision of email only. The emails have become the highlight of my day, and I have to mentally reprimand myself not to check them every hour for his response. The only time my resolve cracks is when I am lying in bed at night, alone. The desire to hear his voice is so strong that I've now started to put my phone in the other room to avoid the temptation of calling him.

"Have you two shared dirty emails yet?" Layla asks with an evil smile as we sit in our normal booth at O'Malley's three weeks later. It seems that as of late, my relationship with Cal is the favorite topic of discussion when all three of us get together.

"No, because his assistant checks his email. In fact, I got one from her today under his email letting me know that I might not hear from him for a couple of days as they only have three days left in Las Vegas until production moves to Hong Kong, so he is working twelve-hour days."

"That's just creepy that she checks his emails," Robert says, before ordering another round of drinks for us.

"I understand why she does it, and I actually appreciate her warning me."

"So no dirty emails and you won't call him for some phone sex? What a dull relationship. You're being stupid, Jenna!" Robert reminds me for the millionth time. I shrug my shoulders as I sip my drink, his comment not worth responding to.

"I think she's being smart," Layla chimes in, sending a warning look to Robert that does not go unnoticed.

"Thank you, I do too. I'm just being careful to not let myself get hurt again."

"Of course you would think that. You two bitter yentas are going to grow old together if you keep that thinking up." We laugh at his choice of words, and I try to recall if he has ever mentioned his own heartache in the past.

"Have you not gotten your heart broken before, Robert?"

"Of course, my heart has been completely slaughtered. Once. And yes, it was brutal. But I am in love with love, and I believe that you can find love multiple times. Remember the good times with that person. Remember the reasons why you aren't together. You repeat the cycle until you find the one whose idiosyncrasies are livable, and you can't imagine life without them."

He makes it sound so simple. Like snapping your fingers can turn off your emotions to proceed with life. The brain doesn't work that way. I am convinced it completely wants to mind fuck you if you let it. I'm done giving the power of my feelings to someone else. I am in control and I'll decide who will be the worthy recipient.

"All right Yoda, so what do you suggest us bitter yentas do to change our ways?" Layla inquires with a sarcastic smirk on her face. I look at her with raised eyebrows, surprised she asks a question that will produce an answer we all know she won't like.

"Do you think you can handle my answer, Layla? Because you know I only tell it like I see it."

"Bring it! We haven't known each other long. You'll barely scratch the surface," she says with a confident smile.

My gaze shifts back to Robert, who takes a big sip of his drink. Layla thinks Robert is being arrogant and when she does, she enjoys nothing more than to call him out and prove how wrong he is. This is the wrong place and the wrong time for this current challenge, and I brace myself for the possibility of this to turn nasty, as Layla's wounds run deeper than mine. Any topic regarding herself gets quickly dismissed.

"What I am about to say comes from a place of love and not criticism, even though it might come out that way. All statements are just my opinion - an outsider looking in. I love you both so much and just want us all to be happy." He clears his throat before he proceeds. "Layla, you use your curves as an excuse. You have started to believe the lie that you tell yourself that a man showing interest in you only means he's curious what sex with a fat girl would be like. Well, that's bullshit! You had a man who loved you for you, curves and all. He died and yes, that fucking sucks and is unfair. It happens to millions of other people too. Stop using his death as an excuse to not live anymore! You are still alive, surrounded by people who love you, and want to see you happy. You ARE beautiful! You ARE smart, and there are plenty of other men out there who'll want you just the way you are, exactly like your husband did. Stop lying to yourself, thinking we are satisfied with your excuses, because we see through it all. Do you think he would like how you are currently living? If you want to even call it that."

My mouth hangs open, completely shocked at how brutally honest he just got with her. Robert is new to our circle - he never knew Layla before her husband, during her marriage and when he died. But Robert is an old soul despite his youth, and I'm learning that his judge of character is spot on. He's completely right about Layla. She parties and has sex with random men to numb her pain. I have tried to talk to her about it, but she refuses to talk and tells me she's doing just fine. I grab her hand underneath the table and squeeze. I know she wants to run right now, her natural instinct to do so when things get too emotional for her. Her expression stays emotionless, her eyes cold as she looks at Robert.

"Are you done?" she asks in a hard voice.

"Only if you want me to be."

"I think I'm quite done hearing your assessment."

"I don't mean to hurt you, Layla. I'm just trying to be honest. Please believe me when I say that I don't want to say these things to you, but what kind of friend would I be if I continued to be silent?" He softly pleas with her to understand and not be mad, but she only nods at him and looks away.

"Okay, my turn." I change the subject so Layla can calm down and the focus not be on her anymore. Even though I certainly don't want the attention on me, I'm intrigued to hear what he's going to say.

He shifts his gaze to me and gives me a sad smile. "Jenna, you thought you had the perfect marriage, the perfect husband and life. You didn't. There is no such thing. People are flawed. Marriages are flawed and that's how it is. You still have your ex-husband on a pedestal and use him as an example of why you shouldn't move on. You automatically assume every man isn't going to want to be with you after a period of time. That you must be dull or boring. You are neither of those. Your ex didn't change overnight - you both met in the working world, where you both were working long hours. It was your everyday normal. You allowed it to continue because you were focused on your new career and didn't feel guilty that you weren't paying attention to him, because he wasn't paying attention to you. You BOTH stopped being involved in your marriage, using work as your excuse to not spend time with each other. You still work crazy hours and won't stop to make yourself a priority. You don't even try to see what else is out there. And then, someone does show interest in you and what do you do? You play games with him!"

"Oh yes, Jenna, you're most certainly playing games with Cal," he says, acknowledging the incredulous look at my face. "He wanted to continue pursuing you, and you only gave him your email address? What the fuck is that? How is giving him your email address guarding your heart? Be honest, you're emotionally involved with every email you write. Don't lie to yourself by saying you won't be disappointed when those emails stop, because you will be! You think he's going to continue emailing you after a couple more months, if that? You're dangling him on a rope. You're wasting his time, and he'll realize that and the emails will completely stop. And then it'll be too late to pick up that phone to call him. People make long distance relationship work all the time. So what if he's an actor? He's a human being and if you continue with this game, you'll never know if his intentions are true or not." He downs his drink and sits back in his chair with his arm crossed.

"I'm sorry, Jenna, and I don't mean for my words to hurt you either as I love you as well." He looks back and forth between me and Layla. "You both need to let the past stay in the past and not define your future."

We all sit there is silence, looking everywhere but each other. I feel Layla grab my hand and I look over at her. Her eyes are questioning if I'm okay, and I give her a small smile in response. We all look up as our favorite bartender, Nico, stops at our table and places shots of whiskey in front of us.

"I don't know what is going on over here, but you all look fucking depressing. Lighten up, my favorite people! Pick up those shots and let's toast!" We do as we are commanded and pick up the shots as Nico serenades us with one of his favorite Irish toasts.

"May your troubles be less
And your blessings be more.
And nothing but happiness
Come through your door."

We salute each other and throw back the shot, grimacing as the whiskey burns down our throats. We thank Nico as he takes the shot glasses away and leaves us back to our silence.

"I didn't mean to ruin the evening," Robert says as he places some cash on the table and gets ready to leave.

"Robert, you didn't ruin anything." I stand and give him a hug. "Thank you for being honest with me...with us. I know you're coming from a place of love and I am so grateful for that. I know I'm not going to change tomorrow, but I can promise you that I will think long and hard about what you said and try to find ways to improve." I look over to Layla. "Layla, what do you think?"

She looks at us, sighs and gets up from the table to hug us. "I love you both, even when your honesty feels like a knife to my heart. I know I need to work on myself. All I can say is that I will try."

And we end our night out with promises that we pray we can keep.

16

Robert's speech from O'Malley's resonates with me one week later as I take the scenic route on the Riverwalk to meet him and my mother for a business lunch. Cal's emails have stopped, and in their place are apology responses from his assistant. Valerie is always apologizing for his lack of response and has updated me on his arrival in Hong Kong. While I appreciate how great she has been with me, she's not the one I want to hear from. I can't help but think that maybe Robert is right with Cal's interest fading.

Maybe he just wasn't that into you in the first place, Jenna.

I roll my eyes at my own thinking. I don't even know what disappoints me more – Cal, for not trying harder to email me, or how upset I am over a situation I all but predicted was going to happen. Either way, I hate myself for staring at my emails, hoping that every time I refresh there'll be one from him. The madness needs to stop! I need to make a decision of what I'm going to do. I either write him off and enjoy my memories with him in Las Vegas or I attempt to contact him one last time, but this time by phone.

I push the Cal predicament aside as I enter my mother's

favorite restaurant. Around this time every year, we meet to discuss my company's strategy for planning the annual charity gala for the Children's Hospital where my father works. My mother is chair of their events committee and while I am grateful that she got me the gig as it is one of my bigger revenue generators, working with her comes at a price - my sanity. We don't have that smushy sweet, my-mother-is-my-best-friend bond that other families have. Most of the time I can't stand to even be around her. She is materialistic, pretentious, judgmental and drinks more than I would like for her to. I have nothing in common with her and prefer my father's company over hers any day of the week. She is insanely jealous of the relationship I have with my father, yet she is the creator of it. He is the compassionate, loving, and reliable parent. When I told them I was getting a divorce, my father hugged me and told me I deserved better. My mother told me to go after him because he was the best I was ever going to get. Every visit with her is a critique on my looks, my weight, my business - and now my single hood.

"Jenna, dear, I am so glad you are finally here. What took you so long?" Her fake lips pouting as if she's a child. Her hair is up in its signature chiffon, nails and lips perfectly matching the red of her hair. She is wearing a silk blouse, with a pencil skirt and heels. Diamonds sparkle from her ears and hands. Appearances are everything to Pamela Pruitt, and she won't even associate with you if she feels you are not in her league.

"Hello, Mother." I kiss her on her cheek; her perfume is so strong that I make a mental note to change my clothes when I get home. "You look lovely, as usual."

"Why thank you, darling. Is everything okay?"

"Everything is fine, Mother. I took the Riverwalk over since it is a beautiful day."

"Excellent idea, since it looks like your pants are getting a little tight in your rear. Enjoying yourself a little too much, are we, darling?" She winks at me to try to soften the blow of her insult.

Robert starts coughing, no doubt choking on his own saliva that he accidentally inhaled from the shock of her comments.

"How kind of you to notice, Mother. And here I thought I was looking halfway decent today." I peruse the menu to avoid looking at her. My clothes are tighter, but I chalk that up to my lack of working out and my recent poor food choices due to stress. Of course I would never admit to my mother that she is right.

"Now Jenna, I never said you didn't look good. I just said you look like you've gained some weight. Why don't we order so we can start talking business, shall we?" She motions for the waiter to come over to take our orders. We tell the waiter our food selections and proceed to discuss business.

"I am so excited to announce to you our theme for this year's gala." She takes a sip of her wine before proceeding. "Drum roll please!" Robert enlightens her by drumming against the table. "The theme for this year's gala is....Cabaret!" She laughs and claps her hands with excitement.

"Ooh, Cabaret! We haven't done that type of party yet, have we, Jenna?" Robert's gets out his notebook and briskly starts to write.

"No, we haven't and that's actually a really great theme, Mother. No doubt your idea, of course?"

"Of course, darling! Where do you think you get your creativity from?" There is nothing my mother won't take credit for, especially when it pertains to my career. "The board unanimously approved the idea, and we have a meeting next week to go over our budget. So the sooner you can get me quotes, the quicker we can put things in motion." The waiter arrives with our food, and we continue to listen to my mother's vision for the party and throw back and forth some ideas. The hour goes fast, and by the time lunch is done, my excitement for the party mirrors theirs.

"I think we have enough information to reach out to our vendors and possibly get you a quote by the end of this week." I give Robert a questioning glance and he nods his head yes.

"Excellent! I cannot wait for New Year's Eve! It is going to be an amazing event, and we will hopefully raise lots of money. Enough about business, I want to know what is going on with both of you?" my mother asks as the check arrives. We all know this is her way of trying to get any new information about me out of Robert since I refuse to tell her about my life. I grab the check from her to pay and try to answer her as vaguely as possible.

"All is well, Mother. We shoot our first news segment for News Channel 3 in a few weeks, which we are anticipating will bring more new clients and ramp up website activity."

"Have you talked to Tyler at all?" She interrupts me, not caring at all about the exciting new opportunity for my business.

"No, Mother. We're divorced. I expect to never talk to him again." I concentrate on signing the check, not wanting to look at my mother with the disgust I have for her right now for bringing him up.

"Jenna has started dating again though!" I gasp in shock as I look up at Robert and decide to kick him hard underneath the table for his revelation. He grunts and shoots daggers at me.

"What? Jenna! Why haven't you told me? Who are you dating?" My mother actually looks like her feelings are hurt from me not involving her in my personal life.

"Nope, I am not dating anyone. I was for one week, but it looks like it isn't going to work out." Robert raises his eyebrow in question.

"One week? Jenna, that is barely dating and too early to determine if it will work or not."

"He doesn't even live here, Mother." I say with exasperation, tired of the topic already.

"Oh my word, did you meet him online? That is how you get yourself killed, Jenna Lynn!" My mother saying my middle name means she is being serious.

"She met him in first class on her way to Las Vegas!" Robert pushes his chair back to stand, avoiding my second kick to his shins.

"First class?! Ooh, I love first class!" My mother looks back and forth between us, her eyes widening in excitement.

"Yes, I arranged first class for her, so she wouldn't have even met him if it wasn't for me."

"Oh Robert, you take such good care of Jenna. We wouldn't know what we would do without you!" I roll my eyes and want to hurl at the love fest between the two.

"Well, she is the best boss I've ever had! Did she tell you she's giving me a raise next week?" He places his hand over his heart and flutters his eyelids. I laugh out loud with as much fakeness as I can muster since there is zero intention for anyone to get an increase in wages.

"Congratulations! Sounds like business is going well, then?" my mother asks with a raised eyebrow.

"Yes, Mother, it is. In fact, we need to head back for a conference call with our software company to prepare for the potential increase in traffic on our website." I stand up and air kiss each side of her cheek.

"Will you come over for dinner on Sunday, Jenna? Your father wants to resume our weekly dinners as frequently as possible, since you're now too busy to even see us." My mother lays on the guilt trip as we walk her out of the restaurant and wait for her car at valet.

"We'll see, Mother. Let me look at my schedule." We haven't done family Sunday dinners in months due to me purposely making myself unavailable on Sundays. It isn't that I don't want to see my parents - I just don't want to see them that frequently. I am saved by having to say anymore with the arrival of her car.

"Goodbye, my darlings! Chat soon!" She blows us goodbye kisses as she gets into her car and pulls away from the curb into traffic.

"That woman is a hot mess. You two are the best daytime soap opera ever, *dah-ling*!" Robert teases as we head back to my apartment.

"You sure do your best to help instigate the drama." I give him a knowing look, calling him out on his tactics.

"I take offense to that as I was only looking out for you by getting her off your ass about your ex!" I roll my eyes at him playing the victim when he is far from it.

"Whatever, Robert, don't play innocent when you knew exactly what you wanted to tell her."

"Honestly, Jenna, I get sick and tired of hearing her go after you about him. I was hoping her hearing that you are dating again would put an end to it. I apologize, as you're right, it's not my place to tell her about your personal life." I see where his intentions were, but it isn't his business to discuss those details with my mother."Please don't be mad at me, Jenna. I'm gay and you know how we love gossip and drama. I can't help it if it's in my DNA." I shake my head and laugh, entwining my arm through his as we continue walking.

"Since we were kind of talking about Cal without revealing who he was, what IS going on with him?" Robert asks after a couple of minutes of silence.

"I haven't heard from him in almost two weeks. Hate to admit it, but I think you're right." I sigh with resignation.

"I don't want to be right, Jenna. I want you to have a happy ending." He wraps his arm around my shoulders and squeezes.

"Thanks, but my intuition was always telling me it wasn't him, anyway. I should have never given him my email address."

"But if you didn't, then you would be sitting here wondering about the what ifs." Robert knows me well as I nod my head in agreement with him.

"It's time to move on to someone who is going to give you the attention you deserve!" he says with conviction. And yes, I need to. But it is so much easier said than done when someone makes you feel the way that Cal does.

After our conference call, I tell Robert to go home early and enjoy the rest of his evening. I wrap up the remainder of my work, pour a glass of wine and sit on my couch, enjoying the colors of the sunset over Lake Michigan. My thoughts turn to Cal, and I can't shake the nagging feeling that it just doesn't seem like him to all of a sudden stop talking to me. I hold his card in my hand and stare at his phone number. Hong Kong is thirteen hours ahead, putting their time in the early hours of the morning. My internal debate continues as to what I should do:

Don't call, it would be rude to wake him.

He might have his phone turned off, so you wouldn't wake him.

He probably gets up early for work.

He doesn't have to pick up the phone if he doesn't want to!

Call him tomorrow during normal hours.

Call him NOW, as you need closure!

"Ugh!" I dial his number and get up to pace, the anticipation of him answering making my heart race. I would be perfectly happy hearing his voicemail so that I could leave a message and put the ball back in his court.

"Hello?" A female voice picks up on the last ring and I sit down as I suddenly start to feel nauseated.

"Um....Valerie?" I ask, hoping it is her and not some random woman that he is now sleeping with.

"Yes?" Relief spreads through me as she confirms her identity.

"Hi, it's Jenna. Jenna Pruitt. Cal's friend from Las Vegas?" I phrase it as a question, hoping she remembers who I am.

"Hey Jenna! How are you?" Her voice turns enthusiastic as she acknowledges remembering me.

"I am fine, thanks for asking. Sorry if I sound confused, but I wasn't expecting you to answer his phone. Are you in Hong Kong, too?"

"Oh no, I am in Los Angeles. Did Cal not email you about him breaking his phone? I literally just came back from the phone store with his new phone to ship out to him. Your timing is perfect!" She laughs and I feel somewhat better that reality is not what my mind was picturing.

"No, I still haven't heard from him since our last email correspondence."

"Really?" She asks with surprise in her voice. "Jenna, I'm really sorry. I promise you that I have reminded him to email you back!"

"I really appreciate that, Valerie. I understand he's busy, but maybe this is for the best anyway." I can't help the disappointment that laces my voice.

"Listen, Jenna, I like you and I'm going to be honest with you. Cal's career is on the rise, and with that comes people giving him anything and everything he wants. He's a very good actor, and his charm is extremely convincing. Let's just say he's gotten very confident from our days in acting class." I listen to every word she says, completely understanding what she's insinuating. "I know your feelings are probably hurt by his lack of response, but trust me when I say that you want to move on. You're not the first woman he has done this to, unfortunately. Please don't repeat what I'm saying. I'm just tired of watching him do this to good people and he always leaves me to pick up the pieces of these women's hearts. It's disgusting really and if it continues, I'm going to find someone else to work for. I've stayed long enough with him that I've built up my own reputation of being a reliable and trustworthy assistant. I know I wouldn't have a problem finding someone else to work for."

"I am sure you have, Valerie, and I appreciate your honesty. Don't worry about my heart, as it's still completely intact." I reassure not only her, but myself as well. While my heart IS still intact, I can't help the stab of pain it is feeling with the knowledge that I was just another notch on his belt.

"I'm really happy to hear that, Jenna. I'm just so sorry. Maybe he'll prove me wrong and get in touch with you after he gets back from Hong Kong." She sighs with what sounds like complete sincerity.

"Maybe so, but there's no need to be sorry, Valerie. Thanks again for everything and best of luck to you!"

"Best of luck to you, Jenna!"

I hang up the phone and sit in silence to reflect on the conversation. While a small part of me is angry at him for using me, I'm relieved to know the truth and get the closure I need to move on. Still, I can't help but be sad, as I liked him a lot. Probably more than one should have for only knowing someone for one week. If I'm willing to put myself out there in the dating pool again, I know this won't be the last time I'm left disappointed.

"Another one bites the dust!" I toast to myself and take a big gulp of my wine.

Have yourself a pity party tonight and tomorrow, you are completely done with thinking of Cal Harrington.

I take the bottle of wine and decide to commiserate with myself in a nice, long hot bath.

17

The next couple of weeks are so busy that I don't have time to even think of Cal. This time of year is pivotal for us securing Halloween and holiday parties. Our days consist of meetings and answering proposals and conference calls. It is exciting and exhausting, but Robert and I thrive on it. I usually don't like to travel during the months of April and May or accept any new projects that aren't close to our norm, but I cannot turn down the monthly featured news segment and the opportunities that might come from it. The added work has been a welcome distraction and has helped push my memories of Cal to the back burner of my mind.

Today was my last meeting with News Channel 3 before going live tomorrow with our first segment. We discussed the spring party concepts that I'll be talking about and I brought over all the decor to go with each party concept. With Robert being out sick with a stomach bug, Layla was able to help me haul everything over to the studio and set it up.

"What are you going to wear tomorrow?" she asks as we load up my car to leave the studio for the day.

"No clue, and everything is tight on me right now." I am so

bloated from stress that my wardrobe has become limited. I've got to get back into the gym...and maybe wire my mouth shut during my stressful months, as chocolate and wine have been my comfort food as of late.

"Sounds to me like this is the best excuse to go shopping!" I nod in agreement and drive us to the closest mall to find the perfect on-air outfit. Shopping with Layla is always the best therapy, as we have a good time catching up and laughing at some of the outfits we try on. Three hours and five stores later, I have a new dress, shoes, and accessories. I treat her to dinner as a thank you for all of her help today.

"What are you going to do if Robert is too sick for tomorrow?" Layla asks as she takes a sip of her margarita.

"I can do it by myself, but I wanted him there and on camera with me since he's my right-hand man." So in love was he with the idea of being on television that he has had his outfit picked out three weeks ago. "It's no big deal if he misses this first one. We'll have two more trial runs, and if the feedback is good, then we'll extend for a year."

"Don't you love how you put all this work in for only a five-minute segment? It's almost like having sex. All that foreplay you have to go through for an orgasm that lasts only a minute." We laugh out loud at her accurate analogy. "Cheers to that, and may we work hard for many more!" We clink our glasses together and drink.

"Maybe you'll meet some hot news reporter or cameraman to start dating."

I shrug, as the thought of dating anyone right now is as appealing as trying on a new bathing suit in my bloated state - torturous.

"Aren't we supposed to be giving dating a second chance?" she asks as she checks out two men who walk past our table. I just smile and raise my eyebrows at her since she has been the more reluctant one.

"This is why no-strings-attached sex is easier." She catches the eye of one of the guys she was checking out and gives him her best fuck me smile.

"It has its appeal, but even that gets lonely after a while." I watch him salute her with his beer bottle and turn to say something to his friend who looks over at us. If Layla has her way, these guys will be making an appearance at our table soon.

"How have you been doing about the Cal situation?" She turns her attention back to me and looks me in the eye.

"There is no Cal situation. It is over and done with." I break her eye contact, not wanting her to see that it has affected me more than I wanted it too.

"He just seemed so into you. I don't know, I'm kind of shocked by his behavior."

"Hard to truly know someone's character in one week. He could be doing the same thing with someone new right at this very moment." The thought makes me sick to my stomach. I look at my watch and see that it's getting late. I have a big day tomorrow and I need to get a decent night's sleep. I signal for the check from our waiter so we can leave.

"Jenna, I think we are about to have company." She slowly smiles at the men making their way to our table.

"Not tonight, Layla. We are leaving. Together." I sign the check and get up out of my seat. I grab both of our coats and hand hers to her. She stares at it and looks back at me.

"Come on, Jenna. These men might be our future dates." I look over at them and see the glint in their eyes, the fakeness in their smiles. They are two sexual predators spotting their next conquests.

"These men only want to fuck, Layla, and you are NOT doing that tonight." I stare at her until the men reach our table, daring her to defy me.

"Ladies, mind if we join you?" the taller one of the two asks and starts to pull out the empty seats at our table as if we said yes.

"Sorry, boys, but we were just leaving." I grab hold of Layla's hand and drag her to the door as she blows them a kiss and waves goodbye to them.

I wake up bright and early the next morning, my previous feelings of excitement now replaced with nervousness. I decide to take the day off of work and pamper myself with a massage and mani/pedi before reporting to the news station at four o'clock. I call Robert to see how he's feeling, hoping that he's better enough to make an appearance.

"The throw up has ceased, but the activity from my backside has not stopped. I'm so disgusted with the human body right about now." I laugh despite the grossness of it all and tell him to stay home. "I really want to be there today, Jenna. I'm sorry! Forward the phones to me, as I can still work from home even if it might be while I am on the toilet." He sounds miserable and I truly feel bad that he's going to miss our debut on television.

"Don't worry, Robert, there are going to be other chances for you to be on. Just feel better and don't bring that crud anywhere near me."

"There are no guarantees that I haven't already gotten you sick. There, I warned you! I truly hope you don't get this, as I wouldn't wish this upon my worst enemy. Well.... I might wish this upon my ex." I'm happy to hear that, despite not feeling well, he hasn't lost his humor. A sign that he is on the mend.

After I hang up with Robert, I go about my day of pampering and before I know it, it's time to leave for the station. I get dressed and drive myself over there where I'm greeted by the sight of Layla waiting for me outside.

"You came!" I run up and hug her, so thankful that she was in town this week to be here with me.

"I wouldn't miss this for the world!" She follows me into the station, where we are escorted into a dressing room. I meet briefly with the entertainment reporter who'll be introducing my segment, and we go through the questions she plans on asking so I'll have my answers ready. With only having five minutes, we need to be on time with our cues and keep our answers short and to the point. After she leaves, hair and make-up artists come in and get me all dolled up. Between their work and the outfit Layla picked out for me, I look chic and professional. With my confidence soaring, I squash down my fears as we're escorted to set and I stand at the indicated marker. I take a deep breath when the countdown begins and put a genuine smile on my face as the light on top of the camera turns red to indicate we are live.

Five minutes breezes by and before I know it, the segment is finished. As soon as the red light goes off, everyone starts clapping and my nervousness starts to subside.

"Great job, Jenna! I have a feeling we're going to get very good feedback about this segment. I'll schedule a conference call with you next week to discuss next month's segment and the results we get in." The producer shakes my hand and exits the studio.

"You were amazing!" Layla squeals as she hugs me tight. She helps me pack up my decor and we load it back into the car. Once that's finished, we head to dinner to celebrate.

"Oh my gosh, I'm so happy that's over with!" I laugh when we finally get seated.

"How do you feel about it all? You looked beautiful and you sounded so polished and smooth."

"I actually feel really good and think it went great! I think the parties we chose had enough detail to grab the audience's attention and make them curious on what to do next. They announced our website at the end, so we'll analyze the online traffic tomorrow." Robert made sure the page was updated with the new segment content by the time I was done. I cannot wait to see if those figures increased during the timeframe I was on.

I look down at my phone as congratulatory text messages

come in from Robert, my parents and some other friends who saw the segment. I am on cloud nine right now and can't believe how hard work can pay off with so many opportunities. I look over at Layla and grab her hand from the table.

"Thank you so much for being my best friend and caring enough to be here with me tonight. There's no other person I would rather be celebrating with." I squeeze her hand and lean over to kiss her cheek.

"Girl, I got my make-up professionally done tonight for you. Don't waste my money by making me cry!" She smiles as she blinks the wetness from her eyes. "We need to make a toast!" We lift up the champagne flutes that she ordered and I smile in anticipation of the epic toast I know she is about to deliver.

"To you, boss babe! May your success continue to bring you much happiness, lots of money and more hot men to your bed!" *From your lips to God's ears,* I pray, and laugh as we clink our glasses together in hopes the good wishes come true.

18

"Jenna....Jenna...I need you to open your eyes for me...Jenna?"

I am startled by the loud voices that feel like they are screaming in my ear. I try to open my eyes, but my eyelids feel like they have weights on them. I open my mouth to talk back to this person, but sharp pains shoot up my throat and I quickly close it.

"Jenna...can you hear me?" The voice sounds like Layla's. *Why is Layla here?* My body starts to shake and although I feel cold, the shaking seems to be coming from the hands that are holding me.

"Stop shaking me because I'm about to throw up all over you." I croak out, my throat hurting so badly that I never want to talk again.

"Here's a bucket!" I register Robert's high-pitched voice. I manage to open my eyes slightly to see their worried faces hovering over me. I groan and try to lift my arm to cover my face, but my arm won't move.

"Jenna, we need to get you to the hospital. I think you're extremely dehydrated from the stomach flu." I start to shake my head no, but waves of dizziness crash into me so I stop any voluntary movement.

"Robert, stay with her while I call downstairs to have them retrieve her car. Jenna, I have a cup of Gatorade with a straw. I need you to SLOWLY try to drink a little." I watch Layla put the cup on my nightstand and leave the room. Robert sits me up and hands me the cup. I manage two small sips and that's all I can handle.

"What day is it?" I ask, unable to remember. The only thing I remember is going to dinner with Layla to celebrate the success of my first news segment and then immediately feeling sick once I got home. I figured my stomach wasn't agreeing with the greasy Asian food we consumed, but as the night progressed, I started to feel worse. That was Thursday.

"It's Saturday afternoon."

"What? What happened to Friday?" I try to remember what happened yesterday, but the pounding headache that's hammering behind my eyes makes it hard to think of anything. I vaguely remember numerous trips to the bathroom due to both ends of my body being in use, and sleeping in between those trips.

"You sent me a text saying you weren't feeling well, that you think you have what I had, but I didn't have it as bad as this. When you didn't pick up your phone or respond to my numerous texts this morning, I got worried and decide to check in on you. You scared the crap out of me when you wouldn't wake up. You started moaning, so I called Layla and she came over. Have you been drinking water?" Robert asks, as he brings my drink back to my lips for me to try to take another sip.

"I don't know." Usually I am good with drinking water and being conscious enough NOT to get dehydrated, but every trip to the bathroom seemed to drain my energy. I take one more sip of my drink and shudder at the taste.

"Car is downstairs, let's go!" Layla comes back in the room and they both help me stand up. "Do you want to change or go to the hospital wearing that?" I look down to see that I'm in pajama pants and a thin tank top that leaves no imagination to what my breasts look like.

"Can someone please grab a sweatshirt from my bottom drawer? I just need to cover up the girls." Robert complies and helps me put it on. We step out into my living room where I am completely blinded from afternoon light. Layla grabs my sunglasses and purse and we slowly make our way downstairs.

Once we arrive at the car, Robert adjusts the passenger seat to recline and helps me get in. I hold onto a bucket while Layla drives the short distance to the hospital. After giving the keys to the valet, she wheels me into the emergency room with the wheelchair they provided and gives the administrative registration clerk my information and insurance to check me in. A triage nurse sees us to take my vitals and records any answers I can give to her questions. Fortunately due to the time of day, our wait is brief and I am taken back to the treatment area. I am seen by the attending physician who asks me questions while examining me. I answer as many as I can, with Layla filling in more of the details for me.

"It sounds like you have a stomach bug or food poisoning along with severe dehydration. I do want to run some tests to rule out some other options. Let's get you started on IV fluids first, though. I will be back." He leaves the room to go talk to the nurses.

"Can she get another blanket? She won't stop shivering." Layla asks the arriving nurse, who grabs one from the bottom of a cart and pulls it over me. I smile weakly at Layla, so thankful that she is here with me as I wouldn't want to be here by myself with strangers.

"My name is Jackie, and I am one of the nurses on call. I am going to start you on an IV to help with your dehydration. I will need to draw some blood from you in order to run some tests. Is that okay?" I nod my head and keep my eyes closed, knowing that the sight of blood will make me throw up. She pulls up my sleeve and swiftly draws the amount she needs.

"Do you think you can give me a urine test?" she asks and I shake my head no as I have zero desire to pee or try to stand up because of my dizziness.

"Can you tell me your last day of your menstrual cycle?"

"I think I am currently on it." Go figure that puking and pooping my brains out would not be enough for my body to handle.

"What do you mean by you 'think'?"

"It's been abnormal." I proceed to tell her about it and she records it all on my chart.

"I'm going to run these to the lab. They're slightly backed up, so it might be a little while. You should start to feel better soon from the IV. Why don't you just try to relax and I will be back shortly." She leaves and I immediately fall asleep.

I am woken up by Layla when the physician arrives. I don't know how long I was asleep for, but I immediately feel better than before.

"Looks like the IV is doing its magic as you have regained some color in your skin and clarity in your eyes. How do you feel?" The physician asks as he re-examines me.

"Better." Despite still feeling cold, the shivering has stopped and my headache has lessened. I am able to focus more without getting dizzy.

"Good. Since you were exposed to someone else with the stomach flu, I will rule out food poisoning. But I am not entirely sure if it is the stomach flu or hyperemesis gravidarum."

"Hyper what?" I ask, not understanding a word he just said.

"Severe morning sickness."

I grunt and shake my head no, wanting to quickly rule out the option of a baby. "Nope. Not possible. My doctor told me I can't get pregnant due to my abnormal uterus. So, stomach flu it is!" I look over at Layla, who is watching the doctor closely.

He frowns and looks over my chart. "Well, that's interesting, because according to your blood test, your hCG levels indicate that you are pregnant. Have you been sexually active recently?"

"Yes, but we used condoms each time." I start grasping for any excuse that will help prove I am not pregnant, even though I know condoms are not 100% effective.

"Unfortunately, condoms can rip or tear, and the likelihood of you even knowing they are is small. Why don't we do an ultrasound to confirm?" He nods to the nurse, who leaves and returns with a portable ultrasound machine. "Can you recall the last day of your menstrual cycle?"

"I thought I was currently having my period."

"That might be from the baby implanting itself in your uterus or from your cervix as extra blood collects there and could be coming out. Let's just say you aren't currently in your cycle, do you remember the time before this?"

I try to recall the last time I had my period and I immediately suck in my breath, realizing that it was before my trip to Las Vegas. Stress causes me to have irregular periods, so not getting my period when I'm stressed out doesn't usually alarm me. I grab my phone out of my purse to look at the calendar.

"March 18." I swallow and look at Layla, whose eyes widen.

"And when were you last sexually active?"

"The last week of March." I look at my calendar again to confirm the dates I was in Las Vegas.

"Okay, so if you are pregnant, that would put you around 7 weeks. The ultrasound will confirm everything."

While the nurse preps me for the ultrasound, my eyes are glued to the screen, hoping this is all a mistake. The screen starts to show what looks like water. As the doctor proceeds to move the wand around, a black hole suddenly appears with something small in the middle.

"There we are!" He looks at me with excitement of proving that he was right.

"It looks like a hole. Are you sure that isn't an organ?" With not understanding how this can be a baby, I'm not convinced that he knows how to work the machinery.

He takes a pen and points to the screen, "This is the gestational sac that is filled with amniotic fluid and that little gray thing is the baby. Let's listen to see if we can hear a heartbeat." He reaches over to turn a dial and a loud thumping fills the air.

"Wh..what is that?" I stutter, not wanting to believe what I am seeing or hearing.

"That is the baby's heartbeat and it is beating at 105 beats per minute, which is very good." He proceeds to write everything from the screen down on my chart and turns off the machine. I stare at the black screen, the words 'PREGNANT' in red warning letters flashing through my mind.

"I don't understand. Why would my doctor tell me I can't get pregnant?"

"Are you sure he said the word 'can't'? With the miracles we have seen of women beating the odds and getting pregnant, I would be surprised if those were the exact words."

I think back to that painful day years ago. "You're right, those weren't his exact words. His exact words were that it would be 'hard' to get pregnant."

"Well, as you can now see, doctors are human and are sometimes wrong." He smiles and extends his hand. "Congratulations! I hope this is happy news for you. You need to go buy prenatal vitamins and start taking those today. Continue to rest and drink plenty of fluids to stay hydrated. On Monday, call your obstetrician so you can get an appointment right away to be seen and schedule your future appointments. If you're still throwing up and become dehydrated again, come back and see us."

"Thank you." I weakly whisper and watch as he leaves to complete my discharge papers. Panic starts to set in and I immediately start to feel claustrophobic.

"Jenna?" I turn to look at Layla with questioning eyes and slowly start to shake my head.

"No....No...this can't be happening!" I say in denial, not understanding why I am pregnant now and not when I was married.

"It's okay, Jenna...it's okay." Layla hugs me and I hold on tight, tears starting to stream down my face as my whole world feels like it is caving in on me. The nurse walks in and I wipe my cheeks, ashamed for her to see my tears of sadness.

She goes over my discharge papers with me and repeats the instructions that the doctor just told me. I sign the papers and we are free to leave.

The car ride home is silent as I watch the outside world in a trance. Layla must have sent Robert a text because he is there to greet us when we pull up to my building, his expression somber. They help me out of the car and walk slowly with me to the elevators, the lift up to my floor painfully quiet. As we enter my apartment, I look around as if I am seeing it for the first time, noticing all the things it lacks that didn't matter before. *Can a baby even live here?* There are children in the buildings, so clearly I am overreacting.

"Why don't we have a girls' day? We can watch movies, eat junk food and have a slumber party!" Robert claps his hand, his voice overly enthusiastic.

"I'm not hungry." The mere thought of food makes me to want to vomit. "I think I want to be alone, guys."

"I like the movie idea!" Layla hastily replies.

"Great, let's pick a movie." Robert briskly walks over to the TV and turns on Netflix. He starts to flip the movies and laughs. "Oh my gosh, wouldn't it be funny if we watched '*Knocked Up*'?"

With the look of horror registering on our faces, he immediately stops laughing. "Too soon to make a joke about it?" Robert usually is on point with inserting his comedic comments to lighten the mood. This time he failed.

"What the fuck is wrong with you?" Layla angrily stalks towards him. "Give me that remote!"

"I'm sorry! I was just trying to lighten the mood. I didn't mean anything by it."

"I'm going to go throw up now. I'll be back. Pick a suspenseful movie." I retreat to the sanctuary of my bedroom and shut the door as Layla continues to ream Robert on his insensitivity. I go to my bathroom and splash cool water on my face, hoping I'll wake up from this dream. I dry my face and decide to lay down on the bed. I turn to my side and hug my pillow as tight as I can when my vision starts to blur with the tears that need to be released as my new reality sinks in.

I am going to have a baby.... a baby I never thought I would have.

I am going to be in charge of another human being's life.

I am going to be a single mom.

I lose the concept of time as I cry my sorrows into my pillow. I feel the bed shift and strong arms wrap around me as Layla lays down in front of me and holds me. I feel hands rubbing my hair away from my face and realize Robert has gotten behind me. Having both friends here to comfort me makes me not feel so alone and my tears start to subside. I try to gain control of my breathing and eventually the three of us lay in silence, holding onto each other.

"What am I going to do, guys?" I break the silence by communicating my thoughts out loud.

"We're going to have a baby! You're not alone, Jenna. We'll be here with you every step of the way." I feel Robert nodding at Layla's words.

"I love you both so much, and while I thank you for that, I don't think you understand the undertaking of a baby."

"Doesn't matter – we're doing it together," she says firmly. I let her words sink in, knowing that I won't hold them to their promise as they need to live their own lives and not worry about helping me.

"What about Cal? Are you going to tell him?" Robert softly asks. So engulfed in my own emotions, that I haven't given any thought of him. Considering we haven't talked in weeks, would he even want to be part of the baby's life?

"I'll contact him after I make it out of the first trimester. No reason to tell him now, in case something happens." They don't say anything to this, and I use their silence as affirmation that I'm doing the right thing by not telling him yet.

"Let's keep this between us for now, okay?" I plead to them, needing to think and be in denial for just a little bit longer.

"Okay," they say in unison. We hug each other tighter, and I can only pray that this baby will strengthen our bond and not divide it.

"Never did I ever think I would be laying in bed with two straight women. This is a gay man's worst nightmare of a three-some!" Robert breaks the silence and uncontrollable laughter permeates the air, all three of us laughing at the image of what we must look like.

"Come on guys, let's go watch a movie!" Layla says as our laughter dies down. I let Layla and Robert take me in the other room to distract me for a couple of hours.

19

My reaction to my pregnancy might mirror what one's reaction would be to the news that they have a terminal disease - horror and denial. I refuse to believe that I'm pregnant and I demand that Layla and Robert not even talk about it to me, let alone anyone else. I go about my days pretending that all is right in my world, but then become horrified when I can't fit into any of my pants. I can already tell that my wardrobe will consist of dresses until winter. The nausea has started to subside, but the constant fatigue forces me to take daytime naps, which are completely inconvenient for my professional life.

Is my reaction to all of this messed up? *Absolutely!*

Should I be grateful that I can even get pregnant when I thought I couldn't? *Yes!*

Do I feel guilty every time I feel ashamed of being pregnant? *You bet!*

As I walk home from my 12-week doctor's appointment, the souvenir ultrasound photo of what looks like a little alien safely hidden in my purse, I realize that I need to start facing my future. I need to start making a plan for myself...and for my unborn child. It's still hard for me to be excited about the fact that I will be a single mother, but I need to accept my fate. I also need to decide when I'm going to tell my parents. Oh yeah, and the father of my child. I groan out loud and decide to do what I do best right now - ignore the situation.

It's too gorgeous of a summer day to go back inside, so I make a beeline for the beach to get some vitamin D and people watch. I sit down on the stairs, take my shoes off and inhale the fresh air off the lake. I close my eyes and smile, basking in the warmth of the sun's rays. *Ahh, this is exactly what I needed right now.* I almost start to nod off when I hear a baby squeal with laughter. I open my eyes to see the cutest little boy running in the sand, his parents chasing after him. He's wobbly on his adorable chunky legs, and his smile reveals two top and two bottom teeth. His father catches up to him, scoops him up and throws him high in the air, making the boy laugh even harder. Both parents look adoringly at him, kissing him every chance they get. They are the perfect image of what a family should look like.

Will I look at my child like that? Will Cal be happy to hear he is going to be a father? While I can't answer the first question yet, I can get the answer to the second question. It's time to rip off the band-aid and call him. I look at my watch to see that it's early afternoon. If he's in Los Angeles, then it's lunchtime. If he's in back in London, then it's nighttime. Either way, this would be the perfect time to make the call. With a sigh, I put my shoes back on and take one more look at that perfect family I was watching before. The little boy is now sitting on top of his father's shoulders while the mother strolls next to them along the shore. I need to give Cal that option of wanting to be in his child's life. I get up and walk back to my apartment.

When I arrive, Robert is packing up his bag to leave. "There you are! I was starting to get worried about you. Everything okay?"

"Yes. I spent a couple of extra minutes thinking at the beach."

"What did the doctor say?"

"He said I was pregnant," I say sarcastically, but with a smile. Robert just rolls his eyes at me as he shuts down his laptop. "He said that everything looks good so far, and I have to see him every month for the next four months for an ultrasound and to check my cervix due to my abnormal uterus. After that, I won't need any ultrasounds until the last month to make sure the baby is in Operation: Get Out of Uterus position. Oh, and I got my first photo of the baby." I take the photo out of my purse and hand it to Robert. "It's apparently the size of a plum."

He looks at the photo, looks at my belly and then places the photo against my belly and shakes his head. "That is just freaky. Crazy how you can see it is starting to look like an actual human and not a tadpole. What are you doing to do with this photo?"

"I don't know. Put it away? Why are you asking? Do you need to keep it to remind yourself not to knock anybody up?" I joke, not really understanding his question.

"I think you should put it on your refrigerator."

I look at him strangely. "Why would I want to do that?"

"So you'll finally get it through that head of yours that this shit is real! Jenna, we need to start planning the future!" He throws his hands up in the air with exasperation.

"I know this is real, Robert. I just needed some time. In fact, I was going to call Cal right now."

"Really?" His expression filled with shock. "Good! It's like if you have an STD, your partner has the right to know. He really needs to know about the baby, Jenna."

I blink my eyes at him and stare as my brain tries to digest what he just said. "Did you just compare a baby to an STD?" I shake my head and rub my forehead, concern taking over my confusion. "Is there something you aren't telling me, Robert? Did someone give you an STD?"

"Nope, I'm clean as a whistle! Just horrible at analogies!" A blush colors his cheeks from embarrassment. "On that note, wish I could stay for this but I have to run by the storage unit to pick up the decorations for next week's news segment... and I have a hot date tonight." He smiles slyly.

"You do? With whom?" A pang of jealously jolts me, wishing that I had places to go and people to meet.

"Oh, some guy I met at the gym." He waves his hand downward as if this wasn't a big deal.

"The gym? Since when do you go to the gym?" I look at him closely and notice that his face does look thinner, his clothes fitting him looser.

"Since the day you came back from the hospital saying you were pregnant. I need to get healthy so I can be around a long time for our baby," he says with sincerity as I start to tear up from his words. I walk toward him and hug him tightly.

"Thank you, friend. I love you so!" I kiss his cheek before pulling away.

"I love you too. We told you that you're not going to be alone and Layla and I mean it. Now go call Cal, then call me after to tell me what happens. Good luck!" He squeezes my arms and leaves the apartment.

I take a deep breath, square my shoulders and march into my room. I sit down on my bed next to my nightstand and pull out his card from the drawer. I wondered why I felt the need to keep his card after we stopped talking, and now I'm grateful that I did. I close my eyes and pray that this will all go well.

I dial his number and once again feel disappointment when Valerie's voice comes through the other end. "Hi Valerie, it's Jenna Pruitt." I say with a business-like tone.

"Hi...Jenna, how are you?" Her voice is mixed with reluctance and surprise.

"Is Cal around? I really need to speak with him."

"No, he's not available right now and Jenna, I really hate to tell you this, but Cal has started dating someone serious. I thought from our last phone conversation that you were moving on as well?" Her voice gets slightly condescending, which only adds fuel to my anger.

"That's fine. He can date whomever he wants, as I don't care. Something has happened that I really need to speak to him about."

"Jenna, with all due respect, why would he call you back when he has a new girlfriend? I just don't..."

"Valerie, I am fucking PREGNANT, so that is WHY I need to talk with him NOW!" I snap into the phone, my temper gone from her excuses.

"Wh-WHAT?!" She stammers loudly, shock registering in her voice.

"I'm twelve weeks pregnant and I'm just calling to let him know about it," I say calmly, reminding myself that she is not to blame for his actions and I shouldn't be taking my anger out on her.

"No offense, but how do we know that it's his? Hollywood actors are always having women falsely claiming that they are pregnant with their child."

I laugh bitterly at her and choose to ignore the fact that she is implying I might be lying. "I am one hundred-percent positive it is his, as I have not had sex with anyone else since then."

"We can't prove that until a paternity test is done, which we will demand to do once the child is born. Did you not use protection? Were you not on birth control?" she asks, her voice laced with disgust.

"Not that any of this is even your business, Valerie, but we did use protection. Condoms can tear without your knowledge. And I had no reason to be on birth control at that time," I say bitterly, wishing even more that this was being discussed with Cal and not his assistant. I take a deep breath to calm down before continuing. "Valerie, I'll be more than happy to do a paternity test when the baby is born. This has been a shock for me as well, and I'm being honest when I tell you that I do not want ANYTHING from Cal. I don't want his money, I don't want to be in the tabloids, nothing. I just wanted to do the right thing by letting him know so he can decide if he wants to be in this baby's life or not. That's all that I want from him." I sigh with resignation, hoping she understands.

She is quiet for a few seconds before responding. "I understand. I'm sorry, Jenna."

"Yeah, so am I," I say softly, tired from the emotions and the headache that is pounding my temples.

"I'll talk to him as soon as I reach him. You should be hearing from him soon."

"Thanks, Valerie." I hang up the phone and lay back against the bed, completely drained from that phone call. If this phone call was emotional on me, I don't want to imagine how it's going to be when Cal calls me back.

One day later:

To: Cal Harrington
From: Jenna Pruitt
Subject: Please call me!

Cal,
Hope you are doing well. I talked with Valerie yesterday over something very important that I need to discuss with you. Please call me as soon as possible.

Best,
Jenna Pruitt

Two days later:

To: Cal Harrington
From: Jenna Pruitt
Subject: I REALLY NEED YOU TO CALL ME!

Cal,
PLEASE...I'm begging you...it is IMPERATIVE that you call me back.
Jenna

Three Days later:

To: Cal Harrington
From: Jenna Pruitt
Subject: EMERGENCY! PLEASE CALL!

Stop being a coward and fucking call me already!

Text message from Valerie the next day after last email:

VALERIE: Hi Jenna. Cal has received your emails and he tells me he plans on calling you back today. I'm so sorry, Jenna! He's being a complete asshole. I have never seen him like this. I'm thinking of you and hope you're feeling good.

Email the following day after text from Valerie:

To: Jenna Pruitt
From: Cal Harrington
CC: Valerie Lewis
Subject: Current Situation

Jenna,

My assistant has discussed with me the reasons behind your emails and phone call. While I would hope you wouldn't try to deceive me for monetary gains, I'm not in the position to be present in the child's life. My current focus needs to stay on my career. A paternity test will be conducted, and if the DNA matches, then financial arrangement shall be made.
Please contact my assistant once the child is born.

Best of luck to you,
Cal Harrington

I stare at his email in absolute shock. I read his words over and over again, each time is another slash to my heart. Not because he is rejecting me, but because he is rejecting his own child. I can't fathom how someone would not want to be part of their own child's life. I recall him mentioning to me his desire for kids in the future - was that all a lie? I roughly brush away my tears, determined to never shed a tear over this man again. My heartache turns to immense hatred and I vow to never waste another moment, thought, or even breath on Cal Harrington ever again.

To: Cal Harrington
From: Jenna Pruitt
CC: Valerie Lewis
Subject: re: Current Situation

FUCK YOU!

20

Six and a Half Months Later

"All these women who say they feel beautiful being pregnant are full of shit!" I huff, trying to catch my breath from walking around the mall. It's New Year's Eve, one day before my due date, and I'm beyond ready for this baby to arrive. I am well above the twenty-five to thirty pounds they recommend you gain - more like forty-five pounds on my 5'5 frame. I haven't had a good night's sleep in seven months and everything aches. I feel like I have been completely lied to when it comes to pregnancy. Everyone paints this picture that all things are glorious after the first trimester. *LIES!*

No one tells you about round ligament pain.

No one tells you about the constant pressure on your bladder.

No one tells you about the back pain.

No one tells you about the hemorrhoids.

No one tells you about the acne.

No one tells you about the wet dreams being so vivid, you wake up screaming your orgasm.

Okay, so this may not be a bad thing.

Is every woman different when it comes to their pregnancy symptoms? *Of course*. Am I being overdramatic? *Yes*. But by the time I reached the seven-month mark, I was over being pregnant. I didn't even start to look pregnant until I was six months, the infamous round belly just showing up one day and completely freaking me out. I didn't care if people thought I was gaining weight, but looking pregnant was different. I didn't want anyone out of my tight knit circle to know I was having a child out of wedlock. I stayed inside most of the time and hired extra event coordinators to be on-site managers for our booked parties since Robert couldn't be at every party by himself. I hid behind the decor tables during our news segments to hide my belly. Fortunately, the producer was understanding with my wanting to keep my pregnancy private. During the day, I act confident about my impending motherhood, but alone in bed at night, I feel anything but. While I should have wanted to be the poster child for successful women doing it all on their own, I felt more like Hester Prynne with the scarlet "A" on my chest. My mother's reaction to my pregnancy didn't help my confidence in my ability either.

I went to my parent's house for dinner one Sunday evening during my fourth month of pregnancy. Despite my best efforts, she couldn't help but notice my weight gain and wouldn't stop her incessant chatter about how concerned she was and that something could be wrong with me, blah blah blah. So, I decided right then and there to shut her up and put myself out of my emotional misery of telling them.

"Something is wrong with me, Mother. I am pregnant." I gulp down my water as silence fills the room and both of them stare at me.

"Oh Jenna, why do you have to make a joke out of everything? This is not funny." She continues to cut her steak while my father puts his fork and knife down, crosses his arms against his chest and continues looking at me. Our bond together is so tight that I know he can sense I am telling the truth.

"I'm not joking, Mother. I am eighteen weeks pregnant. The baby is due on New Year's Day."

My mother's mouth drops open and she goes back and forth from looking at me to my father, waiting for someone to say something. My father presses his mouth into a thin line and looks down at his plate to avoid showing the disappointment that has now entered his eyes.

"Who is the father, Jenna?" he asks quietly while fiddling with his wineglass.

"The father wants nothing to do with the baby, so I will be raising my child by myself." I place my napkin on the table and stand, deciding it is time to leave.

My father's head shoots up. "The hell you will, Jenna! That man needs to take responsibility and at least pay child support." He bangs his hand against the table, jostling the silverware and wine glasses, his eyes darkening from anger.

"I want nothing to do with him, Dad." I smile sadly as my father closes his eyes and balls his hands into fists.

"How could you, Jenna! How could you do this?" My mother shrieks as tears stream down her face.

"Oh, that's right, Mother, because I purposely put holes in the condom we used so I could ruin YOUR reputation." My voice laced with heavy sarcasm as I push my seat in. "So sorry for continuing to be a disappointment to you."

"Watch your tone, young lady!" My father glares at me while my mother gets up and moves behind his chair, placing her hands on his shoulders.

"Don't worry, Mother, my little secret will stay safe with me. I don't need anyone's help! Feel free to keep your distance so your reputations will stay intact." I turn to leave and walk to the front entrance, slamming the door shut on their pleas to come back.

The following day, my father showed up alone on my doorstep, telling me he would never abandon me and that everything is going to be alright. My mother seems to need a little more time as I have not heard from her since.

True to their word, Layla and Robert have been there for me every day of this pregnancy. They came to my twenty-week doctor's appointment and were enthralled by being able to see the baby via ultrasound. They convinced me to not find out the gender so that it would be a surprise. I can't stand surprises and the suspense has been a constant fight among the three of us due to my desire to want to decorate the nursery. They planned a getaway trip when I was twenty-eight weeks pregnant to Fort Lauderdale for the three of us since I refused a baby shower and have made sure I have not had one stressful workday. They even came to all of my baby classes with me, which were hilarious because of Robert's horrified expressions at watching the birthing video. Their enthusiasm for this baby has helped lessen my doubts about doing this all by myself.

So here I am, ready to have this baby and trying every old wives' tale to see if I can make it come early. The idea of this baby coming after its due date makes me want to cry, so I try to walk faster but waddling like a penguin as I do now makes it that much more difficult.

"Jenna, slow down! You are going to pull those delicate ligaments! How much longer are we going to keep walking? We have already walked over a mile and I need to start getting ready for your mother's party." Robert whines and looks at his watch. "You already have eaten spicy food for lunch and now the walking. Nothing is happening! And I am sorry, but don't you even dare ask me to have sex with you to try to force that baby out!" The expression on his face is so appalled at the idea that I can't help but laugh out loud.

"Robert, I am not THAT desperate for the baby to come out." I look at my watch to see that it is getting late for him. "Fine, we can leave but we need to stop at the drugstore first so I can buy castor oil."

"Castor oil? Good god, Jenna that's almost as bad as being desperate enough to have sex with a gay man! You're going to shit your brains out! No, I draw the line on this!" He slashes his hand in the air as if really trying to draw a line.

I shudder at the visual, but am determined to still try it. "My mother used it for me and I came out just fine."

"Your mother is bat shit crazy and probably has a deal with the devil! She got lucky as it doesn't work on everyone and I read it can be dangerous for the baby. Please don't do it, Jenna." He grips my hand and squeezes so I would look at his face to see his concern.

"How about this, I will only take half of the recommended dose, okay? Maybe even less than that. And I will take it once Layla arrives to babysit me." I joke as the two of them have not left me alone these past three weeks. Layla will be coming over to spend New Year's Eve with me while Robert is at the party. The plan is to have a nice dinner, watch the ball drop and have a sip of champagne. *I am nine months pregnant, one sip is not going to hurt the baby and I deserve it!*

"All right." He grumbles. "But I still don't like this idea!" We stop at the drug store and I buy the castor oil and a small bottle of root beer to drink with it and we head back to my apartment.

Four hours later and I feel like a proud mama watching her son go to the prom as Robert comes out of my guest room, looking impeccable in a three-piece black tuxedo. My eyes tear up at how proud I am of him. While I would love to blame these tears on my pregnancy hormones, I think I would have this reaction even if I wasn't pregnant. He has really stepped up both personally and professionally to help me juggle what my new life is going to be like. He's become the little brother I never had. I would literally be a mess without him.

Layla whistles and walks a slow circle around him. "Look at you, you sexy thang! You look marvelous!"

"You really do, Robert. You look amazing! The baby thinks so too as he won't stop kicking since you walked back in."

Robert places his hand on my belly and we watch my belly ripple like a low wave on the lake. This is the best part of being pregnant - feeling the baby kick and move inside of you.

"I'm still waiting for a small hand to come out of your belly and fist bump me." He laughs and shakes his head. "Stop calling my princess a 'he'. You know you're having a girl for me to spoil."

I groan at the thought, really hoping for a baby boy who looks just like me with the only thing inherited from his father are his height and magnificent blue eyes. "If it's a girl and she's anything like me, I will have gray hair before I am forty!" We all laugh at the thought of another sassy Pruitt girl in this world.

Robert stops laughing and his face gets serious. "I don't know if I can handle Pamela without you." He grips my hands and squeezes.

"You'll be just fine. Everything is ready to go. Besides, she's always liked you better than me anyways. Maybe she'll try to hook you up this time with someone since I won't be there," I say with a hopeful smile. My mother loves playing matchmaker and has taken it upon herself at every single one of her parties to put eligible, successful bachelors in my place.

"With your mother's tastes, I will definitely be coming home alone."

"You better be coming home alone since you are sleeping here!" I nod at Layla's words, really hoping he wouldn't do that.

"Layla, unlike you, I have zero desire for both of you to hear me get down to business. So, before I leave, I want to watch you take that castor oil to make sure you do what we agreed upon."

I nod and head to the kitchen. The directions on the package say one to four tablespoons, so I decide to only do the one. Robert and Layla both read the packaging and watch me pour the one-tablespoon into my root beer.

"Bottoms up!" I toast to them, take a swig and immediately start to gag at the horrible taste and texture of the cocktail.

"That's what you get for wanting to get my baby out early!" Robert laughs at me as I make gagging noises.

"It's only one day early and this is revolting! I can't finish this!" I pour the remaining liquid down the sink drain, regretting my decision to take it.

"Can you do me a favor and please try not to poop anywhere else besides the toilet? I love you, but I really have no desire to clean up turd." Layla shakes her head at the thought.

"I don't think anything will even happen since I did the lowest dosage and didn't even finish it."

Two hours later, Layla and I are eating dinner when all of a sudden I feel a wave of nausea and I start to sweat. I feel a sharp pain and I gasp out loud, holding my belly.

"Jenna, what's wrong? You're completely white as a ghost!" Layla grips my hand with worry.

I run to the bathroom, having to hold my belly and my butt as I make it just in time to relieve myself. It seriously was exactly like the scene with Jeff Bridges in *Dumb and Dumber.*

"Are you okay in there? You've been in there an awfully long time." Layla knocks on my bathroom door to check on me.

"Yeah, I'm okay, besides being traumatized by the power of castor oil." I hear Layla laugh as she leaves my room. I take a shower, finish my dinner and settle on the couch to start watching the New Year's Eve festivities.

I cry out loud in my sleep as an intense cramp ripples from my back to my abdomen. I sit up in my bed and hold my belly, praying that this is not another onslaught of the effects from the castor oil. The pain slowly subsides and I look at my clock to see it is three o'clock in the morning. We've been asleep for almost three hours. I decide to get up to see if Robert has made it home yet. I look over at Layla, who's sleeping next to me, to make sure I don't disturb her. I tiptoe out into the hallway to see the guest bedroom door is still open, indicating he has not arrived home. I go back into my room and lay back down. I'm about to fall asleep when another sharp pain grips my abdomen. I sit up and start to do my breathing exercises while counting to see how many seconds the pain lasts. As soon as it's over, I take a deep breath and look at my phone. It has been ten minutes and it felt just like the first one.

I get out of my bed, grab my phone and go into my bathroom to look on the internet to check if these are true contraction. As soon as I get into my bathroom, I feel a tightening, then hear a popping sound and water rushes down my legs onto the floor. *Oh shit, my water just broke!* I look down in shock as we were told in our birthing class that most women's water does not break like it does in the movies. I grab some towels to clean up the mess and go wake up Layla.

"Layla, my water just broke. It's time." I shake her to try to rouse her out of her sleep.

"What?" She grumbles, clearly not enjoying being interrupted.

"Time to go. My water just broke." I turn on the lights and see her shield her eyes from the brightness.

"Your water broke?" She asks with a confused look on her face.

"Yes, it's time to get dressed." I pull out my going to the hospital outfit and start to put it on.

"Oh, shit!" Layla throws back the covers and races around the room to get dressed, finally understanding what's happening.

We're ready to go in five minutes and just as we're about to leave, Robert walks through the door, looking exhausted.

"Whoa, why are you ladies up?" Shock registers on his face as we greet him in the living room.

"It's time to have the baby!" Layla says, excitement gleaming from her now awake eyes.

"Really?" Robert looks over to me for confirmation and I nod. I grab my purse and suddenly stop in my tracks as another contraction hits me. I lean against the wall, hold my belly and breathe rapidly. Robert and Layla just stare at me, their eyes growing wide as they watch me. The pain finally subsides and as I take deep breaths, I look around my apartment, feeling like I am missing something.

"Where are the car seat and hospital bag?" I open the hallway closet and don't see them there.

"I put them in the car before I left today just in case that crazy idea of yours with castor oil worked. I can't believe it worked, by the way. That baby better be fine, Jenna!" Robert wags his finger at me in warning.

"Well, let's go find out!" We head downstairs, get into my car and make the short drive to the hospital. I have another contraction in the car before I am wheeled into the hospital. Robert registers for me and after having to sit through two more contractions in the waiting room, we finally get a room in labor and delivery.

"When do I get my epidural?" I pant as another contraction rips through me. The on-call doctor and nurse are monitoring my contractions and the baby's heart rate as I breathe through the pain.

"Your contractions are strong, so we can go ahead and start you on an epidural. Let's check your effacement and cervix."

"Oh, thank god!" I breathe out as the pain slowly decreases.

"You're 100% effaced, but your cervix is only halfway there. Let's give it another hour to see if you progress, and if not, we'll put you on Pitocin."

Five minutes later, the anesthesiologist comes in and discusses the epidural, the insertion, what will happen and any side effects. He waits for another contraction to pass before inserting the epidural. Once he's finished, I breathe a sigh of relief and lay back against the hospital bed. The nurses and anesthesiologist leave the room and for the first time, Layla, Robert and I are alone.

"I can't believe we're here," I say as I look around the hospital room.

"Are you scared?" Layla asks. I look at her in silence before answering.

"Not yet," I smirk, not wanting to get all worked up over the unknowns. "Let's not even think about it. Robert, tell me ALL about the party!"

Robert goes into detail about the party, how much money they actually raised and how my mother did try to set him up with someone. "He was bald and wrinkly, but had lots of money she told me!" He laughs and shakes his head. "Honestly though, she looked sad. She didn't have that normal devilish Pamela Pruitt twinkle in her eye. I think she really misses you."

I swallow the lump in my throat and shrug. Despite all of her craziness, I can't deny that I do miss my mother. According to my father, she feels I should be the one apologizing for my behavior that night. I inherited my mother's stubbornness as I don't plan on apologizing anytime soon as I believe she is the one who owes me an apology. I have come to terms that this is her loss and she has the power to make it right.

An hour passes and the doctor comes back in to check on me. "Doesn't look like much progress has been made. Let's go ahead and start the Pitocin." The nurse nods at the doctor and leaves the room. "It is going to be a long day with this being your first baby. Try to get some sleep while we wait." She looks over at Layla and Robert. "Why don't you two go get something to eat or some coffee while Ms. Pruitt tries to rest?"

"Robert, go home. You are exhausted. Layla will call you if anything changes." Robert looks from me to Layla with worry in his eyes.

"Are you sure?" He asks and I nod my head. "Okay, but Layla, you BETTER call me or we are no longer friends!"

"Stop being so dramatic, you know I will! I'm going to pull out this chair bed and go to sleep." She nods toward the chair that pulls out into a twin bed.

Robert gives us each a hug goodbye and leaves. The nurses help pull out Layla's bed and provide her with a blanket and sheets.

"How are you feeling?" The nurse asks as she checks the contraction monitor print out.

"Epidurals are amazing!" I say, my eyes ready to close from exhaustion. She just laughs and tells me to rest. I look over at Layla to see she is already fast asleep. I close my eyes and drift off.

But I quickly learn that "sleeping" in a hospital is a bit of a joke. They wake me up to check my progress every hour. After the third time, I am green with envy that Layla is sleeping through all of this.

"You are progressing nicely," the doctor says. "I am predicting maybe another two to three hours and we can start turning off the Pitocin, lowering your epidural and begin the pushing process." She leaves the room and I close my eyes to try to go back to sleep.

Not twenty minutes later, I hear the door open again and I can't contain my exasperated sigh of annoyance for my sleep being interrupted. I open my eyes to find my parents staring back at me. My father is next to my bed, smiling, while my mother is at the foot of the bed, holding a vase of beautiful flowers, her gaze hesitant as she waits for my reaction at their arrival.

"Hi sweetheart, how are you feeling?" My dad pushes my hair off my forehead and gazes at me lovingly. Robert must have called them, which I'm grateful he did.

"I'm just tired. They put me on Pitocin and think that within the next two to three hours we should be good to go." I look over at my mother and nod to her. "Hello, Mother."

I watch her wipe away a tear and clear her throat. "Oh Jenna, I'm so sorry! I wasn't thinking clearly that night and should have been more sympathetic. This situation just wasn't what I wanted for you." She sighs and shakes her head. "No matter, I shouldn't have placed blame and I apologize." She comes around to my other side, puts the vase of flowers down and grips my hand.

"My baby is having a baby and that is such a beautiful thing. If you think about it, this is a miracle since you had so much difficulty before. Robert called us and told us you were here and I just couldn't bear the thought of missing the birth of my first grandchild. Do you mind that we're here?"

"No, Mother, I'm very happy you are here." I squeeze her hand and she throws herself at me, hugging me as hard as she can. She pulls back and looks at me with more tears in her eyes and places her hand on my belly. "I sure can't wait to see this little one." She looks behind her and gasps in surprise, not seeing Layla when she first walked in. "How is Layla even sleeping through all of this?"

"I'm not, I am just basking in the glow of the reconciliation." She opens her eyes and we all laugh at her dreamy face.

My parents sit down and tell me about the party and what a wonderful job Robert did. I beam with pride at hearing these words because my mother is a harsh critic, so if she is happy then it must have been wonderful. "He really did a wonderful job, Jenna. He deserves a raise."

I nod my head, thinking about all that he's taken on these past months. "He sure does."

The doctor chooses that moment to come back in. After I introduce her to my parents, she checks my progress.

"Wow, well, it looks like we are going to be ready quicker than I thought. You are 100% dilated. We are going to remove the Pitocin and lower your epidural so you can start feeling your legs again."

"Will I feel those awful contractions again?" Dread seeping into my voice at the memory of how painful they are.

"You'll feel a lot of tightening, but nothing like the pain you have without an epidural. We'll give you another hour for the medicine to start wearing off. You get to choose two people to be in here with you. Are those two people present?" She asks as she looks around at everyone, who are staring at me.

"I would like my mother and best friend here." I turn questioning eyes to my mother who has her hands to her mouth and nods her head yes.

"I better call Robert. Mr. Pruitt, do you want to come with me to get some coffee for you and Mrs. Pruitt?" Layla asks my father. He nods his head and leaves with her. My mother smiles down at me and moves back so the nurses can start prepping for the birth of my baby.

Two hours later, tiny screams fill the air as I deliver a healthy baby girl. Everyone is hugging and crying as the nurse takes her away to record her vitals and clean her up. I move my head back and try to see around the nurses who are taking care of me and the baby. Layla is taking pictures of the baby and I am anxious to hold her.

"She's beautiful like her mommy!" My mother says as she watches the baby get washed up. Her screaming continues until the nurse swaddles her in a blanket and brings her to me.

As she places her in my arms, everyone in the room fades as I stare at my daughter. I'm in complete awe at her perfect tiny nose, her perfect tiny lips, and her perfect tiny chin. I don't realize that I'm crying until a tear splashes on her face, causing her beautiful face to squish up, ready to scream at the intrusion. I quietly shush her and she opens her eyes at me. It feels like I am looking into her soul and at that moment, I am beyond thankful that she is mine.

"So, this is what true love feels like." I smile down at her and kiss her forehead, ready to start my new life with her.

21

Four Years Later

I hear my bedroom door slowly open, the pitter-patter of feet against the carpet. The bed shifts slightly and I feel a hand brush the hair away from my ear.

"Mommy," she whispers into my ear. "Time for you to wake up."

I moan softly, pretending to be asleep as I'm curious to hear what she's going to say. I've actually been awake for an hour, staring up at my ceiling, trying to map out the busy day ahead of me.

"Wake up, lazy bones!" Her tiny voice gets louder and she pushes her hands against my chest. I throw my arm over my eyes and bite my lip to prevent the smile that wants to form on my face.

"Mommy!" She says as sternly as she can. "You need to wake up and make breakfast! I need to go to school to see my boyfriend."

"What?" I throw my arm off my face and pound the bed, the movement startling her. She starts to laugh and I proceed to tickle her, wishing I could bottle that sweet sound up forever.

"Boyfriend? What boyfriend? You are not allowed to have a boyfriend!" I continue to tickle her, her feet almost kicking my face as she falls back against my legs in a fit of laughter. I scoop her up and hug her to me. This only lasts briefly before she is pushing herself out of my arms.

"Uncle Robert met him and says he approves! I don't know what that word means but he was smiling so that must mean it's good. So do I get to keep him?" She asks, her eyes getting wide.

"I need to meet him first before I decide on that. And we don't 'keep' people, silly!" She doesn't pay attention to me as she runs in her room to get ready.

I help her get dressed and then start making breakfast in the kitchen. Breakfast is my favorite meal with Avery. I love watching the expressions that cross her face as she watches television while eating. The cliché saying of how time moves faster when you have children is pure truth. It seems like yesterday I was in that delivery room. *How has it been four years?* I stare at my baby, who is looking more like a little girl every single day. And every day the same thought crosses my mind as I stare at her:

She looks exactly like HIM.

Dark hair, pale skin and those famous blue eyes. She has my bone structure, so people tend to say she looks like me. But if they knew who her dad was, they would be singing a different tune. I am not surprised at all by the irony of it and it certainly does not alter the fact that I am irrevocably in love with her. I don't think about Cal Harrington anymore, but I can't ignore his image when it is staring back at me from a magazine cover in the grocery aisle line. His career has risen and he has become one of the elite actors in Hollywood. I'm sure he doesn't think twice about the child he has in this world and every time I do see an image of him, hatred rears its ugly head. I wish I could let go of my hatred towards him, but I can't seem to. I look over at Avery as she announces she is done with breakfast and can't even fathom not wanting to be part of her life.

I bring my thoughts back to reality and get us both ready to walk her to school. I was fortunate to find a highly rated child care facility within walking distance from our apartment and we love it even if I do want to throw up every time I write the outrageously expensive monthly tuition check. Professionally, my company has been doing the best it ever has been. The monthly news segments have been a hit and we've gained some new high profile clients from those segments. But with more publicity comes more demand and with Avery now in my life, I had to think of ways to work smarter as I refuse to be an absentee mother. We stopped accepting new corporate parties for the months of November and December and put all of our attention on our current client's parties. I converted my dining room into a small office area for Robert and our new part-time assistant. I have scaled back my travels and only accept speaking engagements for conferences that will pay me the most money. When my workday ends at 5 p.m., my full attention is on Avery until she goes to bed and then I stay up and work on blog posts for our children theme parties. I have made friends with some of the other parents at Avery's school and often use Avery and her playmates as my models for the photos we put up on the blog of our themed parties. Some of those blog posts have even been featured in national entertainment magazines, which have increased sales for our online shop that sells the decor to these parties.

My professional life even crossed over into my personal life when I met the man I am currently dating. The captain's wife for the local professional hockey team saw one of our news segments and called to hire us for her son's birthday party. It was there that I met Jax Morrow. I wasn't looking or even interested in dating anyone, but I couldn't resist his charm or persuasion to go out with him. It isn't just because of his good looks, but the way he looks at me and how it makes me feel. Being around Jax made me start to desire men again, a feeling I hadn't felt since Cal. Jax is divorced with a daughter of his own and is in his last years of playing hockey for the Blackhawk's minor league team. In the beginning, our relationship was casual because he plays majority of the time in Rockford, which is two hours away, and spends his summers with his daughter in Canada. Our relationship consisted mostly of phone calls and seeing each other on the weekends when I'm available to go to his games or if he has an off weekend to come to Chicago. This has been working out perfectly for me, but as we've been spending more time together, I sense that Jax wants more and I don't know if I am ready to give him that yet. Avery is my world and I won't let any man take my attention from her. As long as I have her, nothing else matters.

As I look down at my daughter while we walk to school, I realize how truly blessed I am in every aspect of my life and I pray it stays that way.

After dropping her off and going for a run, I went home and got dressed for my busy day at work. Robert and I just left a meeting with a current client whose holiday party we are starting to plan for. With an hour to spare before we have to pick up Avery from childcare, we decide to get a cup of coffee at our favorite local coffee shop. We place our order and find a seat while they make our drinks.

"That meeting went really well. I just absolutely love winter wonderland parties!" Robert sighs, as I nod in agreement. They are my favorite parties to do as well. The theme is so easy and can be so elegant and majestic. "Too bad that CFO is married," Robert murmurs, referring to the CFO of the company we just had the meeting with. The CFO attends every meeting, making sure his Human Resource Director does not go over budget.

"Speaking about love lives, what's going on with yours?" I ask, as he has not mentioned anyone old or new recently.

"Oh, you know, just meeting people who only want to have

fun! " He says as he shrugs his shoulders. "Unlike Layla, I get their names and sometimes have repeat customers. But business has been slow recently," he says with a laugh.

I smile but am distracted by his reference of Layla. Layla seems to have only gotten worse with men. She went back to online dating, which only lasted a hot second. She claims she doesn't have time to go out on dates and it's just easier to meet men out and do whatever she is in the mood for that night with them. I am all for women being sexually liberated, but Layla is doing it for the wrong reasons. Especially when she purposely doesn't want to know the names of her partners. She uses this as her motive to shield her heart. I completely understand her reasoning, but I can't help but be very worried about it.

I feel my phone vibrate as the waitress brings our drinks. I lift my phone out of my pocket to see Jax is calling me. It is very unusual for me to hear from him during this time of the day, so I decide to answer the phone to see if he is okay.

"Hello?" I answer as Robert looks at me to see who it is.

"Hello, gorgeous!" Jax says, "What are you doing?"

"I'm having coffee with Robert, what are you doing?" I mouth who it is to Robert. "I can barely hear you with all the background noise. Where are you?" I cup my hand over the phone so he can hear me better.

"I'm having lunch with some of the guys, but I wanted to let you know that I got called up for tonight's game. One of the guys got hurt at practice today and since a lot of guys are out sick, they had to call me and a defenseman up as replacement." My stomach tightens a little bit as I anticipate what he's going to say next. "Can you make the game tonight if I leave you a ticket at will call?" My intuition being right on par.

"Well, with such short notice, I don't know if I will be able to get a babysitter that quickly. Besides, it's a school night and the game ends too late for Avery to attend," I quickly say before he can suggest she comes with me. Despite her only being in childcare, I try not to schedule anything during a school night. That time is for her and I.

"I can watch Avery!" Robert says loud enough for Jax to hear him, a twinkle in his eye as he looks at me.

"Robert just so kindly offered to watch her, so I guess I'll be there." I give Robert a look indicating that I am not to happy that he made the offer without me thinking about it.

"Tell Robert thank you and I can't wait to see you, baby!" His voice gets low and sensual.

"Me too. Have a safe drive." I say goodbye and hang up. I look at Robert, who is continuing to look at me strangely. "While I truly appreciate you offering to watch Avery for me, it would have been nice to think about if I wanted to go tonight. I have so much work to do and you know how I feel about being away from her on school night."

"Oh, Jenna, I SOOO see your game." He looks at me with a sly smile playing on his lips.

I narrow my eyes at him. "What are you talking about? I don't play games." I blow on the hot coffee, curious as to why he would say that.

"That man is so in love with you and you are going to crush his heart into a million pieces." He leans back and crosses his arm, shaking his head at me.

"You're crazy! Why do you think he's in love with me? I give him zero reasons to be. I put my career and my daughter before him and have made that very clear from day one. I don't show PDA and don't do anything nice for him. I barely ever make the drive out to Rockford. Who would be in love with that?" I skeptically look at him while taking a sip of my coffee.

"Because he sees what all of us see. A hard working, independent and financially secure beautiful woman. You are exactly what men are looking for. Especially with that magically tight pussy of yours."

I spit out my coffee all over our table at his statement and continue to choke on the remnants that remain in my throat. Laughing, Robert stands up and pounds on my back to help me. I brush him off and he leaves to retrieve some napkins. I glance up and notice our surrounding tablemates looking at me with disgust. "Sorry, hot coffee," I mutter out in complete embarrassment. Robert returns with napkins and a glass of water. I grab the water, take a big swallow and help clean up my coffee spit. Once we are done, the waitress comes over and removes the used napkins and replaces them with fresh ones. I sit in silence, staring at Robert and wonder where his mind goes sometimes.

"What?" he asks, "It's the truth." He smiles, shrugs and takes a sip of his coffee. "I hope you didn't get any of your coffee throw up in my drink." He looks at his cup quizzically.

"If I did, you deserve it!" I pause before saying my next thought. "So why do you think it's tight and magical?" I look at him with a smile on my face, now being able to laugh at his terminology.

"You had a child, Jenna, and you've been obsessed with working out and taking care of yourself since then. Before Jax, you hadn't had sex since Cal. All those years of no sex and doing kegels daily so you won't piss in your pants every time you laugh and sneeze equals a magically tight pus..."

"Okay, okay, no need to say the 'p' word again!" I hiss at him, completely comprehending his meaning so he won't say my least favorite name for women's anatomy in public again. He knows I hate that word, along with the "c u next Tuesday" word and deliberately says them all the time to get me riled up.

He throws his head back and laughs at my reaction. "Oh my gosh, this has been the best coffee talk ever!" He continues to giggle as I give him the evil eye. "Oh, come on, Jenna! Let's be honest with ourselves, shall well? You have not dated anyone this long since your ex-husband. Why do you think out of ALL the men that have been put in your path, you give a hockey player a chance? Let's see..." he taps his finger against his mouth while looking up in mock questioning, "is it because he is not local, travels all the time and is never in one place? Seems to me that is your golden ticket to not have to put any effort into the relationship. And since you don't, if he decides to screw one of the many puck bunnies that comes his way, you won't bat an eyelash or shed a tear when saying goodbye to him. You haven't even mentioned him to any of your other friends and the only way your parents know is because Avery told them mommy had a boy who wasn't me over for dinner." He leans in closer to me to make his final point. "You are using him. Obviously for sex, because why else would you continue taking his calls? Just stop denying that you don't play games with people, because until you tell him exactly why he is in your life, you, my dear, are a hypocrite." With that, he sits back and continues drinking his coffee.

I lean back in my chair and continue to stare at him while his words sink in. For Robert to feel the need to call me out must mean one thing – he likes Jax Morrow more than he lets on. "I don't think I'm using him for sex. I do enjoy his company when I'm with him. I just like that we don't have to be together all the time. I like not having to answer to anyone. I like that I still get my alone time, especially with Avery. He's not asking for anything more right now, so if everything is going well, why do I need to make changes to our relationship?"

"Summer will be here soon - what if he asks you to come to Canada? Or he stays here this summer and asks his ex-wife if their daughter can come here? Are you ready for that?"

"He knows I won't spend a whole summer in Canada. And why do I need to think about things that may not even happen?"

Robert shakes his head at me. "Don't lead him on, Jenna."

"I'm not intentionally trying to lead him on!" I say with exasperation. "I don't think he's in love with me. You do! Besides enjoying calling me out at any opportunity that comes your way, let's just say that I am using him for sex, which I'm NOT, why do you even care? Pot calling the kettle black, don't you think?" I raise an eyebrow at him, deliberately reminding him of his many one-night stands.

"Can't you see the pedestal I have you on? No one took a chance on me like you did. You're my mentor, my idol. I will protect your honor with all that I have. I actually like Jax; I think he might be good for you. I just want that happily ever after for you." He grabs my hand and squeezes.

I place my hand over his and squeeze right back. "We all deserve happily ever after's, Robert," I say, with tears in my eyes as his words touch my heart. "Thank you, dear friend, for your honesty and loving me like you do. I feel like I'm the lucky one for having you put up with me, not only as your boss, but as your insane friend. And you put up with my kid, and we all know how she's as crazy as her mommy!" I say with a laugh, wiping the runaway tear that fell from my eye.

"That crazy little monster has me wrapped around her little finger," he says while blinking the wetness out of his eyes. "Just like her mommy." He takes his other hand, pats my hand on top of his other one and removes them from my grasp. "Seriously though, you do need to think about the future and if it includes Jax. By the way, does he come back to your place when he is in town?"

"No, the team has a hotel room for him every time they call him up and he stays there until they tell him that they are keeping him up for the remainder of the season, which he would then find an apartment, or they send him back down."

"So you're having hotel sex, huh? Kinky!" He wiggles his eyebrows up and down at me.

"Sorry, kid, you're not getting any graphic details out of me." I laugh at the disappointment on his face.

"C'mon, Jenna, he's so cute and I now have to live my sex life vicariously through you, which I never thought would happen!" He whines, which makes me laugh even harder as I wouldn't think he would have to either.

Not really wanting to talk about my sex life, I decide to change the subject. "Are you going with Layla to Las Vegas this weekend?" Like myself, Layla has refused to go back to Las Vegas since our last trip there and has managed to find someone else to go for her since then. Unfortunately for her, her boss is demanding that she go this time and she's asked Robert to go with her.

"I promised my realtor friend to help him with an open house this weekend. Even though I still want to go to Las Vegas, I don't think I want to go with Layla and be left by myself while she canoodles with men."

I nod in agreement and can't blame him for feeling that way. "We need an intervention with her, but I honestly don't know what it's going to take." I shake my head, upset with how Layla is choosing to live her life.

"Let's talk about this while we walk to go get Avery." I look at my watch to see that it is indeed time to go, especially since I need to get ready now for my evening with Jax.

22

I am running back and forth between rooms, tearing up the beds, the couches, rummaging through my desk, trying desperately to find my phone.

"Remind me never to let Avery touch my phone!" I yell at Robert while he watches me destroy my apartment.

"You say that every time you can't find it. Let me send it an alert with the find my phone app," he says with a bored expression on his face.

"Why didn't you do that in the first place?" I say with an exasperated look on my face. I have been searching for a good five minutes already. We were going to walk to our meeting, but now we'll have to hail a cab in order to make it on time. I hear the alert sound going off and follow it to Avery's room, where I find the phone at the bottom of her toy chest. I come back out and wave it in front of him, but he's distracted.

"What's wrong?" I ask, the expression on his face filled with concern while looking at his phone.

"Layla said she was in New York this week, right?"

I stop to think as she's been traveling a lot for work these past couple of days and I haven't talked to her since. First she was going to Las Vegas this past weekend, then she was coming home on Sunday night only to fly right back out on Monday for New York. "Yes, she should now be in NYC. Why?"

"Well, her phone is showing up at her apartment." He turns his phone to me, confirming that it's registering live at her apartment. "She wouldn't lie to us, would she?"

I stare at his screen and blink, hoping that technology is just playing tricks on us. We all have the same phone carrier and accepted each other's invitation to track each other in case of emergencies. "Restart your phone, maybe it's a glitch." He turns his phone off and on, but the status on her current location remains the same after it reboots. I decide to call her, where it rings once and then goes to voicemail, indicating she declined my call. I go to my text messages as an incoming text comes in from her.

Layla: Can't talk right now, in a meeting. Will call you later.
Me: Are you still in New York?
Layla: Yes

"Call to reschedule our meeting!" I tell Robert and run into my room to grab her spare house key from my nightstand drawer. While Robert calls our client to reschedule, fear and anxiety start to overtake me. Layla has zero reasons to lie to me and the last time she did, it was catastrophic. We get downstairs and walk out to find a cab sitting on the corner outside of my building. We give the driver her address and ask him to hurry. Despite the drive only taking us ten minutes, it feels like an eternity. Memories come flooding back from years ago when I got the call from her housekeeper to come over, that something was wrong with Layla. When I got there, the ambulance had already arrived and she was unconscious, laying on a stretcher due to a deliberate overdose. I struggle to hold back my tears, praying that she is not back in her dark dungeon of hell that she was so unfairly forced into when her husband died. She only lies when she is back in her dark place.

The cab pulls up to her building and I tell the driver to keep the change as I inadvertently throw money at him trying to hastily get out of the cab. The doorman greets us with a smile, knowing who we are and who we are seeing. He doesn't bother calling her to ask if he should send us up since we are on her approved guest list. We give no indication of anything wrong as we simply smile back at him and make our way to the elevators. Robert squeezes my hand as the elevator reaches her floor. We exit and walk briskly to her apartment, the carpet muffling the sounds of our footsteps. We stop in front of her door and I'm about to put the key into the key way when Robert stops me.

"What if she's having sex?" he whispers.

"Then we will exit quietly and hope we aren't noticed." I slowly turn the key to unlock the door and gently push open. We take off our shoes before entering so that the hardwood floors don't announce our arrival. We silently close the door behind us and stop in the entranceway to listen for any sounds. All we are greeted with is silence. We tiptoe forward to find the kitchen and adjoining living room littered with empty boxes of pizza, candy wrappers and wine bottles. We look at each other and walk towards the master bedroom. The door is open, so we can see that the lights are off inside it, no sounds indicating she might be having sex. Robert starts forward into her room.

"Get back!" Layla screams as she jumps out of the doorway, swinging a baseball bat.

"AHH!" Robert and I both scream and fall to the floor.

"What the fuck are you guys doing, sneaking up on me like that? I almost hurt you!"

"What the fuck are you doing here and not in New York like you said you were?" Robert yells back at her as we get up off the floor and try to catch our breaths. This whole scenery would have been laughable if there wasn't something else going on.

"How did you guys know I was here?" She avoids looking

directly at us as she goes into her room to put the baseball bat underneath her bed.

"That doesn't matter. What matters is why you felt the need to lie to us?" We follow her into her bedroom and I cross my arms over my chest, waiting for an explanation. Part of me doesn't even care anymore as all I want to do is hug her tight, relieved to see that she is okay. "What's going on, Layla?"

She turns on the lights, sits down on her bed and sighs. She looks like she hasn't slept in days. Purple bags appear underneath her eyes and her hair is up in an oily messy bun. She is wearing baggy sweat pants with an oversized shirt. She looks up at me, bites her lip to keep it from quivering and looks down at her hands that she is wringing in her lap.

"I did something bad." She whispers and I immediately kneel down in front of her and grab her hands. Robert sits down next to her on the bed and puts his arm around her.

"Layla, whatever it is, it's going to be okay. We're here and will get through this together." I assure her, desperate for her to believe me so she can fight whatever internal battles she is struggling with. My mind races as I try to think of what she could have possibly done for her to be reacting this way.

"We can't help you unless you tell us, honey." Robert sweetly rubs her arms up and down and gives them a reassuring squeeze. She looks back and forth between us and swallows. We sit there together in silence before she decides to proceed.

"I told someone." She looks at me when she says this, holding her breath for my reaction. At first, I don't comprehend what she's referring to and can only think that maybe she's talking about her overdose. Then realization of her meaning hits me when the tears start to fall from her eyes. Layla never talks to anyone about her overdose and she refuses to shed any tears in front of people about herself. I slowly stand up, her grip on my hand tightening so I wouldn't let go. We stare at each other, her eyes silently communicating to me my biggest fear.

"Told someone what?" Robert asks, confusion written on his face as he looks to one of us for an answer.

"About....about...Avery." She stammers, her shoulders starting to shake from holding back her sobs.

"Okay....." I slowly say, trying to remain calm. "How did she even come up?" My brain wants all the gory details while my heart is screaming no and to run.

"As you know, I was back in Las Vegas this weekend for another sponsored party. Well, I met this guy there. He seemed really nice and of course, he was good looking. He asked me if I was married with kids and I said no, only a beautiful goddaughter." She takes a deep breath before she continues. "We were drinking heavy amounts of alcohol and having a great time together. I asked why he was in Las Vegas and how he got into the party and he said his work sent him as he's a celebrity photographer. I asked him which celebrities he has photographed and one of the names he mentioned was Cal's."

She pauses to gauge my reaction so far. "Continue," I command.

"I don't remember much of the evening as we were taking a lot of shots, but....but apparently I told him how I hated Cal and he asked why and well, I guess I then proceeded to tell him everything that happened between you and him." She pauses and looks down. "Even the part where he said he didn't have time to be in her life."

I stare at her, as the breath I didn't even realize I was holding in slowly comes out. "Maybe he was just as drunk as you were and doesn't remember your story," I meekly say, holding onto hope that I'm right.

She shakes her head no, gets up and heads to her dresser drawers. She pulls out a folded note and hands it to me. I unfold the note to read its brief lines:

Thanks for the great time and amazing sex.
Best of all, thank you for the story that is going to make me a lot of money.
XOXO

I close my eyes and crumble the piece of paper in my fist and let it fall to the floor. Robert picks it up and reads it. He gasps and covers his mouth.

"What does that mean, making a lot of money off the story?" Robert asks, despite knowing the answer.

"He's going to sell the story to the tabloids." Layla voice shakes.

I am scared to open my eyes to look at her as I am trying to control my anger, but the devil inside of me wants to rage against her so she can feel how deeply she has just cut me with her unintentional betrayal.

"He has no proof. The story won't get far," but even Robert doesn't sound very convinced.

"Jenna, I am so so sorry…I…"

"You need to call him and tell him you made the story up." I open my eyes to look at her, surprising myself with how calm my voice is.

"I can't," she whispers "I don't have his phone number." She cries harder as she starts to completely unravel.

"What's his name? We can Google him right now. Hopefully, we can find him and call his office".

"Jenna…" She trails off, her voice filled with despair. "You know I don't pay attention to names!" Her face blushing to a deep red.

"FOR FUCK SAKES, LAYLA, HOW THE HELL DO YOU NOT REMEMBER THE NAMES OF THE MEN WHOSE DICKS HAVE BEEN INSIDE OF YOU?!" I explode, not being able to hide anymore my disgust toward her lack of self-care.

"Jenna!" Robert yells in shock from my outburst.

"I've got to get out of here!" I turn on my heel and walk toward the door.

"Jenna, please don't leave me!" Layla wails as she comes after me, grabs hold of my arm and turns me around. I grip her biceps and look into her anguished eyes.

"Listen to me, Layla. I know this was an accident. I know that if you were sober, the topic would have never come up, but you've got to let me go right now. You just rocked my whole world! I need some air, some time to process what is happening. I love you, but please, leave me alone for right now." She releases me and drops her hands in defeat.

"Don't follow me." I warn and point to Robert. "You stay here with her tonight." I run out of her apartment toward the elevators. As soon as I get in, I try to catch my breath, but my chest aches from the pain of the imaginary knife that just got plunged into my heart. Tears start to blur my vision and run down my cheeks as I run out of the building, the concerned yells of Layla's doorman running after me becoming fainter the farther I run. My body's natural instinct leads me to Avery's school. I sign her out, not caring that she hasn't even had her nap yet as all that matters right now is her.

23

It has been two days since Layla's revelation and today I am feeling somewhat better, that maybe everything is going to be okay. The first person I called was my lawyer, who put me in touch with one of the best child custody lawyers in the state. After that phone call, I called my parents.

"Cal Harrington, the actor?" my mother asks while my dad stays quiet on the line, trying to digest everything I just told them.

"Yes, Mother."

"YOU had sex with THE Cal Harrington?" Skepticism lacing her voice.

"Yes, Mother!" I close my eyes and take a deep breath as my patience deteriorates with every word that comes out of her mouth.

"Jenna, darling, you know you don't have to lie to us if it was some stranger that you had drunk sex with and forgot their name."

I immediately hang up on her, questioning once again how we could possibly be related. While my relationship with my mother has been so much better since the birth of Avery, she still has her moments where I want to be anywhere else but in her presence.

My father calls back from his cell phone and we discuss what to be prepared for and how to keep my mother away from talking to the gossip columns. My father always knows how to make me feel better and he reassures me everything will be okay. It still didn't help me get a good night's sleep though.

The following day, I was ready to see Layla and asked Robert to bring her over. We cried, hugged and strategized on the what if scenarios.

"Do you really think this is going to be that big of a story?" I ask, as we watch Robert finalize setting up the Google alert on Cal.

"He's a huge movie star now, Jenna. If the reporters report the story correctly, it isn't going to look good in his favor that he didn't want his own child. He'll contact you to save his career," Layla says confidently. I look at Robert, who nods his head in agreement. The thought of having to see him makes my stomach hurt.

"Ugh, I just don't even want to deal with him," I groan and cover my face with my hands.

"Yes, but you do realize that at some point you are going to have to face him?" Robert looks at me with a sad smile on his face. He's right and I understood that one day he was going to be back in my life. I was just hoping it was when Avery was requesting to find out who her father was, preferably when she was a teenager or an adult, and could see him without me. But life has once again thrown me a curve ball and at the end of the day, all that matters is that my daughter is safe, happy and is with me.

I am walking back to my apartment from checking in on Robert, who is the site manager for tonight's event that we are planning. Originally I was supposed to be, but Robert agreed to take my place at the last minute so I can go to Jax's hockey game. Jax, who is still left in the dark about who Avery's father is. It has been five days since that day in Layla's apartment and so far, things are radio silent. The anticipation is absolutely killing me and a part of me wishes the story was out already so we can go on with our lives while the other half wishes it was going to remain a secret. I need to tell Jax and I had the opportunity on the phone last night, but I just couldn't dampen his excitement at being told he was going to play the last remaining month of the season here. Quite honestly, I don't even know what to say. All I ever told him was that Avery's father was not in the picture and never would be. Now, not only is there a chance her father might come into her life, but he is a world famous actor. My stomach starts to hurt again from the thought of his reaction as I know it won't be good. I decide to call him, hoping his voice will make me feel better.

"Hey, babe." He answers on the third ring, sounding very groggy.

"Were you sleeping? I'm sorry, why did you pick up?"

"I'll always pick up when I see that it's you," he sweetly says. "Are you walking?"

"Yes!" I shout while a horn blares loudly. "I am just walking home and I wanted to see how your day was going, but we can just talk later after the game."

"No, let's talk now as I don't want to stop hearing that sexy voice of yours. In fact, why don't we have phone sex so that way I am so charged up to see you tonight, that I will score four goals to get my sexual frustration out until I'm inside you."

I laugh, knowing that he is completely serious. "I think I need to torture you just a little bit longer and wait since you MIGHT get the real thing tonight."

"Might? I better get that sweet thing tonight as well as a blow job."

"If you score four goals tonight, you will definitely be getting a blow job," I confirm, giving him more incentive to play well.

"I am so hard and wide awake. I think you need to make a

detour to my hotel right now. It'll be good for the team and the outcome of tonight's game." I laugh and I glance at my watch to see what time it was, entertaining the thought of going to see him now as he would be a welcome distraction. I look back up before answering and stop dead in my tracks. My breath catches in my throat as I see a wide-angle lens pointed directly at me. The photographer looks up from behind the lens, goes back down to shoot some more photos of me, then proceeds to put the camera back in his bag. He slowly starts to walk toward me. He has two bags, one on each shoulder. He pulls the flap over the top opening to discreetly hide the camera he was using. If I hadn't caught him earlier and just saw him in his current state, he would look like any other young professional walking outside. He is wearing a tight charcoal colored long sleeve V-neck shirt with black skinny jeans and black converses. His clothing does nothing to hide his well-toned body. His caramel color hair is long and styled just past his ears. As he makes his way closer, I am in shock to see how good looking he is.

"Jenna? Hello? Are you still there?" I faintly hear Jax talking to me.

"I...um, sorry Jax, but I have to go. I'll see you tonight." I end the call and look around at my surroundings. Unfortunately, there's no one else on the street to help me if I need it. I ponder whether I should backtrack my steps, not wanting this man to follow me home. *Maybe he'll walk right past me?* I open up my purse and rummage through to try to find my sunglasses to shield my eyes, only to come up short as I left them at home. I grab the small bottle of mace for protection instead. Before I have time to decide what my next move is, he stops right in front of me.

"I see I've been caught!" He flashes me what would be to other females a devastatingly handsome smile. "Hello, Jenna Pruitt, I am Chase." He puts his hand out for me to shake.

I just stare at him, not believing that he knows my name or that he thinks I would ever shake his hand. His green eyes sparkle in amusement as he realizes I will not be reciprocating his handshake.

"I'm not offended that you won't shake my hand. Smart girl. In fact, you should start trusting no one who comes your way."

"Sound advice coming from the likes of you," I say in disgust as I start to walk, not knowing if I want to continue in the direction I was going or detour somewhere else to get away from him. "Where are you from, Chase?" I ask, trying to distract him with small talk so he won't pay attention to the road we just turned on as all I want to do is get into the security of my building.

He thinks about this before answering. "I'm from Victoria, British Columbia."

"You're quite tan for a Canadian." I look him up and down with confusion on my face as I was not expecting that answer.

"Why, thank you!"

"That wasn't meant to be a compliment," I scoff, annoyed that he is smiling at me. I stop walking and turn to him. "Listen, Chase, I think Canada is a fantastic place and it's probably time you go back home to the motherland before I press charges against you for stalking."

He throws his head back and laughs as if I've said the funniest thing in the world. "Now, Jenna, we just met and you and I both know that you have no proof that I am stalking or harassing you as we are just two people taking a stroll, chit chatting on this beautiful day."

I grit my teeth, trying to hold back my temper that's ready to explode. "I would really appreciate it if you would respect my privacy and leave me alone."

"I wish I could, Jenna, but unfortunately, your story is circulating and photos of you are about to bring in a lot of money. I just can't pass up that opportunity." He pulls his sunglasses off of his head and brings them down over his eyes, looking like a model off the runway. "I just wanted to quickly introduce myself to you as you're going to be seeing quite a lot of me. I'm being completely honest with you when I say that I mean you no harm and you have zero reasons to be afraid of me."

I laugh bitterly at his lies and start to walk, making a quick left onto a different street, hoping he will keep going straight.

"There are a lot of bad people about to come to town to take your picture. And when I say bad, I don't mean their quality of work. They're bad men, not caring that you're a human being. They just want their money and they will do whatever it takes to get it."

I pretend not to hear him so that he doesn't see the panic his words are starting to cause me. I turn down another street, this one less crowded and more residential and pick up my pace to try to out walk him. Instead he picks up his pace too, gets in front of me and turns around to walk backwards so he can make sure I am looking at him.

"Jenna, I need you to listen very carefully to me and take my advice. Let these guys have their shot. Don't block your face, don't flip them off, and don't wear a disguise. Those tactics will anger them and they'll come after you even harder. They'll say horrible things to get a rise out of you. They want you to mace them," he nods towards the mace I am holding. "Better yet, they love it when people get physical with them. Don't do any of it. Just stay quiet and let them get their photo. The more quality photos of you they can sell, the more money they make, and the more they will leave you alone. They'll eventually leave when the next big scandal comes around. Just whatever you do, don't engage with them. Particularly a man named Danny Salari. He'll go after you and your daughter."

I stop short at the mention of my daughter and ball my hands into fists. "Don't you fucking go near her!" I scream into his face. He raises his eyebrows at my reaction and holds his hands up to try to stop me from coming closer.

"I NEVER photograph children, nor will I ever. I am just

warning you about Danny as he is a scumbag." He lowers his hands once I back away from him.

"And you aren't?" I taunt, wishing he would just leave me alone.

"Despite what your current opinion is of me, I am considered to be one of the more reputable photographers. I keep my distance and will never get in your face. Most of the time you'll not even notice that I am around."

"That's just creepy," I say, suddenly feeling exhausted from the emotions that are coursing through me. We get to the next intersection and stop to wait for the light to turn green to walk.

"Why are you telling me all of this? What do you even care?" I ask, feeling defeated by the inevitable that I have tried to avoid for the last four years.

"It's obvious that you're not after Harrington for his money, otherwise you would have gone public about having his baby years ago. You're an innocent and unfortunately, you have no idea what is about to come your way." He runs his hand through his hair and seems frustrated. "Every trusting relationship you have is about to be tested. It doesn't matter if it is with a family member, your assistant, friends or even your boyfriend. Money and power bring out the devil in people. Trust NO ONE, Jenna! Most of all Cal Harrington himself." Without another word, he nods and walks away, leaving me to ponder his words.

24

Twenty-four hours later and the rest of the paparazzi descend upon Chicago. Like a pack of wolves, they sit outside my building, hoping to get a photo of Avery and me. They got one shot of us this morning as we were about to walk to school. One of the doormen tried to help shield us, but the flashes were blinding despite the protectiveness of the glass wall. Avery and I got right back on the elevator to go into the safety of our apartment. Her questions were then endless - *Why are we staying home, Mommy? Who are all of those people? Why are they taking our picture?* So overwhelmed was I that I ignore her questions, and tell her with fake enthusiasm that we are going to have a mommy/daughter day at home.

Not only have the paparazzi invaded my life, but everyone else that matters to me. They knew who Robert was, and hounded him with questions when he arrived here this morning. Fortunately, he has spare clothes in Avery's closet as he plans on sleeping on the couch for a couple of days until things die down. Layla is in Los Angeles for work but her own doorman called her, saying there were some men outside asking questions. She calls or texts every couple of hours, keeping us up to date about how the story is all over the news since we won't turn on the TV with the exception of a movie for Avery.

I told Jax everything last night after his game. Needless to say, his reaction was exactly what I thought it was going to be - he was shocked, angry and then hurt. He stormed out of the restaurant we were eating at and won't return my calls, which has been frustrating and disappointing. When I texted him to ask if he still wants me to accompany him to the team's annual charity event tomorrow night, his only response was yes and to be ready by 7 pm. I wouldn't be surprised if he officially breaks up with me after the event is over with. The only person enjoying this newfound attention is my mother, but that's not surprising. She makes sure she is dressed to the nines and welcomes the idea of her picture being in magazines and newspapers around the world.

I stare out at Lake Michigan, hoping the peacefulness of the lake will help inspire me to think of ways on how to deal with the chaos outside. We can't stay in here forever, especially not with a child who will grow bored. We've watched two movies, eaten lunch and it is only 2 p.m. Our days of walking everywhere may be limited, but I can still drive us out of here since we have our own parking garage in the building. I toy with the idea of maybe staying at my parents' house, but I don't want to draw the paparazzi out to their suburbia neighborhood.

"Hey, should we go swimming today?" I ask Avery with excitement as I remember we have an indoor pool in the building.

Her eyes get big with excitement. "Yes, Mommy!" she screams loudly and starts to laugh. I smile at her happiness and get up to find her bathing suit and cover up. She runs into the living room and I hear her say, "Uncle Robert, we're going swimming!", and she races right back into the room so I can get her dressed. After she's finished, I head to my room to get myself ready when I see Robert talking on my cell phone, his face pale.

"Yes, that's fine," he says into the phone and hangs up.

"What's wrong?" I ask, my heart starting to pound in my chest at the severity of the look on his face.

"Cal is here."

I stare at him, not wanting to believe what he just said. "What? NO! How can that be? How would he even know where I live?" I start to pace, panic seizing me.

"Anybody can find out where you live. All they need is your name and city."

"But, he didn't even call to ask if he can come over!" I whine, my vision being clouded by tears.

"Jenna, he doesn't know your phone number," he reminds me, his voice soft and soothing. He walks over to me and grabs my hands to stop my pacing. "Look at me, Jenna."

As I look at him, a lone tear falls down my cheek, the dam that holds back my emotions about to burst. "I'm not ready for this, Robert. This wasn't how I envisioned our first meeting to be. I don't have my lawyer here and I certainly didn't want him to see Avery yet," I say, frantically. "Why did you let him up?"

"I let him up because it is better to face him sooner rather than later and in a safe environment. You need to try to keep this amicable, Jenna."

"He can't have her, Robert! I won't let him take her away from me," I whisper, not believing this is finally happening.

Robert grips my hands tight and squeezes. "He won't. We won't let him, Jenna! Courts usually favor the mother and you have his email proving he didn't want to be part of her life. You have so many people who will testify on your behalf if it even comes to that."

We hear the knock on my door and my eyes widen. I grip Robert's hands tighter and start to shake my head.

"Pull yourself together, Jenna! You are a warrior. You've been doing this without him and are more than just fine. Don't let him intimidate you! You can do this! Everything is going to be okay." He pulls me in for a tight hug and kisses my forehead.

"Okay, okay, okay," I mutter and wipe the tears from my eyes. "Please go be with Avery and try not to let her out." He nods and goes to her room and closes the door.

I slowly start walking to the door, combing my hair out with my fingers. I look down at my workout clothes, wishing I was wearing something more confident and smart looking. I arrive at the door and take a deep breath. *You can do this, Jenna*! I swiftly open the door without looking through the peephole. Standing in front of me is a beautiful older woman and the first thing I notice about her are her eyes. They are that familiar blue that I see when my daughter looks at me. I then look into the other set of eyes behind her – the ones that have been haunting my dreams.

"Hello, Jenna," Cal says with his throaty sexy voice, that voice that brings back intimate memories. The years have been kind to Cal, if anything, making him even more handsome. His curly hair is cut short and styled with gel. His clean-shaven face has matured, his jawline even more chiseled than I remember. Faint small lines appear around his eyes, which only seem to highlight their beauty. He is wearing a fitted gray peacock coat, a cobalt blue sweater underneath it and denim jeans. I can't contain my eyes from traveling the length of his body, nor can I believe that after all this time and everything that has transpired, I still find him so damn hot.

"Cal," I say with a nod, trying to keep my cool, "how kind of you to show up without calling."

"My lawyer did try to call your work line, but no one answered," his tone cool, his eyes like glaciers - cold and hard - as they assess me up and down. This information does not phase me since reporters have been clogging our phone line for any information they can get about me.

"We've been bombarded with calls from reporters so that line goes straight to voicemail. Nice to see that you are finally doing your own dirty work for once by showing up in person though." I make the first jab, not being able to contain my resentment toward him. The more I look at his sexy face, the angrier I get with him…and myself for how I am reacting to him. I look to the woman standing in front of me for distraction. "Hi, I'm Jenna. I'm assuming you are Cal's mother?"

"Oh yes, Rosalind Harrington, but please call me Rose," she says in her equally throaty, but feminine, voice. She thrusts out her hand for me to shake. "Thank you for accepting to see us on such short notice, Jenna. I've seen so many pictures of you the last two days, and I must say that you are even prettier in person."

Surprised by her compliment since I just insulted her son, I shake her hand back and am about to say thank you for her kind words, when Cal rudely interrupts. "You were wondering if you were going to hear from me? Cut the bullshit, Jenna, how could you NOT hear from me? This story is everywhere, and your timing of planting it is brilliant. I brought my mother here to be a witness for the paternity test and then we will be leaving. My lawyer will be in touch with you once the results are in."

"Excuse me, but did you just accuse me of selling this story to the media?" So shocked am I by his accusations that I don't even realize I'm still holding onto his mother's hand.

"Bloody right I am and don't lie about it! I know your business has been doing well, and that this piece of information can bring your company into the spotlight you have been hoping for. One week together never brought out your calculating, manipulative bitch side." His eyes rake up and down my body in disgust.

"Calvin! There is no need to be rude until we get the facts straight!" his mother chides, actually looking appalled at his behavior. I let go of her hand as if she has burned me. I stare at him with malice, his comment unleashing my pent up fury towards him.

"How DARE you!" I hiss, my anger mounting at each breath I take. "How DARE you come to my house, accuse me of lying and planting this story to boost my business! I would NEVER use an innocent child like that! Unlike you, I don't want the spotlight! I never wanted the story to be made public. Once you refused to be part of her life, I was done with you! I never wanted to hear or see you ever again!"

"What the fuck are you talking about?" he growls. "I never knew about a baby until you went to the tabloids. I would never refuse to see my own child!"

"Look who is lying now!" I yell. "How convenient that you have forgotten the email you wrote me stating that if the baby was yours, you have no time in your life for it. You even copied your assistant on it."

"Valerie? When did you talk to Valerie?" His face looks confused as if he has amnesia.

"When did I NOT talk with Valerie? I ALWAYS talked with Valerie because you never picked up the phone yourself. Did you forget that you told me that she handles your phone calls when you are on set working? Every single time I called you, she picked up the phone. She even started to respond to my emails when you stopped. You were too much of a coward to talk to me. Never again, Cal! I am done with your bullshit and lies! You can talk with my lawyers."

"Jenna, there seems to be a huge misunderstanding." He plants his foot between the door and the casing and grasps the edge of the door, preventing me from slamming it in their faces. The color has drained from his face and his mother has her hand over her mouth, and is looking at him with despair. Normally I would have asked what is wrong, but I don't give a shit about how this man is feeling. He needs to feel somewhat of the pain that he inflicted on me.

"You bet there's been a huge misunderstanding, and it's that you think you can waltz into our lives four years later just because the story has been made public, and now everyone knows you are a deadbeat dad!" He flinches at my words and my confidence soars. "I will not let you take my child away from me. I have been doing just fine without any help from you! I don't want YOUR money OR YOU in our lives. It's one thing to not want me, but to not want your own child? And then to finally show up only when the story will affect your career? DISGUSTING! I would never have slept with you if I would have known what a despicable human being you are. I want you to get the hell out of my life, YOU FUCKING ASSHOLE!"

My chest is heaving and I am sucking in my breath as if I was just held under water. I am so furious that I don't care that I cursed and called him horrible names in front of his mother. As I wait for him to lash back at me, I notice that they aren't even looking at me anymore. They are looking down to their right side of me. His mother has tears in her eyes, and Cal just has a look of utter astonishment on his face. I realize who they are seeing. I don't have to look down to know that she is there. I close my eyes, and I can feel her hand on the back of my thigh. I reach for her hand and look down at her. Her face confirms that she has heard the yelling – her lips are pouting and quivering, as if she is on the verge of crying. Those beautiful blue eyes watery. I give her a reassuring smile and squeeze her hand. This makes her feel better and she turns her gaze towards Cal and Rose. She is staring at them just as they are staring back at her. *Can she tell she has the same eyes as them? Does she see herself in his face?*

"I'm sorry, Jenna, I tried to keep her in her room, but she heard the yelling and got upset." I turn around to look at Robert, who looks helpless.

"Mommy, you need to get ready for swimming." She starts to pull my hand back inside the apartment. "Let's go have some tea first since it makes you feel better." She suddenly stops and places her little fists on her hips. She looks at Cal and screams as loudly as her four-year-old voice will let her, "STOP YELLING AT MY MOMMY, YOU FUCKING ASSHOLE!"

25

It figures that the first time she repeats curse words, it would be in front of Cal and his mother. I can just picture them testifying in court against me, saying what a horrible mother I am for teaching my daughter curse words. I'm trying not to laugh at the outrageousness of it all by biting my lip.

"Avery," I say, as I get down to her level and look in her eyes, "Mommy didn't mean to call her friend that bad name that you just said. Please don't repeat after me, ok?"

"What bad words, Mommy?" Avery asks, looking confused.

"The bad words that Mommy said." Trying to make her understand without saying those exact words again is trickier than I expected.

"Silly Mommy, I didn't say any bad words! I was just calling him by his name. You said his name was fucking asshole," she says in her sweet little voice.

I hear a giggle, and look up to see Rose's hand over her mouth, stifling her laughter.

"Unfortunately, that is not his name." *It has been my name for him though!*

"You called your friend a bad word, Mommy?" she whispers

with a shocked look on her face, not believing that I did something bad.

"Yes, I did. Mommy was a little upset and should not have said those bad words. It was an accident, and I will try very hard not to do it again."

"Mommy, you need to say you are sorry to your friend," she says with big round eyes.

Damn it! An apology is the last thing I want to say to this man. To make matters worse, Cal is standing there with a twinkle in his eye and a smirk playing on his lips, thoroughly enjoying this scenario. He deserves every bad word I choose to call him. I want to punch that smug look off his face.

"Yes, Avery, Mommy will apologize to her friend," I say with a big sigh, "Cal, I'm sorry for calling you those bad words." *Not really!*

"Apology accepted," he hunches down to Avery to introduce himself. "Avery, my name is Cal and this is my mother, Rose."

"Rose? That is my middle name, Avery Rose Pruitt!" she announces with excitement.

Both Cal and his mother look at me, their eyes questioning if her middle name is for his mother. I nod confirmation as that was the only thing I was willing to give her of his when I named her.

"Your name is beautiful, Avery. We came all the way from London to play with you."

"London? Do you know Wendy, John and Michael? They live in London. Do you see Peter Pan flying to their house?" she quizzes them, showing off her love for Peter Pan.

"Yes, Avery, I know all about Peter Pan," Rose says, "Can I join you for tea and tell you all about them?"

"Yes, you can. Mommy, let's go!" she says, as she starts to pull me towards her room.

"Avery, your mommy and Cal need to talk about some things. Is it ok if you show me your room and you and I have tea together?" Rose looks at me for approval.

I nod my head yes. "Go ahead and have fun with Rose, Avery. She flew a long way just to have some alone time with you. Mommy will be in her office talking with Cal."

"Okay, Mommy. Let's go, Rose!" Avery grabs Rose's hand to take her to her room and stops to introduce her to Robert. "Uncle Robert, this is Rose. She knows Peter Pan!" She excitedly says. "C'mon Rose, c'mon Uncle Robert, I will race you." She takes off toward her room ahead of them.

I turn my attention back to Cal and realize I have not officially invited him in as he is still standing in the doorway. I turn to my side and wave my arm, gesturing for him to come. He nods his head and enters. I look out into the hallway when I hear a door slam, but see no one walking around. I shut the door and walk toward the living room.

"Are you the infamous Robert, Jenna's assistant?" I hear Cal ask Robert with his hand extended out for a handshake.

Robert blushes and shakes his hand back. "That's me! Can I get you anything to drink or eat, Mr. Harrington?"

I look at him with murderous eyes. Why in the hell is he playing lap maid to the devil? I have no doubt that his big boy panties just got all wet from looking at Cal.

"Please call me Cal and water would be great, thank you." Cal takes off his coat and Robert grabs it for him, as if he is his butler.

I follow Robert into the kitchen and whisper into his ear, "I need you to go into my bedroom and call my lawyer to see if I can set up a meeting with him tomorrow. And stop being so fucking nice to him. He is the enemy!"

"Sorry!" Robert whispers back, "he's just so hot, Jenna!" I roll my eyes in disgust and head back into the living room with Cal's water while Robert proceeds to my bedroom.

"Why don't we go into my office?" I lead the way and shut the door behind him once he has entered.

"This place is nice. How long have you lived here?" he asks while looking around my office.

"Ten years," he looks at me in surprise, "my grandmother left it to me." Not understanding why I felt the need to tell him that, I rub my palms against my legs, sweat starting to form on them due to my nervousness. Deciding not to want to look directly into his eyes when talking, I turn my back toward him and look out the window.

"So, help me understand how this has all been a big misunderstanding?" I look over my shoulder at him when I don't get an immediate response.

He lets out a long breath and rakes his hand through his hair. He takes a sip of water and begins. "Do you remember how I told you how Valerie and I first met?" I nod my head and he continues, "I really didn't think anything of it when she told me she should handle my phone calls and emails while I was on set. She made it sound like it was the professional thing to do and that all assistants did that. I never bothered to ask my fellow actors if this was normal, nor did I ever notice any missed calls or emails. Fast forward to when I met you. I told her we were emailing, and that hopefully you would soon be calling as well. I told her that you were a priority in my life, so to please make sure I knew about any missed emails or phone calls that she might see before I did. She never in the past acted jealous over anyone, so I had no reason to be suspicious of her. I believed her when she told me you hadn't emailed or called, especially with how reluctant you were with keeping in touch when we went our separate ways. One time I thought I caught her talking to you, but she denied it, and said she would have told me if you called. Then my phone conveniently broke, and she got me a new phone with a new phone number. All of my contacts were in the phone, so I again had no reasons to be suspicious. She said my emails had been hacked into, which is very common for this industry. I asked her to send you my new email address and she told me she did. As time went on and I didn't hear from you, I resigned to the fact that it was only a fling. Again, I had zero reasons to think anything was amiss." He moves to stand next to me to look out the window.

"In order to prepare for one of my movies, I had to be in a certain kind of shape, so the studio hired a trainer for me. The trainer happened to be a female named Geri Roberts. Valerie was on vacation when I had my first meeting with Geri. She was gone for one week and had not met or known about Geri. The only detail she knew was that I was going to be working out with a different trainer other than my own. When Geri called wanting to talk with me, Valerie told her I would call her back, but never gave me the message because she had no idea of Geri's relevance - just that it was a female that she had never heard about. This went on for almost two weeks. Geri finally complained to the studio about how I never returned her calls, when I had been waiting to hear from her. I thought SHE was the unprofessional one. When I found out that Geri had been calling me all along, I questioned Valerie, who in turn confessed that she was in love with me. I fired her, and had a restraining order placed against her. That was two years ago."

I close my eyes and cross my arms. As his words slowly fill the pieces to the puzzle, my emotions are completely overwhelmed.

I am angry with him for believing her when she told him I didn't call.

I am angry with her for lying to him and denying my daughter her father.

I am scared that having Cal in our lives will bring these types of crazy people to us.

I feel betrayed by Cal thinking I was the type of girl who would use our child to heighten my career.

I am mad at myself for caring what he thinks of me.

Sensing my despair, Cal stands in front of me and grabs my arms, which forces me to look into the turmoil playing in his own eyes. "Jenna, you've got to believe me when I tell you that I had no idea that you were still trying to contact me."

"So YOU were not the one who write that email saying you didn't want to be in Avery's life?" Skepticism laces my voices as I still have a hard time believing that he has known nothing about this.

"No, I stopped seeing emails from you BEFORE I left for Hong Kong."

"What?" I say, with shock, "there were more emails after that. She must have deleted them before you logged on to see them and obviously, your account wasn't hacked at all. She probably changed the login information so you wouldn't check for yourself." I shake my head in disbelief as I've never known someone to be that cunning. "I have every single email correspondence in a file that I can give you if you want to read them."

"No," he lets go of my arms and rakes his hands roughly through his hair. "I don't need to see them. I believe you, Jenna. Do you believe me though? I know we don't know each other that well, but you've got to believe me when I say I would never have abandoned you both if I had known the truth."

Either the pain reflecting in his eyes is real, or he is the best damn actor on the face of this planet. "I don't know what to believe, Cal," I say softly, still feeling that I'm in some sort of nightmare right now.

He starts to pace around my office like a tiger locked in a cage, "I can't fucking believe this! I can't believe I have had a child for the last four years and had no idea about it. That fucking, conniving bitch!" he spats. "She is lucky I already have a restraining order against her." He suddenly stops pacing and looks at me. "How did the press find out about Avery if you didn't tell them?"

I look down at my hands, trying to phrase my words carefully without darkening Layla's reputation. "Long story short, Layla told the wrong person at the wrong time."

"Why would Layla tell someone?"

"Does it even matter at this point? It was an accident."

He ponders this and looks out the window and then back at me, his eyes having a dangerous glitter to them. "So if she didn't inadvertently tell this person, who then went to the press, I still wouldn't know about Avery?"

I give him a knowing look and watch as his jaw clenches with anger.

He turns his head at the sound of Avery's voice as we see her and his mother coming out of her bedroom through the glass of my office French doors. We watch in silence as she shows Rose her shopping cart of fake food and her little kitchen that is close to the real kitchen. Rose has a look of pure bliss on her face as she sits and listens to her granddaughter play.

"I'm sorry, Jenna," his voice thick with regret, "so very sorry for all the lies that were told to you. I'm sorry for not being there for you when you were all alone dealing with this." Before I can react, he pulls me into his arms, hugging me to his chest. I keep my arms at my side as I don't want to touch him. I don't want to feel that hard chest under my cheek. I don't want to smell that damn intoxicating cologne of his that is making me remember things that I don't want to remember. I try to push away from him, but he's crushing me.

"Please let go of me." He releases me and backs away from me and grumbles, "sorry."

A part of me is relieved to hear his words, but the other part fuels my anger. I don't want his pity as I think I have done a pretty damn good job raising Avery on my own. I did have some help from my parents, Layla and Robert, but in no way does that compare to Avery having a father. I have hated him for so long and now that the truth is known, I don't know what to feel towards him. "When do you want to do the paternity test?" I quickly change the subject to get back on point.

"It isn't necessary. She looks just like me."

"Yeah...she does," I say with a sigh.

"I would like to come back tomorrow with my lawyer to

discuss legalities. I need all of her vital information so that I can add her to my will and create some bank accounts for her. We also need to discuss my visitation rights when I permanently move to Chicago." His tone of voice changes to one of all business.

"Wait, you're moving to Chicago?" I ask, dumbfounded. This was the last thing I was expecting to hear.

"Of course I'm going to move to Chicago. We're starting to shoot my new movie here in a couple of weeks, so I'll be in a hotel at first, but then I'll find a place to buy. This is where you live. I would never imagine uprooting her when I can be flexible. I would like for her to visit my family in England with me as well."

"She's never been on a plane before. This is all going too fast... I...I can't deal with this right now." I take a step back and decide to sit behind my desk.

"I want a relationship with my daughter, Jenna, and I will need your help with that," his tone becoming more firm.

"These things are going to take time, Cal. She doesn't even know you exist!" My head starts to hurt even thinking about how to tell her. *Hey Avery, you know that man you called a fucking asshole? That's your daddy!*

He narrows his gaze at me. "What do you mean? You told her she doesn't have a father?"

"She knows she has a father, but I didn't tell her who her father was. All she was told is that her daddy does not live with us and works all the time," I say as I rub my temples.

He ponders this for a minute. "Well, thanks for not telling her I was dead," he says, begrudgingly.

"There's no reason to lie to her. I knew one day she would want to know about her real father."

"Does she currently have some sort of father figure?"

"Just my dad and Robert. I am dating someone, but he isn't present much in her life right now."

I think I see a small flicker of relief in his eyes, but I could be imagining it. "Ah yes, the hockey player?"

I nod my head yes, wishing he didn't know about him. I see Robert hovering in the kitchen, looking at me and I excuse myself from Cal.

"What did my lawyer say?" I whisper as I meet him in the kitchen.

"He said he can meet exactly at 9 a.m."

"Okay, let me see if that works for Cal." I walk back into my office to find Cal texting on his phone. "My lawyer can meet tomorrow at 9 a.m. Is that too early for you and your lawyer?"

"That should work," he confirms and glances at his watch. "We need to get going. Oh and this time, I will need your phone number," he says with a smirk. I frown at the idea, but know that I have no choice in the matter. We exchange numbers, and walk out of the office to join Avery and Rose in the living room.

"Thank you for playing with me, Rose. I had so much fun!" She throws her little arms around Rose's legs. Rose kneels down and hugs her tightly. My heart swells with pride at my daughter's sweet gesture and I can't help but feel somewhat relieved to see Cal's mother so open with accepting her.

"Thank you so much for letting me play with you, Avery." With the help from Cal, she gets back onto her feet and gives me a hug. "Thank you!" she whispers in my ear. She pulls back and I nod in return to her.

"Will it be okay if my mother spends time with Avery tomorrow while we have our meeting?" Rose gasps in delight at the suggestion, while Avery jumps up and down in excitement.

"Avery is usually in school by then." I look at Robert who nods his head, understanding that I was going to ask if he would stay with them if I kept her from school. "I can keep her home in the morning for you to spend time together." A part of me is very hesitant to even do this considering I just met Rosalind Harrington, but I feel I would be viewed as the biggest bitch if I said no.

"Thank you very much," Cal says with a slight smile. Avery and

I walk them to the door. "Until tomorrow," he nods goodbye while Rose waves and they walk out.

I breathe a sigh of relief as soon as I close the door behind them, suddenly feeling utterly exhausted.

"God, that was intense," Robert says as I head into my room to get dressed for the pool.

"It sure was," and I proceed to tell him everything later on that evening after Avery is asleep.

26

Cal and his mother arrive early the following morning, bringing us breakfast and presents for Avery. While they spend time playing with her, I finish getting ready, deciding to look professional in a white silk blouse, charcoal grey pencil skirt with a wide black belt and black heels. I pay careful attention to my hair and make-up with adding simple jewelry to finish my look. Satisfied, I take a couple of deep breaths to calm my nerves, grab my purse and head out into the living room.

"Mommy, you look pretty!" Avery announces, and I blush, feeling the heat from Cal's eyes as he checks me out.

"Thank you, honey. Now Avery, I need you to make good decisions and listen to Robert and Rose while Mommy is gone, okay?"

"Yes, Mommy, I will be so very good that you will want to buy me a present for my good behavior."

I smirk at my daughter's smartness and bend down to give her a hug and a kiss. "Maybe I will. We'll see."

"I rearranged your schedule today so you don't have anything planned until 5 p.m.," Robert says, as he hands me my sunglasses and hugs me goodbye.

"What's at 5 p.m.?" I rack my brain, trying to remember, as I would never plan an appointment that late normally since I usually have to get Avery from school before then.

"Hair and make up for the Blackhawks' charity gala."

"Oh! I forgot," I say slowly, as I start to feel guilty with the knowledge that I haven't even thought about Jax.

"It's okay, Jenna. I've got you covered. Go focus on your meeting." I nod and put the subject of Jax in the 'to worry about later' compartment of my brain.

"I have a car waiting for us if you're ready to go?" Cal asks softly. We say our goodbyes and head to the elevator in silence. I step into the elevator and lean against the wall opposite him. I watch him push the lobby button, and can't help but admire how good he looks in his three-piece suit. I shift uncomfortably in my heels, telling myself it is from them and not my reaction to how sexy he is.

"Just to warn you, there are a lot of paparazzi downstairs. As soon as the elevator doors open, put your sunglasses on. Follow my lead to the car and do not say anything to them. Understand?"

"Can't wait!" I sarcastically reply as I put my sunglasses on. The doors open and I gasp in shock to see close to twenty camera lenses being pointed in our direction. I regain my composure and keep my face neutral as I follow Cal out. I hear our names being called even before we make it outside.

"Jenna, over here!"

"Jenna, where are you going?"

"Cal, are you and Jenna together?"

"Jenna, we need to see your beautiful smile!"

"Cal, are you moving to Chicago?"

The clicking of the cameras and asking of questions are constant, the reprieve coming once we are safely inside the car and drive away. I see Chase standing away from the rest of the paparazzi, looking at his screen to see what kind of shots he got. I turn around to look behind us and see them jump into cars and taxis to follow.

"Jenna," Cal's strong voice brings me to focus, "I need you to let the driver know the address of where we are going."

"Yes, sorry, that would really be helpful, wouldn't it?" I nervously giggle and give the driver the address. I look out the window, only to find that the paparazzi have caught up.

"How do you get used to this?" I can't believe he deals with this every day. This is exactly what I don't want for Avery and myself.

"It will die down, Jenna. These paps do not like being outside in the cold weather." I study him to see if he is joking or not, but his face betrays nothing.

"Winter isn't for another couple of months – they'll stay here that whole time?" I ask incredulously. That's much longer than I was hoping for.

"Afraid so. Just always keep your head down, let them get their shot of you and don't tell them anything."

We pull up in front of a building, and are immediately boxed in with paparazzi cars in front, to the side and in back of our car. They leave their cars running, get out and swarm like bees over to the side where Cal is opening the door. He smiles, and waves at them, and then extends his hand to help me out of the car. I grip his hand while getting out, fighting the urge to use my purse to shield my face. Cal places his hand on the small of my back and leads me inside the building where both of our lawyers are waiting to escort us upstairs to discuss Avery's future.

Sometime later I sit in my dining room, reminiscing about my meeting with the lawyers with Layla while Robert gives Avery a bath for me. I am all fancied up in a navy, long beaded lace cocktail dress with a V-neckline, and my hair pulled down into a low bun at the base of my neck. I am ready for my night with Jax, and am just waiting for his arrival. He confirmed via text that he will arrive at 7 pm and nothing else. It's been a day full of all kinds of emotions, and having to deal with the drama of Jax and his feelings is the last thing I really want to do tonight.

"So let me try to understand this, because Cal's name is not on the birth certificate, he technically has no rights to Avery?" Layla asks while making us a drink in my kitchen.

"Right, so we had to sign a voluntary declaration of paternity and then once that is processed, he has parental rights. I'll have primary physical custody of Avery, but we'll share joint legal custody in order for him to be involved in the decision making aspect." I was hesitant at first to agree to joint legal custody. I have no idea if Cal and I have different beliefs on how she should be raised and giving him that kind of power scares me. He has so much catching up to do on learning about her, that I feel he might never truly know what is best for her. Especially since he still won't be around much due to his job.

"Is he going to pay you child support?"

"I don't want his money, and I put up a fight during negotiations that I didn't want child support. I finally agreed to have him retroactively pay for these past four years. They want me to provide a list of what I think my expenses were, but I don't know how I am going to accurately report that since I didn't keep track. All I care about is that Avery is taken care of, and with the amount of zeros they were throwing around, she'll be a very rich girl when she reaches twenty-five." I shake my head at the thought of how much money she will inherit.

"I love you, Jenna, but I think you're being pretty stupid for not taking child support payments. What are his visitation rights?"

I shrug at her, deciding it's not worth discussing again my strong feelings of why I don't want a dime from him. "Nothing is set in stone, but when he's in town, he'll get her every other weekend, on Christmas Day, every other New Year's, and he's requested all summers in England with him and his family." I peek at her from over the rim of my glass as I take a sip of my drink.

I'm still in denial that there's a chance I won't be seeing my daughter for most of the summers. The only time she's away from me for long periods of time is when she spends weekends at my parents' house and that's usually once a month. Even then, I miss her as soon as I drive away. I can't even imagine the hot mess I will be her first summer away from me.

"ALL summers? No way! I need time with my tinker bell too!" Layla huffs, as she spends a lot of time with Avery during summer time. "How could you agree to that?"

"I agreed to two out of the three months, and I can't deny her seeing her father. I want her to have a relationship with him. Who knows if she's going to be able to even handle it?"

"Or maybe we plan a girl's vacation every summer to England during the time she is there?" she says with an evil grin on her face.

"Now that sounds like a brilliant idea!" We laugh and toast each other when Robert comes back in, smiling like the Cheshire cat.

"I swear, the soap opera that is your life just keeps getting better and better."

"What do you mean?"

"Jax and Cal are on their way up - in the elevator together!" He claps his hands together in excitement. "I so wish I could be a fly on the wall in that elevator!"

"How do you even know this?" I ask, looking around for my phone to see if I had a missed call from the doorman.

"I have your phone, silly, and I answered the call to let them up. Let's take a bet who will be the one looking all hot and brooding due to meeting the other man who has had sex with Jenna? Cal or Jax?" He looks between Layla and me with way too much enthusiasm for this subject.

"I say Cal!" Layla answers.

"I say Jax!" Robert responds back to her.

"I say I'm not taking part in this stupid bet! I'm going to go put my jewelry on." I head into my bedroom and shut the door, wanting a couple of minutes to myself before I have to put on a fake smile and pretend all is fine, when really it isn't. *Let's get this over with!* I take a shaky breath, square back my shoulders, and go back out to the living room.

I step out just as Robert shuts the door behind Cal and his mother, who are standing in the hallway, watching Avery run into Jax's open arms. He picks her up and holds her high. The look on Cal's face is one of envy, and it makes me wonder when he's going to want to start having alone time with her. He stares at them a little longer until Layla comes out of Avery's bedroom.

"It's nice to see you again, Layla. May I introduce you to my mother?" Cal makes the introductions and tries to lean forward to give her a hug, but Layla stops him before he can do so.

"Sorry, Cal, but I've hated your guts these past four years and really don't know how I feel about seeing you. No offense, Mrs. Harrington." she smiles at Rose, but removes the smile once looking back at Cal.

"Seems to be the consensus in this place." Cal smirks and looks behind her at me.

"Well, can you blame us?"

"No, I can't. And even though I'm sure at the time you thought it was devastating, I'm forever grateful to you for telling whoever you told about Avery." He goes in for the hug anyway, and all Layla can do is stand there, her arms held to her side, not knowing if she should hug him back or not.

"Wow, Avery, look at your mommy. Isn't she gorgeous?" Jax says, all eyes reverting to me now. I smile and focus all my attention onto Jax, who looks handsome in his black suit and tie. He carries Avery over to me where he hugs me with one arm and whispers, "I've missed you." He then kisses me full on the lips, clearly trying to send a message.

I pull away with a nervous giggle and look at Robert for help. "Has everyone been introduced?"

"Yes, we rode the elevator up and Jax introduced himself to us then," Cal responds, and then proceeds to purposely check me out in such a blatant way that I feel Jax grip me tighter by the time Cal's eyes reach back up to mine.

"Yes, but I wasn't expecting to be introduced to Mr. Harrington tonight. Better now than never!" Jax laugh is so forced that I can barely contain from outwardly cringing.

"That's my fault for surprising you with a visit. We're leaving tonight, and I just wanted to say goodbye one more time to Avery," Rose says, as she steps forward.

"Leaving tonight?" I ask, eyeing Cal for an explanation, as he never mentioned anything today.

"My mother needs to get back to London, and I have to be in Los Angeles this week for business. I will be back next Monday, and we can spend some time together then to discuss our future," Cal says with a sly smile, his innuendos surely meant to only rile Jax up even more. I look away from him to see Robert's shit-eating grin, clearly enjoying the pissing contest between the two men.

"Will I ever get to see you again, Rose?" Avery asks with big, sad eyes.

"I hope so, Avery. Maybe this summer?" I tense as Rose looks up at me, but I refuse to confirm since Avery still doesn't know that Cal is her father and what going to London would actually mean.

"Oh Mommy, can we?" She looks at me with so much excitement that I hate to tell her no.

"We'll see, Avery. Mommy has to go. Give me a hug and a kiss!" I hold her tight and get a nice, wet kiss planted on my mouth. Her lips start to quiver with the realization that I'm leaving. "Look at all these fun people who are here to play with you tonight," she looks around the room and smiles. I put her down and continue to give hugs goodbye to Layla, Robert and even Rose.

Cal is the last obstacle before reaching the door. I stop in front of him to say goodbye when he leans in and kisses me on the cheek. "You look beautiful," he whispers, sending shivers down my spine. I take a step back and glare at him, which only makes him chuckle. "I'll call you when I'm back." He extends his hand out to Jax for a handshake, which Jax takes.

"Good to meet you, Cal. I'll see you when you get back!" Jax smiles as he reaches around me to open the door and gently pushes me out.

We walk in silence down the hallway to the elevators, but once inside, Jax lets his charade of being lovey dovey go.

"The man has balls to eye fuck you in front of me. ME! Your boyfriend! How do you expect me to put up with that shit without punching him, Jenna?" He angrily rakes a hand through his hair.

I put my hands on his chest to try to calm him, "I'll talk to him, but Jax, you were trying to flaunt us as if we're this perfect family in front of him. That wasn't fair to him either."

"If this relationship is going to go any further, then one day we might be a family and he's going to have to get used to that!" I just nod my head, not wanting to discuss any possible future together right at this moment.

We arrive at the lobby and only get a few steps in before flashes ricochet off the glass windows from the paparazzi. He grabs my hand, and we hurry to make it to the safety of the car that is waiting for us while they continue to call out our names. We get in, and the driver pulls away and merges into traffic.

"Listen, Jenna, I know I haven't handled this very well and I'm sorry. I know this has been hard on you." He pulls me into his side and kisses me on the lips. I'm happy he has apologized and I deepen my kiss to show him my appreciation.

But as soon as we get to the event, Jax disappears with his teammates and starts drinking, leaving me with the other wives and girlfriends who bombard me with questions about Cal. I suddenly feel as if all eyes are upon me, talking about me, watching me. I feel sick to my stomach and try to find refuge with someone I trust, but that someone was Jax and he's choosing not to spend it with me. I am relieved when the program for the evening begins, hoping it will distract me from my uneasiness. Jax continues to drink and barely eats dinner. By the end of the evening, I have to ask his teammates to help me get him into a taxi due to him being intoxicated. We arrive back to his hotel without any paparazzi around, and manage to make it up to his room.

"Please don't be mad at me," he mumbles as I get him into his bed, "I just love you so much." And with that, he passes out.

I stare at him, deciding that I'm not going to lay into him about this tomorrow, as he deserves the horrible hangover he's going to have, and the wrath of his head coach when he doesn't perform as well for tomorrow night's game.

I kiss him on the forehead, turn off the lights and head home.

27

The news stories of Cal and I continue into the following week. Most of the stories seem fabricated from 'anonymous' sources, but one story has an anonymous source quoting my exact words to Cal his first day on my doorstep.

"Seems to me one of your neighbors was listening in, and decided to cash in on the exclusive," Robert says, as he reads through one of the many magazines he bought with Cal and I on the cover. "I think this one is by far my favorite though. Jenna in a LOVE triangle!" He laughs as he hands me the magazine that has photos of Cal, Jax and myself in a triangle.

"Utterly ridiculous!" I look with disgust at the magazine. I am very disappointed that one of my neighbors would even do that to me, but as Chase warned me, money makes people do things you wouldn't think they would normally do.

"The good thing is that there aren't many photos of Avery. Mostly just you."

"Yes, but they've been hounding her school, and the principal and the other parents are getting very angry. They've requested a meeting with me on Monday to discuss 'other options'. I think they're going to kick her out." I have been scrambling to find another childcare, but the choices are slim with most places having wait lists.

"Do you think little miss over there is starting to wonder anything?" Robert asks, nodding toward Avery, who is in her room playing. Cal calls her every night before bed to talk to her. The first night was the most awkward with both of them not really knowing what to say to each other, but since she has opened up more to him, their conversations have started to last longer.

"No, not yet. She only asks why everyone is taking our photo. Cal did tell her about tonight so I thought it would be fun to have a watch party." Cal will be attending the Oscars, and while I have zero desire to see him looking handsome in a tuxedo with other just as good-looking actors and actresses, I thought it would be fun to make it special for Avery to watch.

"And what about Jax? How is he handling all of this?"

"Not that great. The media scrutiny has affected his performance. Since he is not playing as well, he has been benched. They are on a ten-day road trip, so maybe being out of the city and not seeing me will help."

"Why won't seeing you help?"

"I think seeing me reminds him of why he's under scrutiny in the first place."

Robert just rolls his eyes at me and laughs. "Jenna, if that's the reason, then that boy needs to go."

"I thought you liked Jax?" I ask, with a questioning smile.

"Not if he is going to be a big douche bag! Besides, I think I like Cal more." He smiles with a sly look.

Now it is my turn to roll my eyes at him, "Of course you would! He is famous, after all."

"I don't care about the fame. Cal just has to look at you and I can tell he's pure wickedness. Yum-my!"

I laugh at his craziness and go to the kitchen to start making our snacks for the show. I give Avery a bath and get her in her pajamas so as soon as we see Cal on TV, we can go to bed.

"Avery, come sit with Uncle Robert so we can look at all the pretty dresses on the red carpet," Robert calls from the living room. Avery runs out there to join him while I grab the snacks. I sit down with them, and pass around the popcorn as we see beautiful actresses and handsome actors walk the red carpet. We talk about which dresses we like best, and wonder why some actresses made some poor wardrobe choices.

"Look, there's Cal!" Avery yells when the camera pans to him. He looks devastatingly handsome in his tuxedo. And with him is none other than Cora Gregory. She is stunning in an emerald green off the shoulder dress that is molded to every curve of her body. Her dark hair is left down in loose waves and she is wearing gold jewelry. They are the most perfect looking couple in Hollywood. Recalling our conversation in Las Vegas about her only being a friend, I wonder if he was lying to me as they look too beautiful together not to be a couple.

"Who's that with Cal, Mommy?"

"That's an actress named Cora." I keep my answer vague, not wanting to influence my daughter with my opinions on her.

"Avery, I think you need to ask Cal if she's his girlfriend the next time you see him." I give Robert a shocked look, not believing he's asking a four-year-old to find out the gossip.

"What?" he shrugs, "it would be an innocent question coming from her."

"That is true," I agree, and hate to admit that I am equally as curious.

We're slow to get up in the morning, tired from staying up late as Avery wanted to watch more of the show. Fortunately, I don't have any meetings scheduled until the afternoon, so we take our time eating breakfast and getting ready for school. I open the door for us to leave and am startled by the sight of Cal.

"Ah! You scared me!" I place my hand over my heart, which is beating at a rapid pace.

"Cal!" Avery jumps into his arms to give him a hug. This is the first time she has shown Cal any affection, and I'm completely transfixed by the sight of them together.

"Sorry! You opened the door before I could knock."

I shake my head from looking at them and try to focus. "Wait, how are you even here? We just saw you on TV last night in Los Angeles."

"I took the red-eye back. It's time to start getting settled here." He looks at Avery and then back at me. "Where are you ladies going?"

"I am taking Avery to school and then working out."

"Can I go to school with you?" Cal asks as he tickles her stomach. She giggles and tries to swat his hand away.

"Sure, you can come. It probably would be good for you to see where she goes. Oh, and the principal wants to talk with me today about the paparazzi. She and the rest of the parents aren't happy."

He draws his eyebrows in concern and nods his head. "Yes, let's meet with her so we can discuss some solutions."

We take the elevator down to the garage and get into my car. "Nice ride," Cal says, admiring my Land Rover. I strap Avery into her car seat and get into the driver's seat.

"Thanks. It was the only thing my ex-husband gave me that I decided to keep." The car was one of his sorry-I-am-not-paying-attention-to-you-gifts when we were married.

At first, I was hesitant to keep it since I live in the city and don't necessarily need a car, but it has been very convenient to have and I'm glad I decided to keep it. "How was last night?" I ask, wanting to change the subject. I pull out of the garage, and see one paparazzi car waiting to follow.

"It was good. Tiring, but good. Nice to see some people I haven't seen in a while ,and a lot of great movies won."

"Cal, was that girl in the green dress your girlfriend?" Avery asks, and I am so proud of my girl for remembering to do so. Not that I should care since I have Jax.

"That is my friend Cora and no, she is not my girlfriend." I keep my eyes on the road, but feel his gaze on me for a reaction. "You'll get to meet her and my friend, Sean, very soon."

"Yeah! I love meeting new people!" Avery says and we laugh at how cute she sounds.

"Wow, we're here already?" Cal asks, as we pull into the parking lot, paparazzi waiting for us by the entrance. They quickly got used to our morning schedule of waiting for us at school to get a photo.

"Yes, normally we walk to school, but they've been making it difficult to do so." I nod my head toward the paparazzi. "Avery, put your sunglasses on. You can say hi to these men if you want too, but let's keep the sunglasses on, okay?" She puts on her sunglasses and is ready to go.

As soon as we get out of the car, they start taking pictures and calling our names. We walk to the front entrance and go inside. Avery takes Cal's hand to show him where her room is and introduces him to her teachers.

"Will you be picking me up too, Cal?" Avery looks at him with hope in her eyes.

"Absolutely, sweetheart." He kisses her on the check, and we leave her room to go have our meeting with the principal.

"Mr. Harrington, what a nice surprise to see you today. Thanks for coming as well. As I was saying to Ms. Pruitt, the photographers have been very disruptive to our environment, and myself and a lot of other parents are very concerned about this for our safety. If this doesn't stop soon, we're going to need Avery to find another school."

"I completely understand, Principal Hayes, and am very sorry for the disruption. I will provide a full-time officer at the door until things calm down, as well as make a sizable donation to the school. We're appreciative of all the hard work you and your staff do for our children. Again, I apologize for the inconvenience of everything and hope this solution will work for you?"

I expect for her to tell him that won't be enough, but instead she smiles and offers him her card. "That sounds wonderful, Mr. Harrington. Please take my card and call me when the officer is secured, and I will give you our routing number to make that generous donation." She shakes our hands and escorts us to the front entrance.

"Does money always get you out of trouble?" I jokingly ask, as we get in the car and try to avoid looking at the paparazzi. Thank goodness for tinted windows!

"Not with everyone," he gives me a pointed look, and I can't help but laugh at him. *You should not be sitting in a car alone with him, laughing! Think of Jax!* I stop laughing and start the car, but realize I have no idea where we are going.

"Um, where am I going?"

"I thought we were going to work out?"

I look at his clothes that consist of a t-shirt and jeans. "How are you going to work out in that?"

He looks down at himself and shrugs, "I can manage to do weights. Where's your gym?"

"I was going to work out in my building's gym." The idea of him in that small work out room with me is not a good one. Not wanting to sit here in the school's parking lot with all the paparazzi, I decide to start the car and will drive around until he tells me where to go.

"Okay, I'll just work out with you." I stare at him and it sounds innocent, but with this man, nothing is ever innocent.

"Why do you want to work out with me?" I ask, suspiciously.

"Because for one thing, I need to get a work out in, and the second thing is that I think it is important that you and I spend time together as well so we get to know each other better. I think that'll help my progress with Avery if I know and understand her mother better." I think about his logic and while it makes sense, warning bells are going off in my head.

"I don't think that's a good idea, Cal. People will talk and the next thing we know, there will be a story out saying you are living with me. Even though we know the truth, that isn't fair to Jax."

"While I disagree with you, I'm in no mood to argue. Why don't you and I discuss this over dinner?"

"We can't have dinner out together!" I say with exasperation that he would even suggest this.

"Why not? People need to eat," he says matter-of-factly.

"Because it will be labeled as a date by the paparazzi and I can't have that."

"Robert told me there's a restaurant at the top of your building. We can go there and the paparazzi will never know."

"Of course, Robert would tell you that," I say, making a mental note to have a little chit chat with dear ol' meddling Robert.

"I've been talking quite a bit to Robert now that I have his number as well."

"I bet you do," I say sarcastically, not enjoying this new relationship between the two.

Cal just laughs and I realize I'm still driving around in circles.

"You still haven't told me what hotel to drop you off at."

"Yes, I know. I've been enjoying our car ride together." He looks over at me and I see that flirtatious glimmer, the one that used to put my stomach into somersaults. The one that still does.

"I have work to do today, so please, what hotel are you staying at?" I say firmly, not wanting to give him any inkling of the effect he still has on me. I need to keep my guard up with him.

"I am staying at the Ritz-Carlton."

I nod my head and take the car in that direction, needing some distance from him.

"I want to have dinner with you, so we can talk about my

schedule. Filming doesn't start for another two weeks, so I would like to spend as much time with Avery as possible. I want to take her to school, pick her up, go sight-seeing with her, eat meals with her...everything that normal families do with each other. I need you to be there with us for the time being so she gets comfortable with me, and then eventually start doing things with just her and I. I also would like for you to go house hunting with me so you can feel comfortable in the home I pick out for her." I should be happy to hear all of this from him, but instead my feelings turn sad at the thought of her and I not being together all the time anymore.

"Once filming begins, my schedule is going to be limited for the next three months. I'm going to try to work with the director to see if we can shoot more night scenes, but I don't know if he'll agree to that. This is another reason why I'll need your help." Basically, he's asking me to be accessible so that when he's free, Avery can be free. The bitter part of me wants to throw it in his face how he hasn't been accessible to us for four years, but I know that would be wrong. I'm still not quite over the fact that this has all been a misunderstanding.

I pull up to the Ritz-Carlton, and watch the circus of the paparazzi jump out of their cars, waiting to get their photo of us. "I'll work on trying to be accessible for you." I swallow my lump of bitterness and decide to say no more.

"Thank you, Jenna. You truly don't know what this means to me. I'll see you later for school pick up." He nods at me, exits the car and shuts the door. I don't bother to watch if he makes it into the hotel or not as I speed away, needing to get home to work out my frustrations.

28

I've become very good at trying to juggle all the balls in my basket of life over the next month, but as with real juggling, balls will start to drop. Before the start of filming for Cal's movie, he did spend almost every waking hour that he could with us. The routine became normal as he comes for breakfast, goes to school with us, then he works out or makes business calls. After, he meets me at Avery's school to come back home with us, where we eat dinner, play games and read bedtime stories together. I've gotten so used to having him around that I have found myself stocking my refrigerator with his favorite beer and snacks. Now that filming has begun, he still manages to make it to drop her off at school, but sometimes we don't see him until bedtime. One night, he even fell asleep with Avery and I didn't have the heart to wake him and kick him out. She needs to start getting used to sleepovers with him anyway, I kept telling myself as I tossed and turned that night, not knowing why I was expecting to see him in my doorway.

While the stories in the magazines have seem to simmer down, the paparazzi have stuck around, still hounding me any chance they get. Chase always keeps his distance, but his warning of

Danny Salari came back to mind when he called me a bitch for not smiling for them. Since then, I still won't say anything to them, but I have started to smile more and sometimes wave, hoping that will start to appease them enough to leave us alone.

Tonight is the last game of the season for Jax and I am letting Cal watch Avery by himself while I go. Robert will start off the night babysitting since Cal will still be working, but as soon as Cal arrives, Robert will leave. I've been going to every single one of Jax's home games, trying to be the supportive girlfriend, but with him not being a regular in the lineup, his mood swings are more frequent and he's less fun to be around.

Four hours later, not only was Jax not in the lineup, but the team lost their last game. Missing the playoffs by two points, the players were devastated. I drove Jax to his favorite restaurant, but he barely ate and conversation was at minimal. We get back into the car and head back to his hotel. Maybe a night full of sex will cheer him up.

"You can just drop me off instead of parking," he says, his voice monotone, his eyes emotionless. I know he's upset about the loss and how the end of the season went, but I'm still surprised that he doesn't want to spend time with me.

"You don't want me to come up?" I ask, confused and hurt by his lack of attention.

"I can't do this anymore, Jenna. Let's stop pretending that we are in a real relationship for once, okay?"

"What do you mean?" I ask, suddenly very confused by what he is talking about.

"You've never once invited me to stay at your apartment. We've been together for almost a year and I am not allowed to sleep over?"

"Jax, I told you that I didn't want to make Avery uncomfortable if she woke up and saw you in the house. You said you understood!" I explain, getting annoyed that we're going over this again.

"Yet, it's okay for Cal to sleep there, who hasn't even known her that long?" he asks bitterly, his voice so filled with jealousy that I'm finding him quite unattractive at this moment.

"That's her father, Jax! There's no comparison!"

"Does she even know that he's her father yet?"

The car is filled with silence as he's just proven his point since she doesn't and he's absolutely right.

"Jax, I'm sorry…I didn't mean to hurt you," I plead, not wanting this to end like this.

"I know you didn't mean too, but you did." He opens the door to the car and looks back at me with longing and sadness in his eyes. "Goodbye, Jenna." I jump when the car door slams and watch him walk into his hotel with tears streaming down my face.

I drive back home in shock that my relationship with Jax has ended and ashamed of how I treated him. I realize that Robert may have been right - I used Jax and not only did I use him for sex, but I took advantage of his feelings for me without giving them right back to him. All Jax wanted was for me to love him back and I didn't. The realization makes me cry harder and I truly feel horrible for any pain I've caused him.

I get back home, exhausted and disgusted with myself. I open the door to see Cal and Robert sitting on the couch, talking softly so they don't wake up Avery.

"Jenna, what's wrong?" Robert asks, noticing right away how upset I am.

"Jax broke up with me tonight," I whisper, not able to look at either of them. "If you both will excuse me, I'm going to bed now. Please see yourselves out if you don't mind."

"I'm sorry, Jenna," Cal says, and even though he sounds sincere, I don't believe him.

"Somehow, I quite doubt that." I say and shut my bedroom door.

The hits keep on coming the next day, but this time it's News Channel 3 calling, saying they're canceling our monthly news segment.

"Why?" I ask angrily, knowing the answer before the producer needs to say it out loud.

"Right now, Jenna, the owners feel your current situation is a little too scandalous. While the ratings have been through the roof, they want to pull the plug. I'm so sorry, Jenna, as there's nothing I can do."

I hang up the phone, mad as hell at the unfairness of it all. Now Cal Harrington has affected my personal AND professional life and I am sick of it all. I need a release. I need to go have some fun and be around people I trust.

"We're going to O'Malley's tonight!" I say to Layla on the phone.

"Really? We haven't been there in almost a year!" She says, her voice sounding excited.

"I know, but this has been a really shitty week and I need some time with my best friends. I've got to release some of this stress."

"You don't have to tell me twice, I'm game!"

I hang up with her, call Robert to confirm and secure a babysitter since Cal will be working very late tonight and won't see Avery until the morning.

After I pick up Avery from school, I make sure to feed her and get her ready for bed. The babysitter arrives and I get myself ready. I decide on skin tight jeans, with a red low-cut v-neckline blouse and a black blazer to go over it, paired with mesh black peep toe ankle booties. I wear smoky eye make-up and paint red lipstick on my lips. Feeling good with how I look, I kiss Avery goodbye and make my way to O'Malley's.

The paparazzi follow my taxicab and get pictures of me as I exit the cab. Once inside the safety of the restaurant, I find a booth away from the windows and wait for Layla and Robert to arrive.

O'Malley's is exactly what everyone needed as three hours later, I'm feeling better from being in the company of my best friends. They made me laugh, we ate bad food and I was feeling buzzed from the many ciders I ingested. Robert and Layla decide to stay behind as they both started chatting up people while I want to go home and snuggle with my girl.

I walk out of O'Malley's and am pleasantly surprised to find it empty with no paparazzi insight. With my apartment only being a couple of blocks away and other pedestrians on the street, I decide to take advantage of this beautiful evening and walk home like I used to do.

As my apartment complex comes closer to view, I suddenly hear a car screech behind me and a door close. I start to feel uneasy and quicken my pace, my intuition telling me that the paparazzi just found me.

"Well, well, well, look who decided to take a nighttime stroll. Did you enjoy your time at the bar?" Danny Salari walks in front of me and flashes the camera in my face. I stop and close my eyes to readjust them as I was not prepared and forgot to wear my sunglasses.

"Yes, thank you. Please move out of my way," I ask politely as I walk faster around him. Two more paparazzi follow me on my side and continue taking pictures with their flash. I pull my hands up and try to shield my eyes from the side.

"I don't think so, lady, as you owe us a good quality photo," he says, as he flashes his camera again at me, this time lower since my eyes are downward. The flash makes me stop again, the blindness making me unsteady on me feet. I keep walking forward, my building seeming so close, yet so far.

"We've been here for almost two months, every day spending our hard earned money, hoping for one quality shot of you, yet you just won't cooperate with us." Another flash in my face, and I try to shield my eyes and just walk forward watching my feet, but they now have boxed me in, inching closer to me.

"Okay, I'm sorry. How about I give you the photo now?" I pull down my hands and smile, but with the flashing of the bulbs, I can't seem to keep me eyes open. And as more paparazzi arrive, the more blinding the flashes become.

"No, your eyes are too squinted. We need you to open your eyes for us."

"Well if you would stop for a second and let my eyes adjust, they will open!" I snap, getting irritated with them.

I hear them stop and I keep my eyes close, giving them a break before I open them again. They give me two seconds to look around to see my bearings. I smile and then the flashes begin. But this time, they become relentless.

"Stop, I can't see where I'm going!" I cry, but no one seems to care as the clicking keeps going. I try walking forward by only watching my feet, but someone puts their camera down low again, the flash back into my eyes. I lose my balance and fall to my knees.

"Look boys, she's on her knees where she belongs!" They laugh at Danny's crude remark and continue taking photos of me. I start to crawl forward, scraping my hands on the concrete, but they have me surrounded and won't move.

My anger has vanished and is replaced with utter terror. I push my knees and legs to the ground and huddle down, covering my head with my hands, hoping one of them will soon see how wrong this is and call the police.

"Look, she is too drunk to even get back up." I flip them my middle finger and the taunting continues. Scared for my life and not knowing what to do, I start to panic and cry silently, my night turning into a nightmare. I start to tune the taunting out and go inside my own head, rocking back and forth to try to soothe myself.

I have no idea how long I'm on the ground for, but suddenly I hear yelling. A male's voice is shouting, telling them to get back.

"You fucking assholes, what the hell is wrong with you!" I hear someone say. I feel hands on me and I start to shrink inward, my hands hitting their fingers off of me.

"Jenna! Jenna, it's Chase. I'm here to help you! It's Chase, Jenna! I'm right in front of you. Look at my black converses." I hear his panicked voice get closer and closer as I start to tune back in. There are two black converses in front of my knees.

"This is my hand waving to you, Jenna, can you see it?"

My vision is blurred, not able to focus from all of the flashes to my eyes. I see a blurry hand in front of my face and nod.

"Grab my hand, Jenna, grab my hand! I'll get you home!"

I grab his hand and he immediately helps me to my feet.

"Get the fuck away from her, Salari! You're going to pay for this!" Chase lifts me up under my knees and continues to carry me the rest of the way to my building. I wrap my arms around his neck and bury my head into his chest, wishing the noises of the flash bulbs and the clicking of the cameras would stop.

"I didn't do shit - I can't help it if she has had one too many drinks tonight and can't walk. You've got nothing, Canada!"

"What the hell is going on? JENNA! Oh my god, what's wrong?" I hear Robert's worried voice come next to me as Chase continues to carry me.

"She was attacked by the paparazzi. I fucking thought you were with her tonight?" I hear a ding and my mind registers we are in my elevator.

"We were with her, but we thought she took a taxi home, not walked! Oh my god, she's shaking. Is she okay?"

"She's in shock. Why the fuck does Harrington not have a bodyguard on her? This is so fucking typical. Selfish asshole!" I whimper out loud, Chase's anger making me scared.

"You've got to lower your voice, Chase, once we get off this elevator. We don't want to wake Avery and scare her, not to mention these nosy neighbors."

I'm trying to fight against the darkness that wants to overtake me as I try to stay conscious while Chase walks us off the elevator, onto my floor. I hear Robert open the door and tell the babysitter to not say a word.

Chase walks briskly into my room and lays me on my bed. I so want to go hold and sleep with Avery, but no words will come forth and before I know it, I lose the fight and complete darkness enfolds me.

29

I wake up with a start, another vivid nightmare from last night haunting my sleep. Unlike last night's feeling of being the scared prey before a shark attack, this morning I am angry. I'm a lioness ready to pounce on anyone ready to hurt me.

I get out of bed and put my workout clothes on, my need to run out these feelings inside of me before I have a mental breakdown.

I walk out of the bedroom to find Cal and Robert talking softly to some stranger. They all turn and look at me, concern on their faces but something else, as if they have been up to something without my knowledge. I'm immediately on alert. I stare suspiciously at this stranger who's in my home without my invitation. His haircut indicates military, his eyes are cold gray steel as they stare back at me. No amount of clothing can hide his rock hard body. He's stunning in a completely dangerous way. I know the situation is serious since Robert is not drooling all over him.

"How are you feeling today?" Robert asks in a sweet voice that he would use on Avery.

"Fine," I say firmly, shooting him a questionable look. "Where's Avery?" I walk to her room but find it empty.

"I took her to school already," Cal says, his tone of voice all business, his eyes penetrating as he assesses my mood. "Jenna, I want you to meet Mason, your new bodyguard. He'll be with you at all times when you need to leave the house. We're extremely fortunate that he was available on such short notice." Cal nods his thank you to Mason. "I've reviewed his credentials and I am 100% confident that he'll be able to keep you and Avery safe when out in public."

I stare at Cal in silence, my anger toward him mounting to a new level for not consulting me. He never discussed getting a bodyguard, nor did he ask if I even wanted one. He has completely taken away all forms of freedom from me.

I turn to Mason with an extended hand and my most dazzling smile, "Nice to meet you. Do you have a last name, Mason?"

"You may call me Mason, ma'am," he says, his voice just a little too cocky for my liking. He grips my hand in a tight, brief handshake.

"Well, Mason, I do appreciate you being here for my well-being, but you see, there seems to be a slight miscommunication as I was never asked whether or not I wanted you here and no offense to you personally, but I don't need a bodyguard. I am sure Mr. Harrington is paying you generously to waste your pristine skills on babysitting me and my daughter. I apologize on his behalf and wish you the best of luck as I do not need your services." I smile sweetly, turn on my heel and head to the front door.

Three steps in and my arm is grabbed by Cal, who whirls me around to face the fury that is raging in his eyes. "Mason, it seems Ms. Pruitt is ready for a morning run. Please feel free to get ready to join her by changing into your work out attire in the guest bathroom while I have a little chat with her."

Mason picks up a duffel bag from off the floor and heads straight to Avery's bathroom. *How does he even know where it is already? How long has he been here?*

As Cal drags me by the arm to my bedroom, I glare at Robert, hoping he can read my mind as it screams TRAITOR at him. He could have sent me a text message this morning while I was in my room to warn me about Mason and he didn't. Rational thinking Jenna would try to understand why Robert would think it was okay to not tell me what Cal was planning. But rational Jenna is not here right now and irrational Jenna is mad as hell. All I'm thinking about is what a selfish prick Robert is to go behind my back and side with Cal.

I yank my arm out of Cal's grip and walk to my window to try to get as far away from him as I can. Cal shuts the door and all I hear is his footsteps pacing back and forth.

"Jenna, I know you're not stupid enough to believe that you don't need a bodyguard after last night's incident." His voice is harsh and condescending with his insult.

I ball my hands into a fist and turn around, the image of punching him in the face providing immense pleasure. "Well, Cal, I guess in your eyes I AM stupid, because I DON'T need a bodyguard as I feel that last night was an isolated incident and won't happen again as people will hopefully be appalled when they see the images once published."

He closes his eyes and grips the bridge of his nose and takes a deep breath. He keeps his jaw tightly locked, his patience with me obviously on thin ice. "Unfortunately, that is not how it works in the paparazzi world. Last night just fueled their fire and they will be after you even more."

I calmly approach him and look him in the eyes so that he understands how dead serious I am. "I don't know the paparazzi world. I don't know your world. What I do know is that I don't want any part of their world. Just like I don't want any part of YOUR world. You brought this into my life. YOU need to fix it." And with that, I turn on my heel and throw open my bedroom door, not caring anymore what Cal Harrington thinks.

I want MY life back.

He OWES me my life back.

Mason is waiting for me at the front door, the look on his face indicating that his intensions are to escort me on my run.

"Hope you can keep up with me, Mason." I wink at him with a venomous smile on my face as I exit my apartment.

"Ma'am, I'm sorry if my presence is causing any tension between you and Mr. Harrington," he says, as we get into the elevator. "But I did see the images from last night and what they did to you is not acceptable."

"Not your fault, Mason. Completely Mr. Harrington's fault," I say with a sweet smile as we exit the elevators. I stop to think what the best route would be to take, but an idea springs to mind. "Mason, have you ever been in downtown Chicago before?"

"No ma'am, I haven't."

"Well, you are in for a treat! Just follow my lead," I say seriously as I put my sunglasses on and adjust my hat. I notice the paparazzi have been moved behind a police barricade twenty feet from the apartment building's entrance. It looks like there are even more of them than before and a flicker of doubt momentarily flashes through my mind. *Maybe it is good that I'm not running by myself today.* I push that thought aside as this is still all Cal's fault that I don't even have the freedom to go out by myself anymore.

We get outside and start to jog, the paparazzi immediately starting to follow us. Some of them hop in their cars and some start on foot.

"Looks like Princess Jenna couldn't handle us, boys!" Danny Salari says, referring to Mason as he tries to run alongside us. "Wonder how long it will take before she has sex with this one!" he says, getting laughs out of some of the other photographers. I grit my teeth and proceed to run faster. Soon Salari and some of the few who decided to try to run stop following us. The only paparazzi remaining are the ones following us by car. My intention is for us to head into the city on our run. While normally I stay on the lakefront trail for my runs, going into downtown will be my best chance to lose both Mason and the paparazzi.

I run west for half a mile at a steady pace, trying to keep my head straight while my eyes follow the lanes of cars to my left, trying to gage when there will be a break for me to quickly dart through. Finally, I see one and my heart starts racing. Saying a quick little pray of hopes that I don't die, I suddenly veer left and run straight into the oncoming traffic. Car horns blare, tires screech and cars collide as I narrowly make it across to the other side. I hear Mason yelling my name and I take off even faster. I start zig zagging through people, turning right onto a new street, then left onto another new street, trying to see where I can go without being followed. After making another turn onto another different street, I look behind me and see no one that I recognize, but I refuse to take a chance as Mason could have made it across that traffic once those cars stopped. My lungs are screaming, my legs are tired and sweat is dripping down my face as I decide to slow my pace down to catch my breath. I see a huge department store that takes up the whole block with multiple entrances on each of its four streets and run inside. I follow the signs to the restroom, find it and go inside to dry off some of my sweat. I splash cold water on my face and take a couple of sips. Once I have caught my breath, I head to an exit that leads to a different street.

I get out, look up and down the street and immediately spot one of the paparazzi's cars. I start to run, moving as fast as I can, going up and down more different streets, in and out of places that I know have multiple entrances due to their size. I continue my game until I'm so tired that I can't run anymore and decide that I'm done caring about proving I don't need a bodyguard. I head east to the lake and when I see the beach, I immediately run to it. I collapse on the sand and look up at the sky, sucking in as many breaths as I can to calm myself down, but instead of calming dawn, I sit up and start to cry. I wrap my arms around my knees and put my head down and let it all out because even if I wanted to stop, I couldn't. I cry out all of my fears from last night, my anxiety of being chased and the loss of my freedom. I cry until I have no more tears to shed. I take some deep breaths and just stare out at the lake, its soothing waves calming me down.

I realize the gravity of what I just did by losing Mason. I also realize the benefits of having Mason with me, especially with Avery. Now I feel like a fool. Cal is going to be livid and I'm going to have to apologize to him. I groan out loud and am even more mad at myself. I look at my watch and am shocked to see I have been gone for close to three hours. I start to swipe the sand off my legs and grab my sunglasses that I took off.

"That was not the smartest move to ditch your bodyguard, Jenna."

I whirl around to see Chase walking toward me, his long hair pulled back into a ponytail, aviator shades covering his eyes. With his camera put safely away in his bag, I let my guard down, especially with him saving me last night.

"I realize that. I'm not too proud of myself right now," I sigh, actually starting to feel ashamed.

"I can't blame you, though. Hell, I can't even imagine what you are feeling right now." He just shakes his head and looks at the lake.

"Chase, what's a guy like you doing in this business? You seem so nice and intelligent." Not to mention hot, but he doesn't need to know I think so.

"I'm obviously not that intelligent, otherwise I wouldn't be in this business," he jokes with a sad smile. "Honestly, my family situation back home is not good and the money is helping out. Once things are better, I plan on quitting."

"Will you go back to Canada?" I ask, wondering if he has a special someone at home. He's too good looking not to.

"I don't know. I'm kind of digging Chicago." He smiles, "C'mon, I'll walk you back home."

We start walking back to my apartment in compatible silence. As we get closer, we start to see the other paparazzi members waiting for us.

"Get your game face on." Chase recommends as we see Danny Salari leading the pack.

"Thanks again for last night, Chase." I sincerely say as I don't know what would have happened if he hadn't intervened.

"I'm glad I made it there."

"Me, too."

I put my head down as keep moving forward as they surround us both and start snapping photos.

"Wow Jenna, two guys in one day, you sure do move fast. And with one of our own! Canada, how did you get so lucky as to fuck that?" Danny taunts. *Don't say anything, Jenna. Keep moving forward.* My building is in view, the police barricades close.

"Watch your mouth, Salari!" Chase warns.

"What will you do about it, Canada? Absolutely nothing because you are too much of a pussy!"

All of a sudden, I hear a crack and a thud. I turn around to see Danny on the ground, blood pouring from his nose while Chase stands over him and is holding his hand with a pained expression on his face. Chase just punched Danny in the nose and I feel even worse that he did it for me.

"Chase!" I yell, getting his attention to see if he is okay.

"Keep going, Jenna! I'll be fine." He motions with his hands for me to keep going, grabs his bag off the ground and starts walking in the other direction.

"I'm going to fucking sue you, Chase! You asshole! You broke my nose!" Danny screams. I run the rest of the distance to the barricades and breathe a sigh of relief when I enter my building.

My relief is short lived when I see one of the doormen pick up the phone and say "she's here" into the receiver, no doubt letting Cal know my arrival home.

Time to face the music.

30

I creep toward the front door of my apartment, dread and regret making me walk at a snail's pace. I feel ashamed by my actions and don't know how to make it right. I'll just have to apologize to both Cal and Mason and reassure them I won't ever go rogue again. I take a deep breath as I stand in front of my door and slowly open it.

Robert and Mason are sitting on the couch while Cal is standing, staring out the window. All three men look at me as I enter the apartment. I can feel Cal's anger radiating off of him and decide to apologize first to Mason, whose clothes are drenched from sweat.

"I want everyone except for Jenna out of this apartment." Cal growls as he turns around and looks at me. Robert and Mason look at Cal, then at each other, and decide not to leave. For both of them to defy Cal's order must mean Cal is beyond furious.

I swallow the lump that has formed in my throat and start apologizing, "Cal, I..."

"You little fool! Do you know what could have happened to you out there?" he yells, his eyes demanding in fury, the vein in his neck bulging with each breath.

"I'm sorry, really I am. Mason, I'm sorry!" I turn to Mason, who just nods at me, acknowledging my apology without any words.

"What were you hoping to prove, Jenna? Did you know you caused a three-car pile-up with your little stunt?" His nostrils flaring with disgust at my actions.

I feel even more remorseful now and just look down at my hands.

"Tell me, Jenna, what were you hoping to prove?" Cal shouts at me as if I were a child. Although I understand him being upset, I don't appreciate him treating me this way in front of Mason and Robert.

"C'mon Cal, she apologized. Jenna, you won't do that ever again, right?" Robert asks, looking tired from all of the worrying I've put him through.

"I promise, I won't ever do that again." I confirm, hoping that this will calm Cal down and we can move on from this.

"You're damn right you'll never do that again because THIS is why you need a bodyguard, Jenna!" He grabs a large zip lock bag off the table and makes his way toward me.

"NO Cal! She's had enough for today!" Robert yells as he tries to grab whatever is in Cal's hand, but misses.

Cal shoves the bag in my hands and I gasp at the sight of a black-and-white photo of Avery and me. Our eyes have been cut out and there is a gooey red substance all over the photo. The words "DIE" scrawled in the same red substance.

I look up at him, then at Robert, in complete horror, my brain refusing to register what it just saw.

"This," Cal takes the bag out of my hands and shakes it in my face, "is WHY Mason is here! You could have gotten yourself killed today!" he spats at me.

"STOP Cal! You've made your point!" Robert shouts out in frustration.

With my eyes refusing to look away from the image of Avery,

eyeless and bloody, bile starts to rise up my throat and I take off in a run for my bathroom, shutting the door and barely making it to the toilet. When I think my body can't take anymore, the dry heaving turns to wails as I scream and cry at the thought of anyone hurting my daughter. I lay on the floor of the bathroom, my body trembling and heaving with each tear that falls.

Eventually exhaustion takes over and the tears dry up. I continue to lay on the floor in a daze and before long, my inner voice tells me to get up. I stand up and flush the toilet and look in the mirror. My eyes are red, my whole face is puffy and swollen from crying. I wash my hands, brush my teeth and gargle with mouthwash. I untie my hair from its ponytail and decide to go back out there to find out more details of where the photo came from.

Cal is sitting on the floor of my bedroom, his back against my bed, waiting for me. His one knee is pulled up, supporting his arm that hangs over it, while his other hand lays against his thigh. He lifts up his head and looks at me with eyes filled with anguish. I walk up to him and as I approach, he holds out his hand to me. I reach out to grasp it, thinking he needs help getting up, but instead he pulls me down into his lap and hugs me tightly. The unexpected comfort undoes me as I clutch at his shirt and sob into his chest. He rocks me silently, letting the wetness of my tears soak through the expensive fabric of his shirt. We stay this way until my tears end and continue to just hold each other.

"I'm sorry, Jenna. I shouldn't have done that." I hear the regret deep in his voice. "I was scared and angry when Mason came back without you and I needed you to understand the real reason why he was here. Last night's incident just moved up the process of him arriving sooner."

"Why didn't you tell me about the photo? When did we get it?" I softly ask, needing some answers to so many questions.

"It arrived in the mail last week. Robert found it and immediately called me. I went to the police, who got the FBI involved. They tested it for fingerprints, but it came up empty."

"Last week?" I look up at him in disbelief. "Cal, you can't keep these things from me!"

"You're absolutely right, Jenna. But with everything that's been going on, I wanted to shield you from it and hope it didn't happen again. I know that was wrong."

"You have to communicate with me, Cal. I can't be left in the dark about something so serious, despite you wanting to protect me from it."

"Can we make a pact that we'll both work on communicating better with each other?" he asks and I nod in consent, vowing to work on it from my end.

"Good." He leans down and kisses my forehead. I look at those lips and start to remember how they made me feel. Heat starts to pool inside of me and I look up to see him watching me, his gaze alternating between my lips and my eyes. I swallow and lick my dry lips, which make his eyes darken with desire. He bends his head, his lips descending slowly to mine when a knock on my door stops him.

"Cal, your agent keeps calling you." Robert's muffled voice is heard through the door.

"Be right there," he calls. He looks back down at me and smiles.

"Why don't you get freshened up and then come out so we can talk about how we are going to utilize Mason." I nod my head as we untangle our arms and help each other up. I watch him walk out and close my door, deciding that I need to stay away from any physical contact with Cal. *You are fresh off of a break up, Jenna, you are just emotional. Focus on keeping Avery safe!* With that pep talk, I go into the bathroom to take a shower to clear my head.

31

All paparazzi are questioned by the FBI and a restraining order is in place against Danny Salari. He keeps his distance but stares at me with menace in his eyes whenever I see him. He pressed charges against Chase for his broken nose and Chase was arrested, but got out on bail a couple of hours later.

Jax told the paparazzi that he broke up with me and stories are running rampant that Cal is to blame, especially with pictures of us around town together. I can't even keep up with the amount of stories that are being told about me and my relationship with Cal so I don't even pay attention.

I thought it was going to be weird having Mason accompany me everywhere I go, but after three weeks of him being my shadow and personal chauffeur, I have actually started to enjoy it. It is especially nice when the paparazzi start getting aggressive with being in my personal space. Avery, at first, couldn't understand why he was with us all the time, but now enjoys having another adult wrapped around her little finger. Layla now requests to go everywhere I go just so she can stare at Mason.

"Mason, is your love tank full?" she asked him on a day we met for lunch.

"No ma'am," he says, his sunglasses blocking us from seeing his expression.

"Do you want it to be?" she asks with a sly smile and a wink. While Mason usually shows no emotion at all, he couldn't contain the corners of his mouth from lifting in what would be called a smile.

Mason and I are coming back from the grocery store when I hear a strange male voice in my apartment. Cal and a sharp dressed man with gray hair and a beard stand up upon my arrival. *What is Cal even doing here during the day?* I look around for Robert who had to of let them in, but he's nowhere to be found.

"There she is! The woman who's been causing all the uproar!" the strange man laughs and I immediately do not like him.

I give Cal a quizzical look and notice that he seems agitated, his jaw locked, mouth set in a thin line. "Jenna, this is my agent, Philip Logan. We had a break from shooting and Philip wanted to meet you." I shake his extended hand and smile politely.

"Nice to meet you, but I could have met you on set or at your hotel. What are you both doing here in my apartment? Where is Robert?"

"What a lovely home this is too - this view is spectacular! Cal, did you buy this place for her?"

My mouth drops open, insulted that he would think I might not be able to afford this place on my own. "No, I bought this place with the money I make in prostitution." I snide sarcastically. I look at Cal to see his lips twitch from suppressing a smile. "Why are you both here again?"

Philip throws his head back and laughs, "You are a sassy little thing - I love that!" I can already feel a headache forming from the annoying sound. I look behind me as I hear the front door open and close to see that Robert has joined us and is helping Mason put my groceries away. He gives me a warning look to behave, which makes me question even more what is going on.

"Let's sit down, Jenna, and make ourselves comfortable." Philip sits down and I have to bite my tongue from reminding him that this is MY home, not his to make himself comfortable in. With him being Cal's agent, I need to watch what I say and play nice.

"Besides coming into town to check in on Cal and discuss business, I wanted to meet you in person because, well, we need your help." He looks over at Cal who shakes his head at him.

"I told you no, Philip." His tone of voice firm. "Leave it alone."

"My help? With what?" I ask, confused and suspicious of what they could possibly want from me.

"Nothing, Jenna," Cal says, giving his agent a warning look.

"Cal's movie that he shot last year is releasing in two weeks and well, the studio is concerned over the recent headlines that paint Cal in a negative light." His agent turns his full attention on me, ignoring Cal.

"No, Philip!" Cal raises his voice. I look from Cal to Philip, not understanding what is happening.

"The recent photos of you guys together around town looking like one big happy family have been great for publicity and repairing Cal's reputation, but the studio is requesting a little more from you."

"Philip, I don't fucking care what the studio thinks!" Cal interjects, his face red from anger.

"Cal, this is one of the biggest studios in Hollywood, they can crush your career! If you want any kind of future as an actor or director, we need to comply with them." Philip pleads with Cal.

I finally find my voice that was suppressed from shock. "All this time here with us has been for publicity?" I gasp, looking at Cal. I feel like I have just been punched in the stomach. We've been going out more together, Avery and I showing him the city per HIS request. He claimed that since Chicago was going to be his new home, he wanted to get to know it better. So on his days off, we've been taking him to all of the tourist attractions and then our favorite local places. I never doubted for one second his intentions weren't pure, but now with this news coming from his agent, I'm doubting everything and wondering if our outings together have been for the photo opportunity.

Cal looks over at me, hurt registering in his eyes. "Do you really think that, Jenna?" he asks incredulously.

I stare at him, not wanting to believe it, but also not knowing what to believe. My brain is screaming not to trust him, while my heart is saying that he wouldn't do that. Last time I followed my heart, it got scarred.

"What does the studio want from me?" I look back at Philip, wanting to get this over with.

"The studio requests that you attend both the Los Angeles and New York premieres of his new movie, walking the red carpet with him and continuing to look like you're trying to work things out."

"Why?" I question, not understanding how my presence at the premieres will help.

"The studio thinks that Cal will regain the female fan audience if they see you supporting him and that will increase ticket sales," Philip says, looking uncomfortable.

I laugh bitterly and stand up. "You guys are unbelievable," I say in disgust. While most women would be ecstatic to be going to a Hollywood premiere with one of the most eligible bachelors in Hollywood, I consider this request to be one of my worst nightmares. I am being used and all in the name of money and Cal's reputation.

"Jenna, I don't want you to even consider this!" Cal demands, "I will be perfectly fine without the studio's support."

"And if I say no?" I ignore Cal and continue to look at Philip.

"Cal signed a multi-million dollar contract with them for a three movie franchise series. They could pull out and demand the money they already paid him."

"I will gladly give back that money to avoid this bullshit!" Cal spats, raking his hands through his hand while he stands up.

"It isn't just the money, it will affect his career and whether other studios will want him in their future movies."

I look at Cal, who shakes his head at me. "Don't do it, Jenna," he warns and I ponder what to do. I want to selfishly say no and give his agent and the studio a big fuck you. But this is my daughter's father and anything negative against him might affect her. I know that Cal loves his career and if the roles were reversed, I'd be devastated if mine was ruined.

"Everything will be taken care of for you, Jenna. We'll fly Cal's stylist in to take your measurements and get wardrobe for you. His publicist can coach you through what to do the day of each premiere. It'll be easy and maybe even fun for you." Philip glances at me with hope.

"Do I have time to think about it?" I glance at Cal, who throws his hands up in the air and turns around to look out the window.

"Unfortunately, no. They want an answer today. I am sorry, Jenna."

I feel I have zero choice in the matter, a feeling I seem to be having a lot since Cal entered our lives. I sigh with resignation and stand up.

"I'll do it," I say firmly, giving Philip a nod, "but don't ever ask me to do anything like this again." I walk to my front door, needing to find refuge other than my apartment. "I am going to work out in the gym in my building - ALONE!" I look at Mason with a pointed look and slam my apartment door.

The two weeks leading up to the Los Angeles premiere have been a whirlwind of appointments and dress fittings. Cal's stylist came out to take my measurements and go through a book of styles to see what I liked. Cal's publicist flew in to meet with us separately to go over schedules and what is required of me at both premieres. Seems like I'm just arm candy, not having to say a word, just show up with him, let the photographers take my picture with him, attend the parties and come home when the rest of them fly off to the London premiere. Robert works with Cal's assistant on my travel arrangements. Fortunately, I'll only be gone from Avery for two days. Cal will leave three days before for the movie press junket, which means I'll fly there and back home by myself.

I have tried to ignore him for the most part, which wasn't too hard to do with his grueling work schedule, but since today is the day before he leaves, the director gave him the day off and it feels like he is everywhere. He was here this morning with donuts and coffee for school drop off, then he went off to do his own thing, but came back with groceries, announcing he is cooking us dinner and then picked up Avery from school.

"Maybe he just wants to do something nice and simple for you, Jenna," Robert said when I wonder aloud what Cal was up too.

"I don't need him to do anything for me!" I huff, not wanting his kind gestures, not knowing if they are genuine or not.

His dinner was surprisingly delicious and it was nice for once having someone else cook. He offered to give Avery a bath for me and I couldn't help but smile hearing them laugh together and sing songs. He gets her ready for bed and I join them for his reading of a story. I watch him as he acts out the storyline, animating his voice when the story calls for it, taking her imagination to another place. She laughs at his impersonation of a bear and I see what looks like love radiating from his eyes as he looks down at her. He catches me watching him and I quickly look away from him, not allowing myself to be hypnotized by those eyes…or that mouth.

He finishes the story and we kiss her goodnight. We are about to leave her room when she calls back out to him. "Cal, are you my daddy?" she asks, while she looks down and fidgets with her blanket.

Cal looks at me in shock, not knowing how to answer. "What makes you think that, honey?" I ask gently.

"We have the same eyes, silly!" she says in her 'duh, mommy' voice which always makes me laugh.

Cal kneels down next to her bed and holds her hand. "Yes, sweetheart, I'm your daddy," he says, his voice thick with emotion.

She gives him the brightest smile I've ever seen her give anyone. "I knew you would come back one day," she whispers and I suck in my breath, not knowing that she even had these thoughts going through her little head.

He hugs her tight and kisses her. "I'll never be away from you for long periods of time again," he promises, his words angering me as that is a promise he can't pretend to keep.

"Will you sleep with me?" she asks with puppy dog eyes.

"I'll stay with you until you go to sleep," he looks at me for approval and I nod.

I close her door softly and go to the kitchen to pour myself a drink that I immediately down in one gulp. I've got to get my emotions under control. I am relieved that she finally knows the truth, but I am scared that he is going to break her heart. I can't shield her heart from him like I can with my own. *He better not be acting with her!* The more I keep thinking about it, the more worked up I get.

When he comes out of her room a short time later, I am three glasses of wine in and my anger hasn't simmered down. I stalk up to him and try to get right into his face so he can see how serious I am.

"If you break her heart, I will personally kill you!" I growl in a low whisper.

Before I can continue with my rage on him, he grabs my arms and crushes his lips to mine. He pushes me against the wall and pins me with his pelvis, grinding it into me so I can feel his hardness. I gasp against the roughness and he takes advantage of the opening, swooping his tongue into my mouth to clash with mine.

I struggle against him, feeling my body come alive at the memories, all the while my mind screaming no at me.

"Stop," I say as I try to push him off me. I move my head so he can't reach my lips but he just assaults my neck instead, making me moan at the sensations he is shooting down my body.

"When are you going to stop ignoring this, Jenna?" he trails his hands down my arms and slips his hands into mine, holding them against the wall. "You want me just as much as I want you. I see it in your eyes." He continues to gyrate against me, the friction against my core making me want to wrap my legs around him for more.

"No," I shake my head and with as much strength as I can, I push his strong body away from me. "I want nothing to do with you!" I pant, believing my own lies as my body is screaming for him to take me. "I'll go to these premieres with you and continue this CHARADE of being a perfect little family, but when we return we'll start your visitation rights. No more popping into my apartment whenever you feel like it. You don't need me around anymore when you visit her."

He leans in close and smiles dangerously at me. "I see your wall is up, but let me tell you something Jenna, I look forward to BURNING it down." He steals another kiss and abruptly lets me go.

He walks to the door, opens it and turns around to look at me, "I'll see you in Los Angeles," and closes the door softly.

I run to the door and lock it so that he doesn't try to come back in. I turn around, slide to the floor and pull my knees up to my chest. I wrap my arms around myself and pray that I have the strength to protect my heart from him.

32

I take the first flight out of Chicago and due to the time change, I arrive in Los Angeles by 9 a.m. I convince Cal that Mason needs to stay with Avery and my mother, who is taking care of her while we are gone, so I am traveling solo. Cal's stylist meets me at the airport and takes me to my hotel room at the Beverly Hilton.

"We have to be ready by 5 p.m., so hair and make-up will be knocking on your door at 1 p.m. I'm sure you've been up early, so try to get some sleep. Lunch will be ready for you at noon," she says, and leaves me alone until then. I'm in a gorgeous two bedroom suite and notice a beautiful bouquet of white and lavender roses are waiting for me with breakfast in the dining room. I open the card and am surprised to see they are from Cal.

I look forward to seeing you later. Thank you again for being here.
Cal

I inhale the delicious scent of the roses and rip up the card, not wanting anyone to see it and think how sweet he is since I've convinced myself that it's all an act. The closer the airplane got to California, the more my bitterness grew at the purpose of my presence here. I feel like I sold my soul to the devil and I just want to get this over with. I should be exhausted, but instead I'm wide awake, adrenaline pumping and ready to go. I call home to make sure they know I got here safely and decide to work instead of napping.

Lunch arrives and it's the healthiest lunch I think I've ever eaten in my life. "We need to make sure you eat foods that won't make you bloated," Cal's stylist said when she delivered it. *Why even bother eating at all then?* Fresh watermelon, salad with lentil beans and a tall pitcher of lemon water with additional lemons is what I'm served for lunch. I try to normally eat healthy, but on a day like today where my stress and anxiety levels are high, alcohol and chocolate would be on the menu instead. This selection of food darkens my mood. Then I remember the mini bar and a mischievous smile appears on my face with the thought of homemade alcohol infused lemonade. I grab the vodka out of the fridge, take all the lemons out of the water and the lemon dish and grab the stevia packet that I carry in my purse and start mixing. Five minutes later, I take my first sip and sigh in pure contentment.

At exactly one o'clock, Cal's stylist and her team descend upon me. She introduces me to all five of them and tells me what each of their roles will be for the next four hours. She finishes her instructions to everyone and is about to depart when she starts sniffing the air. "Why do I smell alcohol?" she asks, as she continues to sniff around. "Do you guys smell alcohol?" she asks everyone, who shakes their head no. I didn't even realize that plain vodka can smell! One of the stylists, a tall, thin handsome man with gorgeous milk chocolate skin named Kellan, looks at me with a smirk and eyes my drink.

"Nope," I play innocent, not wanting her to take away my drink. "I don't smell a thing."

"Jenna, what are you drinking? I did not order any lemonade." She eyes my drink suspiciously.

"Oh, I made some fresh lemonade with stevia. See, here's the stevia packet." I hold up the empty packet for her to see. She goes to the waste bucket and pulls out the empty mini bottle of vodka.

"And where did this come from?"

"Oh my, looks like housekeeping forget to take the trash away from the last guest," I say, my eyes round with fake innocence and my lie sounding smooth as silk.

"Oh, lighten up, Morgan. It's obvious this poor girl needs a drink, look at all the stress acne on her face!" Kellan says, and I scowl at him for pointing out publicly my flaws.

He throws his head back and laughs. "Child, we are going to have so much fun with YOU!" he laughs. "Let's get to work everyone."

Nails and toes get painted first, then make up is applied and my hair is done with it half up tightly and the rest of my hair fanning down in waves all around me with added extensions for volume and length. Kellan helps distract me from my nerves with hilarious horror stories of other celebrities and wardrobe malfunctions. Morgan pulls out a beautiful Georges Chakra one shoulder, teal Grecian style gown with intricate beading aligning the top. Since it has a built in bodysuit that requires me to get naked for, I take the dress into the bedroom to put on. I say a little prayer of thanks for the snaps at the crotch to make it easy on me for future bathroom breaks. When I walk back into the living room, I am shocked to see most of my right leg coming out of a very high slit in the dress.

"Um, was that slit there when we originally tried this dress on?" I say, not feeling comfortable with the amount of leg I am showing.

"Yes, it has always been there," Kellan says, while he kneels down and helps me into my ridiculously high Vivienne Westwood metallic silver shoes. As soon as he finishes with the strap around my ankles, they all stand back and assess me from head to toe. The silence does nothing to help my increasing anxiety.

"Jewelry!" Kellan snaps his fingers and two stylists rush to him with earrings, bracelets and ring options. All Harry Winston, all incredibly expensive. He picks out the pieces and the stylists rush to place everything on me. Once they're done, they step back and the room becomes silent once more.

"Amazing!" Kellan exclaims and a collective sigh of relief comes out from the rest of the stylists. "Jenna, let's have you take a look at yourself." Kellan escorts me to my room and I stare in awe in the mirror. I don't recognize the woman who is staring back at me. I take a shaky breath, happy to see that I might actually look like I fit in tonight.

"Thank you so much, Kellan! I can't even believe this is me." I laugh at how silly I sound, but it's the truth.

"The canvas was already beautiful, we just had to liven it up with some color," he winks at me. "Let's get your purse and we will start packing up everything to take with us to New York."

He escorts me out to the living room where there is a knock on the door that one of the stylists answers. Cal, his publicist, Sean Lindsey and Cora Gregory all come into my suite looking like the million dollar celebrities that they are.

"It's really good to see you again, my dear." Sean comes toward me first and wraps me in a tight hug with a kiss on the check. "My goodness, you do look ravishing!" He checks me out from head to toe with an evil smile on his face. "Me thinks I need to protect you from the vultures who will want a piece of you tonight." I roll my eyes at his dramatics and look for Cal when Cora walks into my line of vision. Her cool eyes size me up with resentment, but she quickly masks it with fake enthusiasm as she smiles when Sean introduces us.

"It's nice to meet you," I say politely, my guard up from catching her true feelings for me. It's crystal clear that she and I will never be friends.

"It's a pleasure," she says, her voice so sexy that it almost purrs. "Cal has told us so much about you." She half smiles and then slides her arm around Cal's waist, making sure I see her mark her territory.

I smile in humor at her efforts and finally get the chance to look over at Cal. My breath catches at how incredibly handsome he is. He's wearing a black tuxedo jacket with a dark grey dress shirt that has the top two buttons undone, giving a peak of his muscular chest. His tailored black pants shape his legs nicely and end over his black dress shoes. My eyes make their way back to his to find him watching me. His smoldering look making me squirm from the ache his sexy stare is causing.

"Alright everyone, let's go. Limo is waiting downstairs," Cal's publicist announces. I watch Cora snake her arm thru Cal's and turn him toward the door. He looks behind us and nods at Sean, who takes my hand and smiles at me. "Let's go have some fun," he winks and I can't help but laugh at him.

We all get in the car, Cora purposely making sure she sits in between Cal and Sean while I sit next to Cal's publicist, who proceeds to tell us the order of how we'll be walking the red carpet. Cal will exit the car first, stop at the media wall for photos and then wait for Sean, who will then follow, get solo photos at the media wall and then they will pose for photos together. Cora will go next and while she's going, Cal and Sean will start talking to reporters. After Cora will then be me. I'm supposed to stop at the media wall and wait for Cal to join me, who will then come back for me and we'll walk the rest of the red carpet together.

"Jenna, does everything make sense?" She asks me since I am the inexperienced one of the group. I nod and stare out the window, the feeling of not belonging starting to become overwhelming. The car feels stifling and I look around for the air conditioning vents when I notice Cal staring at my exposed leg out of the slit of my dress. His eyes are hooded and as they finally look up at me, I'm slammed with a wave of desire. I gulp and quickly look away from him.

"Is there anything to drink in here?" I ask, my lips and throat suddenly feeling parched by his stare. His publicist hands me a bottle of water and I see him smirk as he watches me drink. *He knows exactly what he's doing to me!*

We pull up to Grauman's Chinese Theater and Cal's publicist gets out first and walks down the carpet, showing the reporters a piece of cardboard with his name on it. She comes back over to our limo and nods, signaling for Cal to get out. He takes one more glance in my direction and gets out.

"Look at that sexy beast!" Sean jokes as we watch Cal stop at the media wall for the photographers.

"He sure is," Cora says, her eyes looking at me with a challenge. I look away from her and continue to watch Cal, mesmerized by seeing him in his element.

The publicist opens the door for Sean to get out to work the carpet. I suddenly feel the air in the car fill with tension and can feel Cora's eyes on me.

"Enjoying yourself?" she asks as she sits back and crosses her long legs. She is wearing a short, black Herve Leger dress that looks like it was painted onto her perfect body. The color of the dress accentuating her feline-like green eyes. I would have said she was the most beautiful woman I've ever seen, but with her soul not matching her exterior, beautiful is the last thing I would now call her.

"Not particularly," I honestly reply. No sense in lying to her when all she wants to do is play games.

"Honesty… how refreshing," she sarcastically says. "Well, let me be honest with you then, dear Jenna. You do not belong in our world. Cal and I were made for each and before you came along, he was starting to realize that. So you and your kid need to keep your distance and everyone will be happy."

I throw my head back and laugh at her craziness. "Oh, you can have Cal! I'm not standing in your way with that. But let's give Cal some credit where credit is due - he can smell a bitch a mile away and still chooses to stay away." I sneer at her, not about to let her intimidate or threaten me. Pure hatred shoots out from her eyes and she is about to retort back when the door opens and the publicist tells her it's her turn to go. She gives me one more malicious look before snaking her way out of the car.

I take a deep breath, feeling proud for standing up for myself, but wanting to throw up at the same time. It's people like Cora Gregory that make me want to be far, far away from the world of Hollywood. I don't understand how Cal and Sean are even friends with her. I look over at the three of them posing in front of the media wall and something about the way Sean looks at her makes me do a double take. *Is Sean in love with Cora?* I shudder at the thought.

I notice Cal's publicist switch cardboards and show the photographers the one with my name on it as she makes her way back to the limo. I freshen up my lipstick and take one more look at myself in my compact mirror. As the car door opens, I say a quick little prayer, hoping I can fake my way through this.

Cal and Sean refuse to sit through the premiere after they introduced the movie to the audience, so we head to the after party early. There are plenty of people in the industry already there as most of them saw a pre-screening of the movie. As soon as we walk in, Cal and Sean are surrounded by people wanting to congratulate them. Cora is not in the movie, her attendance more for publicity and support of Cal and Sean, so she goes off to mingle with other actors who also came out for the same reasons. I'm left to fend for myself, so I head straight to the bar and order a vodka tonic.

I take a sip of my drink and turn around to people watch when

I notice too many eyes in my direction, nothing kind about the looks they are giving me. I sigh as it looks like my evening will be spent hanging at the bar. I turn back around and chat up the bartender since that will probably be the most genuine conversation I have all night with anyone.

Three drinks later and I'm feeling beyond buzzed. I don't know how long I've been left alone at the bar, but I feel that my work here is done. I take some money out of my purse to leave a tip when I feel someone tap my shoulder. I turn around to see Cal's agent with two older gentlemen who look too big for their own britches.

"Jenna, I want to introduce you to the heads of the studio, Patrick Hensley and Michael Morris. Gentlemen, this is Jenna Pruitt." Because I am tipsy, smiling isn't as hard as it was earlier and I return their handshakes.

"Congratulations on the movie," I say, happy to hear that the band is starting to play so it will be harder to carry on a conversation.

"Thank you for coming. Pre-sale tickets have increased in just the two hours of you being here. We appreciate you taking one for the team," Patrick winks and all three men laugh. I stare at them in disgust, feeling I was just degraded amongst the good old boys club. Tipsy Jenna has zero filter and I am about to unleash upon some of the most powerful men in Hollywood when I am grabbed by the waist and hauled to someone's side. I look up to see Sean coming to rescue me.

"There you are! Cal has been looking for you. Gentlemen, if you will excuse us?" he says with his most charming smile. He leads me away but instead of going toward where Cal and Cora are standing, he heads straight for the dance floor.

"What are you doing?" I hiss, the attention from being the only two people on the dance floor the last thing I want.

"I saw the look you gave those men and we cannot have angry Jenna making an appearance tonight. I think we need to liven this place up with a little dancing." He pulls me in close and holds on to me tightly. "Just keep that smile plastered on your face and follow my lead."

I smile brightly and grit my teeth. "I want to go back to the hotel, Sean. I'm done being the pawn in this game."

"To which game are you referring to?" He smiles and nods to someone he sees in the crowd. He swings me around, where I see Cal ignoring Cora as she's trying to talk with him, his eyes trained on us with suspicion.

"Everybody's game, but more specifically, being used to boast Cal's image."

"Cal doesn't give two shits about his image. If he did, then he wouldn't be looking at me so openly with hatred right about now in front of all these industry people." He raises his eyebrows in mock questioning towards Cal, whose jaw visibly locks in anger.

"What about your game, Sean?" I taunt, the alcohol flowing through my veins giving me liquid courage.

"I don't know what you are talking about." I see him smile at another person while twirling me around. He smiles at me as he brings me back into him, pulling me closer than before. I quickly look over at the other end of the dance floor where Cal waits for our arrival, Cora watching him with a sour expression on her face from the lack of attention.

"What about using me as the pawn to make Cora jealous? I saw the way you looked at her earlier. Must be tough to watch the woman you love in love with someone else." I smile as his step falters but he quickly recovers by turning me so swiftly, that I have to hold onto him even harder to keep my balance. "You should have warned me, Sean," I say, as I lean in to whisper in his ear, "because I already told her she can have him."

I lean back to look at him with a flirtatious smile to see that he is not smiling anymore, jealousy burning in his eyes. I suddenly regret my decision to push him, thinking I have gone too far when he dips me down and holds me close. "You want to make them jealous? Then let's give them something to talk about!" He brings his lips to mine in a crushing kiss.

Before I know what is happening, Sean brings me back up to my feet and ends the kiss so abruptly that I nearly stumble back, but am saved when he swings my arms up and the crowd goes wild with their applause. He timed the kiss to the end of the song so perfectly that it looked like this was all planned. He makes us take a bow and the crowd goes even more wild. He wraps his arm around my waist and walks us over to Cal.

"She's all yours," he says to Cal and downs the rest of Cal's drink and stalks over to the bar.

"We're leaving NOW!" Cal hands me my purse, grabs my hand and practically drags me out of the party. I try to get my hand free, but he grips it even tighter.

"You're hurting me!" I hiss, as we get closer to our car. He let's go of my hand and tells the driver to take us back to the hotel. He roughly opens the door and practically shoves me into the limousine.

"What the fuck was that?" he growls after the partition is closed all the way so the driver can't hear us.

"I don't know, ask Sean! He's the one who wanted to dance." I massage my hand, trying to rub out the pain.

"I don't give a fuck about Sean, it's YOUR reputation I care about!" he snaps, raking his hands through his hair.

"My reputation? I thought the whole point in me being here tonight was to save YOUR precious reputation!" I counter, not understanding why he's so angry.

"I'm not the one who looked like a slut kissing another man!"

Rage overtakes me and I pounce on him. I beat at his arms, his chest, screaming and calling him every name I can think, letting all of my suppressed anger flow out through my fists. "I FUCKING HATE YOU, YOU ASSHOLE!" He just sits there and lets me beat him, looking as if he is almost bored. This makes me even angrier and I straddle him so I can get hit him harder. He deserves to be slapped on the face for calling me a slut. I go in for the kill when he grabs my wrists and hauls me against his chest, searing me with his lips.

My struggle against him is pointless because despite my anger toward him for calling me a slut, I want him just as badly as he wants me. He invades my mouth and I kiss him back with even more fervor than expected. He loosens his grip on my wrists and I plunge my hands into his hair, making my tongue grapple even closer with his. I start to moan when he deepens the kiss, sparks of electricity going straight to my core. He breaks free of our kiss and moves his lips down my neck, working his magic on each and every sensitive point until I am panting out his name.

I push his jacket off his shoulders and he leans forward for me to pull it off his arms. I rip open his shirt, not caring that I just broke the buttons off and ruined it. I lean down and start kissing along his neck, down his chest and flick my tongue over his nipple. "Jenna," he moans and grips my head closer. He then trails his hands down my back and unzips the top portion of my dress. I kiss my way back up his chest and go back to his mouth, where everything there feels so right. His kisses light that fire to the explosion and I am ready to feel it.

He pulls down my one shoulder strap and takes my now bare nipple in his mouth. I moan and grind my hips down into his erection, the friction against my clit making me gasp. I can feel him straining against his pants and my hands move to unbuckle them. As soon as he is free, I wrap both of my hands around him and rub up and down his shaft. He lays he head back and starts to pant. "Jenna, you are going to make me come if you continue to do that," he moans as I rub his pre-cum around his tip.

Not being able to take the intense need of having him inside me, I slip my hand inside my slit and unsnap the soaked barrier between my legs. I lift out my skirt and guide him to me, where I slowly slide down on him. I hiss at the delicious invasion, my inner muscles already gripping him tight. I wrap my hands around his neck and crush my mouth to his, my tongue craving his as I slowly start to ride him. The need becomes overwhelming and I throw my head back and bounce harder, faster.

"Fuck, Jenna, you are still so tight," he murmurs as he places his hand on my breasts and squeezes. I moan louder and grip him tighter, the pressure inside me building. He wraps his arms around me, lifts me up to place me on the floor of the limousine and thrusts hard into me. I dig my nails into his ass as he pounds out my orgasm. My release explodes within me and I scream out his name, every emotion releasing out of my body. He collapses on top of me after his own orgasm, his body shuddering from his powerful release.

I was a fool to believe that I was ever going to feel this way with someone else. No one has come close to making me feel the way Cal Harrington does. And as I come down from this amazing high, I notice that the car is stopped outside the hotel and my reality sinks back in. I was asked to come here to PRETEND to be in a relationship with him and here I am ready to give up my heart based on a facade. Shame and guilt crash into me and I push against his chest.

"Get up," I say, needing to get away from him and how he clouds my judgment.

"Jenna, what's..."

"Get off of me!" I scream and he rears back in complete shock at the turn of my mood.

I attempt to zip up the back of my dress by myself, but with my arms being too short, it goes nowhere. I grab my purse, grip the top of my dress to my chest and bolt out of the limousine. I rush into the hotel and decide to take the stairs up to the eighth floor so no one sees me. By the time I reach my suite, I am gasping for air from the excursion. I go into my room and lock the door. As soon as I turn around to head to my bathroom, there's banging on my door.

"Jenna, let me in! We need to talk!" Cal bangs on the door, making the furniture against the wall shake.

"There is nothing to talk about! That was a mistake and will never happen again!" I shout, wishing for him to just go away so that I can deal with my feelings and figure out what to do.

"Open this door, Jenna!' He yells louder and bangs it again with his fists.

"No! GO AWAY, CAL!"

A moment of silence ensues and then a loud bang as I watch in horror the wood around the door knob splinters off and break apart as Cal kicks open the door. The door swings open and he enters my room, his chest rising and falling with each breath he takes.

"If I want you, Jenna, no goddamn locked door will stop me!" he growls. He looks me up and down as I stare at him in disbelief. "Go to sleep. We'll discuss this in the morning." He turns on his heel, walks into the other room and slams the door.

I push a chair against the broken door and throw myself onto the bed where I proceed to cry myself to sleep.

33

A firm knock on my door wakes me from my deep sleep. I look up at the clock to see it is six in the morning and groan at how early it is. I roll over and stare at the ceiling, memories rolling in from last night.

"Jenna?" An unfamiliar voice knocks on my door again. "It's time to wake up. We need to catch the flight to New York." I get up from the bed and move the chair away from the door to see Kellan standing outside of it. He looks me up and down and shakes his head at the condition of my dress. "That's going to cost Cal a pretty penny." He eyes the hole in the door and looks back at me with questioning eyes. "Remodeling are we?" he jokes.

I shake my head at him and rub my eyes. "Do I have time for a quick shower?" I ask. He nods his head and I proceed to get ready. Thirty minutes later, I come out and he has coffee, muffins and water waiting for me. He hands me two ibuprofens with a wink and some water.

"Don't tell Morgan I'm letting you eat a muffin. She would absolutely kill me!" I smile weakly at his joke and devour the muffin, realizing that I haven't eaten since lunch yesterday. No wonder I feel nauseous and shaky as I start to immediately feel better from the food and water.

I take a look around and notice that Kellan and I are the only ones in the suite. "Where is everyone?" I ask, more specifically, wondering where Cal is.

"Most of the crew took the studio's private plane to New York late last night. Cal called saying you weren't feeling well and needed to spend the night, so the studio had the jet fly back to Los Angeles after drop off in New York. Must be nice to have the studio's balls like that!" Kellan laughs. *If he only really knew...*

"It's a five-hour flight to New York and with the time change, we're going to be cutting it close to premiere time. Fortunately they do everything later in New York, so I think we'll be okay. We'll have to get ready on the plane and then a car will pick us up and take us straight to the premiere." I nod my head in acknowledgment, dreading a five hour plane ride. "Cal and Sean are waiting for us in the car, so if you're ready, we can leave now."

"Sean is still here?" I ask, shocked that he wasn't on the plane last night.

"Seems like Sean also was not feeling well last night and decided to depart with you guys," he says with a knowing smile. I smile back and help him load up the luggage cart he brought in with the dresses and luggage for tonight. We take it downstairs and a bellman helps Kellan load it into the awaiting car. I get inside the car and see both Cal and Sean sitting next to each other, sunglasses shielding their eyes.

"There she is, my beautiful dance partner. Did you sleep well, sweetheart?" Sean sarcastically smiles. I put my sunglasses on and push them up the bridge of my nose with my middle finger, which causes Sean to laugh. Cal chooses to ignore me, which is fine with me.

I stare out the window as the car takes us to the airport, wondering how I'm going to pull off another night of this. Fortunately Cal will be headed to London right after the premiere and I will take the last flight home to Chicago, not wanting to spend a night in New York by myself when I can be home with Avery by morning. I let my thoughts drift to last night in the car and marvel at how our sexual chemistry is still so intense, how quickly his sensual lips turn me on with just one kiss and how incredible he feels inside of me......*holy fucking shit, we didn't use a condom last night!*

I don't realize I groan out loud until Kellan asks me if I'm okay. Giving him a fake smile and a thumbs up, I go back to brooding about what a complete moron I am and how Cal Harrington completely annihilates all of my smart brain cells. I am on birth control, but it would be just my luck if I get an STD since I don't know how many women Cal has even been with.

By the time we pull up to the private plane, my mood has blackened from my stupidity and I don't want to be anywhere near Cal. I ask Kellan to sit next to me on the plane, making up a story that I need him to go through how he plans on styling me for tonight. He gives me a questionable look, but complies. The plane is incredible with couches, a large screen television and even a master bedroom with a bathroom in it. I never even knew planes like this existed and just shake my head in awe at the amount of money the plane must have cost. I take a seat in one of the cushy leather chairs, Kellan grabbing the one next to me while Cal and Sean decide to sit in the seats opposite of us. Out of all the places to sit on the plane, it is not surprising that Cal decide to sit in front of me. I pretend to ignore him and concentrate on Kellan as he goes through the plans for tonight. The plane swiftly takes off and we make our way to New York.

I jolt awake from my head falling forward, not realizing that I fell asleep while looking out the window. I glance at my watch to see we've only been in the air for an hour. I look around to see Sean laying on the couch asleep, while Kellan still sits next to me watching a movie on his computer with headphones in his ears. Cal has moved to the lounge chair in front of the plane, his legs stretched out before him, looking like he's asleep but hard to tell with his sunglasses on.

"Jenna, why don't you go sleep in the bedroom?" Kellan says, as he takes his headphones off to talk to me. "I'll wake you up an hour before we land." I nod in agreement, my body and mind so exhausted that all I want to do is sleep. I make my way to the bedroom, shut the door and drift back to sleep.

A little while later, I turn over and cuddle into what I think is a pillow, except it is very hard and has that intoxicating scent that smells just like Cal. I open my eyes to see I am staring at the front of his red cotton shirt, my hand resting on his chest. My legs are completely intertwined with his and his arms are around me. I don't remember him coming in, nor do I remember feeling him get into bed with me. My eyes make their way up to his face, where I find him watching me.

He swallows as he looks into my eyes. "We need to talk," he softly says, his voice husky and low.

I nod, knowing he's right and am so tired of fighting with him.

"I understand how hard it is for you to trust me, given the circumstances you have been placed in. I probably would feel the same way if I were in your shoes. But while you hated me for all these years, I never stopped thinking about you. Anytime I saw someone who remotely resembled you, I always wondered if you were happy. And I can't help but feel that we were given a second chance to try to be together because of Avery."

"People shouldn't be together just for children," I say, trying to ignore the impact his words are having on my heart.

"Do you really think I want to be with you JUST because of Avery? Do you really believe that my desire for you is an act? You're the most infuriating woman I have ever met, yet no woman has ever made me feel the way I do when I'm with you. I want a chance, Jenna! I want you to give me a chance to prove to you that we belong together. That my feelings for you and Avery are very, very real." He wipes away my tears with his thumb and stares in my eyes so intensely that I feel my heart warming, the ice around is slowly thawing. "I want us to start over. I want to properly date you. I want to make you laugh. I want to go on adventures with you. I want to hold you in my arms every night and wake up with you every morning. I just want to be given a chance to TRY."

A knock on the door interrupts him. "Cal, I need to start getting Jenna ready." Kellan's muffled voice is heard through the door.

"I'll be right out," Cal says back to him and continues to look at me, his thumb rubbing my cheek. "Please Jenna....will you please think about it?" he pleads. "If you don't feel the same way for me after some time together, then I will walk away."

I cannot keep denying the fact that it's getting harder and harder for me to protect my heart, to deny that I'm falling under his spell. I've got to stop letting my past experiences dictate my present, despite him having the power to completely destroy my heart. I may not trust people, but I do need to learn to try to trust him.

"I'll think about," I say softly, my heart singing in victory while my head yells in denial. Relief floods his eyes and his smile is almost blinding. "Thank you." He kisses me softly on the lips and before I can try to deepen it, he gets off the bed and let's Kellan come in to get me ready.

34

Four Months Later

Sometimes in life when things are going so amazingly good, you have to stop and wonder, what's the catch? How can this continue? I ask myself that every day when I wake up in Cal's arms, those blue eyes staring at me with all the love in the world. He just said those three massive words to me last week, the magnitude of their weight so deafening that I couldn't repeat them back, but showed him by making love. Every day I try to show him with some sort of action, but I keep holding those words back, understanding that saying them gives him the power of my heart.

Yes, I still have my doubts.

Yes, I still am guarded.

Yes, I am still so very fucked up.

He deserves better, I say to myself one too many times when he sits across from me on a romantic date he orchestrated for us.

He deserves better, I say to myself when I question why he even wants to be with me when I feel so plain compared to the women he works with.

He deserves better, I say to myself when he tells me he loves me and disappointment fills his eyes when I can only smile at him, the words stuck in my throat because I'm still so afraid he's going to shatter my heart into a million little pieces.

Today is another one of those days, every single doubt being at the forefront of my mind. He's scheduled to leave tomorrow to shoot his new movie, moving him to Dubai for two weeks, then to various locations around Europe. This will be the first time we're separated for this long since his arrival in Chicago. We have agreed that Avery and I will try to fly out every two weeks to see him, but even then that might be hard to do.

What if he falls in love with his costar?

What if he falls out of love with me?

God, I am so annoying….so pathetic. This is exactly how I didn't want to feel. I start getting angry with myself, telling myself to shut up and enjoy every moment I have with him. I look at the clock to see I have two hours before I'm supposed to meet him for dinner. He has a romantic dinner planned, having a beautiful dress delivered with a note that said 'WEAR ME TONIGHT' and him formally picking me up, even though he is now living with us in my apartment. He gave Mason the night off since I will be with him and he arranged for my parents to take Avery so that we can have tonight to ourselves.

I'm about to start getting ready for our evening when my cell phone rings and I see Robert's name appear. He is scheduled to be in a meeting with one of our clients, so I pick up to see if everything is okay.

"Hey, what's going on?" I immediately ask when I answer his call.

"I'm an idiot and was working on the client's proposal on my personal computer last night, but I forgot to transfer it over to my work computer, which I have with me, but not my USB file. It's still hooked into my personal computer, which is on my desk. Can you open up the file on my computer and email it to me so I can pull it up for them to see?"

"Sure, I'll just email it to you from my personal account off the web so that way I don't need to eject your USB." I walk over to his desk and open his laptop, find the proposal and email it to him.

"You're a life saver, thank you. I'm probably just going to go home once this meeting is done, if that's okay with you?"

"Of course it is! Enjoy your evening, Robert."

"Will do and I certainly know for a fact YOU will!" He laughs evilly, indicating he knows Cal's plans for this evening.

"You're so good at being a tease."

"Ha, you love it!"

I laugh as I hang up the phone and am just about to close his laptop when a file labeled 'JP' catches my attention. *Why would Robert have a file on me?* Warning bells are going off in my head, screaming not to click on the file, but I ignore them. Robert is very organized and has sub folders within the main folder. I click on the folder labeled 'Avery' but only see important documents that I gave him access too. I click out of her folder and click on the folder labeled 'Cal'. Inside this folder he has more folders labeled 'Emails', 'Press', 'Travel' and 'Chase'. Intrigued as to why there would be a folder about Chase, I click on it. Inside there are two more folders, one labeled 'Photographs' and the other 'Emails'. I click the one that says 'Photographs' and am surprised to see over hundreds of photos in it. I start clicking through them, images of me around the city, oblivious to the fact that I am even being photographed. There are tons of pictures of me the night the paparazzi surrounded me. *Why would Robert have all of these photos from Chase?*

I exit out of that folder and click on 'Emails'. Numerous emails from Chase to Cal, copying Robert with images of me. The body content of the emails list where I was and if I was meeting someone, who I was with. *What the hell?* I click on some more until I open the email with the images from the paparazzi attack. I read Chase's words to Cal that make me stop breathing:

"Tonight should never have happened, Cal! You pay me to follow her, not to be her bodyguard...."

He pays Chase to follow me? I think back to all those times Chase was the only paparazzi around and I was always in awe of how he would find me so quickly, but apparently there was a reason for that. I swallow down the sick feeling I am having and click out of the main 'Chase' folder and go to the 'Press' folder.

Inside are emails from Cal to Robert, instructing him to call numerous news outlets as an anonymous source and supply them stories about me. Stories exactly like the one that I thought were from my neighbors the first time Cal showed up. Stories about my break up with Jax, about Cal and I working on our relationship. All these stories that Cal was the mastermind behind.

I slam the computer shut and close my eyes as tears start leaking down my face. Any trust that I had for Cal is now gone. I am devastated from not only his betrayal, but from Robert's as well. I don't know if Layla is in on this as I didn't see her name on any of the emails and I pray she isn't as my heart can't take any more surprises. I grab my keys, needing to get the hell out of here before Cal comes home, turn my cell phone off and flee the apartment.

I end up at O'Malley's since I haven't been back since the paparazzi attack and need large quantities of alcohol to calm me down and numb away the pain. I sit at the farthest end of the bar and our usual bartender, Nico, comes around to serve me.

"Hello there, lass, whatcha drinking tonight? Where are all your friends?" he looks around as he greets me.

"I want a long island ice tea and keep them coming when you see I'm getting low. As for friends, well, as of tonight, I have no friends." I blink back the tears that are about to spill and look down to try to regain my composure.

"One long island ice tea coming up and of course you have

friends, lass! I'm here for you!" He smiles at me while patting my hand and moves away to make my drink.

Two hours later and I am beyond drunk. I was sucking down those long island ice teas so quickly that by the time I had four, Nico cut me off and water is the only form of liquid I'm allowed to drink. He places a basket of French fries in front of me that I quickly devour.

"Lass, your ride should be here any minute," he says as he brings me my check.

"My ride?" I raise my head from my hands, confused as to whom he would have called and then I remember that he and Layla have hooked up before. "No, I can make it home by myself. I'll just walk." I step off my barstool and immediately sit back down as the room starts to tilt.

"Jenna!" I hear my name and Layla and Robert come into to focus. I start shaking my head no, Robert being the second to last person I ever want to see.

"You," I point my finger at him and spit, "are a fucking traitor!" I slam my hand onto the bar, not being able to control my movements whatsoever.

Robert's eyes get wide with worry. "Jenna, what are you talking about? If this is about not telling you what Cal's plans were for tonight, then I'm sorry. I was only trying to help."

"Were you trying to help when you agreed to go to the press for him with stories about me, Mr. Anonymous Source?" His face pales and he quickly glances at Layla.

"Jenna, let's get you home." Layla says as she moves to my side to help me stand up.

"Are you one of Cal's minions too?" I ask her in despair. She looks at Robert and I already see the guilt in her eyes.

"I knew what was going on, but refused to partake in helping. I am sorry I didn't tell you," she says, looking down at her hands with regret.

"How could you guys not tell me? WHY would you not tell

me?" My voice starts to get hysterical as I feel my whole world collapsing around me.

"The stories were damage control, Jenna! Cal was only trying to protect your reputation from the nasty gossip that was being spread." Robert tries to explain but I shake my head at him, refusing to believe that there is any excuse that would make his actions justifiable.

"I should have been the judge of that! It was MY reputation! I know what is the truth and what isn't!" I yell and people start looking over at us.

"Jenna, please, can we talk about this at home?" Robert pleads as he looks around the bar.

"I am not going home until he's out of my house. Text your new boss and tell him I want him gone."

"You can stay with me, Jenna." I look up at Layla and scoff at her suggestion.

"How can I trust any of you?" I ask, sadness lacing my voice as I realize everyone who I trust has been deceiving me. Out of the corner of my eye I see flashes of light bulbs going off outside and know Cal is here. "Of course, you would tell him that I'm here." I turn to look at Robert. "Do you think about me when you suck his cock as well?"

"JENNA!" Robert shrieks in shock, his eyes starting to well up with tears. "I know you're drunk, but there's no reason to be so cruel!"

"Says the person who stabbed the knife in my back!" I laugh bitterly as I watch Cal walk in, scan the bar and see us. He is wearing a white dress shirt with the cuffs rolled up his forearms, nice dress slacks and dress shoes. His hair is disheveled from running his hands through it and his eyes are filled with worry. He stalks towards me and I curse myself for thinking he looks ridiculously sexy. If I didn't hate him so much right now, I would demand we christen O'Malley's bathroom.

"Jenna, it's time to come home. We can discuss whatever you

think is going on in the privacy of our home." Cal grabs my arms, but I yank it out of his grasp.

"It's MY home! I want you packed up and gone from it. We are DONE!"

"And why is that?" he asks calmly, but his eyes are hard as ice.

"Why? Because I can't trust you! I found everything out, the stories you planted about me, how you pay Chase to follow me! How could you, Cal? Why would you?" The tears that I thought I had under control now fall loosely.

"Everything I've done has been in your best interest! I had Chase follow you to make sure you were safe before we got Mason and I asked Robert to plant those stories because you were getting shredded in the press. You say you don't care about your reputation, but it would have affected your business, how people treated Avery. I couldn't watch that happen."

I shake my head as the tears continue to silently fall, not being able to believe a word he says.

"I will not apologize for my actions, Jenna. The only thing I will apologize for is not telling you sooner. Now let's get out of here."

"How many more things are there that you haven't told me about that were done in my 'best interest' Cal? I'm sorry, but I can't do this anymore." I say with remorse, the pain in my chest so intense that it makes it hard to breathe.

"So that's it? You're going to cast me away for one mistake? I think you're just grasping for any excuse in order to protect yourself because you are too scared to feel anything. You want me gone? So be it," he says with fury. "Help me get her home," he says to Layla. He and Robert form a shield in front of us as Layla wraps her arm around me to hold me steady. Even if I wasn't drunk, I wouldn't be able to walk straight from the tears that are blurring my vision. I shield my eyes with my hands when we get outside in front of the paparazzi. They start shouting our names, asking if I'm okay, if I'm drunk, if we're having a lover's quarrel. I smile at the latter as they will soon find out that we are indeed having a lover's quarrel.

"Jenna, keep your eyes covered and I'll guide you to the taxi that Robert has for us," Layla says, and I try to concentrate on her hands that are firmly placed on my hips, helping me walk straight.

"Here, let me help you with her." I hear someone say and look up to see Chase trying to cover me up with his jacket.

"Ah, well if it isn't my own personal watch dog. You failed at your job miserably tonight, by the way. I think Cal should deduct from your wages," I sneer, shock registering on his face.

"Jenna, I can explain…" Chase starts.

"It's YOU! Get the hell away from her!" Layla screams and pushes Chase away from me.

Cal and Robert turn around to see what all the commotion. "What's wrong?"

"This is the guy!" Layla points a finger at Chase and we look at her as if she's gone mad.

"Yeah, it's Canadian Chase. He's the one Cal is paying to follow me."

"He's the guy who I told your story to in Las Vegas!"

"What?" Cal and I say in unison and in one swift motion, Cal punches Chase in the face. Chase stumbles back and covers his eye.

"You bastard, you never told me that!" Cal roars and goes to hit him again, but is restrained by Robert.

"Cal, get in the cab!" Robert pushes Cal towards the taxi as the paparazzi go furious with taking even more photos.

I stare at Chase in shock as Layla pulls me towards the cab. He shakes his head and then stumbles toward me, his free hand reaching out. "Jenna, I can explain! Please let me explain!" He screams as the door is closed in his face and the taxi speeds away from the bar.

I can't help but start to laugh uncontrollably at the circus that is my life ever since Cal Harrington came into it.

"I can't believe this is so funny to you." Cal looks at me in disbelief.

"Oh, c'mon now, the irony of the puppet master getting played by one of his puppets is very funny," I say in reference to Chase's deceit.

"Cal, she doesn't mean it, she's upset and drunk." Robert says loud enough for me to hear him.

"That's right, traitor! I may be drunk and beyond hurt, but I'm NOT stupid. I'm done with all of you!" I slur, as I slash my hand through the air. "I'm also done with this smell. What is that god awful smell?" I ask, looking around everywhere in the taxi when my eyes stumble upon a box of pizza.

"Oh god," I dry heave, trying to control the bile that wants to rise up out of my throat. "Sir, whatever you do, DO NOT open that box!"

The taxi cab driver looks at me with a questionable smile. "It's my dinner. You should probably have a slice to help soak up that alcohol."

"Please no! If you open that box, I'm going to throw up," I burp, the smell making my stomach start to rumble.

"C'mon, it's just pizza. Here, have a slice." As he opens up the box, everyone in the car screams NO, but it's too late as I empty the contents of my stomach all over his dinner and black out.

35

"Jenna Lynn, it's time to get yourself up!" I moan out against the nightmare I must be having, hearing my mother's voice in my sleep. Brightness starts to radiate behind my eyelids and I groan from the intrusion. My head is pounding and my throat feels dry, screaming its need for water. I hear footsteps in my bedroom, their pace fast as they sprint around my room. The bed shifts and I feel someone grabbing my arms, trying to lift me up.

"Get up, Jenna, we've got to get going. We only have minutes to spare!"

I open my eyes to see that it is my mother, in my bedroom, trying to pull me out of bed. I startle awake and grab her arms, panic seizing me. "What is wrong? Where is Avery?" I look around my room, only to see no signs of my child.

"Avery is with Robert at the pool. Here are some clothes," she throws a pair of jeans and a shirt at me," get dressed, brush your teeth and let's go."

Knowing that Avery is safe, I throw myself back against the bed to go back to sleep and immediately grip my temples when shooting pains from my hangover decide to punish me for the fast movement. "There's nowhere we need to go then, Mother, if she's safe with Robert," I grumble, angry at her for waking me up and leaving Avery in the care of Robert, who I'm still mad at.

"We need to go catch Cal before he gets on his flight."

"Cal is gone?" I slowly sit up and look over at his nightstand, which is empty. The clothes that were hanging up on the travel rack are gone. I look at my clock to see it is 10 a.m., his flight to Dubai was not supposed to be until 5 p.m. Then memories of what I said to him last night come flooding in and I realize why he's already gone.

"I told him I want him out of my life, Mother. Apparently, he listened."

"I know all about last night, Jenna, and we have a small window of time to fix it. Here, take some aspirin." She hands me a cup of water and two pills. I take the pills and flush them down with the water.

"Mother, why are you so insistent of me going after men who are not good for me?" I ask, not understanding why she wants me to fix things with Cal unless it is for her reputation only.

"I was stupid for telling you to go after Tyler all those years ago. You were a smart girl for not listening to me, Jenna, as you were confident in your self worth. The fact remains that I have never been confident with mine and am so very lucky that your father decides to stay married to me, especially when I make poor decisions like telling you that you wouldn't get anything better than Tyler. Tyler was a selfish prick, Jenna," she sits on the edge of the bed and pushes a strand of my hair behind my ears," but Cal is NOTHING like Tyler and you need to realize that."

"But…"

She puts her finger on my lips to shut me up. "Yes, I do agree with you that he should have been honest with you and told you all that had been going on. But honey, every decision that man has made has been for YOU and Avery. He's just trying to protect the two women he loves."

She removes her finger from my mouth to let me speak, "I feel I have lost all control of my life because of him."

"You only feel that way because you're in love with him as well, you just won't admit it because you are scared of getting hurt again," she places her hand lovingly on my cheek. "The bigger risk, Jenna, would be if you stayed scared and miss out on the greatest love of your life."

"I don't know..." I slowly say, her words starting to make sense.

"Do you trust him, Jenna? I mean, REALLY trust him? Because if you truly believe that he'll deliberately hurt you in any way, then we won't go after to him."

I stare at her, realizing that I may have made a grave mistake. "No Mother, I don't think he would deliberately hurt me."

She smiles and squeezes my hands with hers."Then let's go find him!"

I throw the covers off me, grab my clothes and race into the bathroom while my mother says she will get my car and meet me downstairs. It only takes me five minutes before I am running out of the bedroom, calling her.

"I'm on my way down," I say into the phone, but she tells me to wait there. "Why are you-" my voice halts, as the front door opens and Cal walks in. I stare at him for only a split second before I launch myself at him, taking him by surprise.

"You came back! Thank god, you came back!" My voice is muffled by his chest as I hug him as tight as I can.

"I came back because I forgot my passport." His voice is void of any emotion and I realize with despair that he is not hugging me back.

I look up at him with tears in my eyes, hoping that I've not lost him forever. "I am so sorry for last night! Learning that you hired Chase to follow me felt like you didn't trust me, that you were trying to control me and I know that isn't the case. You are only trying to protect me and I was too stubborn to listen." I take a shaky breath while he stares at me.

He grips my arms and pushes me away from him. He walks over to the entryway console, where he sees the passport he left, and puts it in the back pocket of his pants. He stands before me, looking at me with wistful longing before he smiles sadly and shakes his head.

"I don't have enough love for the both of us, Jenna," he states quietly and turns to head towards the door.

I grab his arm so that he can't leave and plead with him, "I DO love you, Cal. I am so in love with you that…that I was just scared! Scared I was going to get hurt again." He rakes his other hand through his hair and I see that there is a glimmer of hope as he starts to show some struggle with his emotions. "Please Cal…..please don't give up on me!" I cry in anguish as my chest starts to ache from the breaking of my heart.

His gaze is intense, as if he's trying to see if I'm toying with his emotions. "How can you love me when you don't even TRUST me, Jenna? We have NOTHING without trust!"

"I DO trust you, Cal, I do!" I try to smile through my tears and nod my head at him, hoping he can see the truth.

He narrows his gaze at me and reaches for my hands. "You really trust me, Jenna?"

"Yes, Cal, I really do!" I say, as I squeeze his hands.

"Then come to Dubai with me, now. You and me for two weeks by ourselves. I'll take care of everything."

I suck in my breath and let go of his hands. I can't just up and leave with him.

He sees my internal struggle and gets angry. "Why do you even hesitate?"

The excuses are all in my head, but won't spill out of my mouth. *I can't leave Avery. I can't leave work. What if you change your mind about me?*

"We'll take great care of Avery, Jenna," my mother says. I look behind Cal and see her standing in the entryway, her eyes red from crying.

"What are you so scared of, Jenna? Avery will be fine with your parents! Robert can handle work! Why can't you just say YES?"

"I....I.. don't know," I stumble with my words, not understanding why I won't let go of my excuses.

"TRUST ME, JENNA!" I flinch as he yells out in frustration, throwing his arms up in the air. "Take the goddamn risk of letting yourself go, letting yourself FEEL, regardless of how you think the end is going to turn out. I KNOW how it's going to turn out if you took that risk on me." He lets his arms fall and looks at me with sadness, "I would be your forever."

Tears silently stream down my face as I watch him walk past my mother to open the door. He stops at the door, turns back to look at me and holds out his hand.

"Last chance, Jenna. What's it going to be?" My eyes plead with him not to do this, but I see the resolution in his face.

I close my eyes and think if I can really do this.

I trust him with our daughter.

I trust him with my life.

I trust him with my heart.

What more is there?

Nothing, Jenna, there is nothing!

I take a deep breath and I open my eyes to look at him, my forever.

I take that step forward.

I place my hand in his.

And I exhale...letting all the excuses go.

EPILOGUE

Eighteen Months Later

I look behind me, up into the crowd, to try to find where Layla, Robert, and their dates are seated. I look for the royal purple of her dress and finally spot them. Robert and his date are huddled together, giving each other flirtatious glances while Layla's date is looking at every other woman but her. Layla has slowly dipped her toe back into the dating world, starting with online dating, and the men she is choosing to spend her time with are douchebags. Even though he isn't looking at me, I can't help but stare in hatred at him, wishing she would have come alone instead of with him. Sensing my eyes on them, they look at me and wave. I wave back and give them a thumbs up and turn my attention back to the stage.

I grip Cal's hand, my nerves about to explode from the anticipation. "Are you nervous?" I ask for the umpteenth time tonight.

He turns to me and gives me that smile that is only reserved for me, the one that makes me weak in the knees. "No sweetheart,

I think you're nervous enough for the both of us." He looks so devastatingly handsome tonight in his tuxedo that he has more than once had to remove my hands from wandering all over his body in public.

I lean into him and whisper seductively in his ear, "You are so going to win."

"I already won because I have you," he whispers and gives me a gentle, yet firm kiss.

As the presenter reads off the nominees in the Best Actor category for the Academy Awards, I can't help but marvel at how far we've come in close to two years together. After I let go of all of my negative emotions of being scared, everything in my life got better. Not only my relationship with Cal, but how I am as a mother to Avery, a daughter to my parents and how I am as a friend.

I clap the loudest after they role a clip of Cal acting in the movie he is nominated for. He laughs at me and kisses me full on the lips as the camera catches our genuine affection for each other.

"And the award goes too..." I squeeze Cal's hand, the suspense about to kill me, along with the drumroll increasing the pounding of my heart. "CAL HARRINGTON, CRIME GAMES," the presenter announces as the audience starts to clap.

"YES!" I scream as I jump up out of my seat and fling myself at him. I grab his face and kiss him with every fiber of my being. He hugs me tight and lets me go so he can walk to the stage to accept his award. I look up behind me and see Robert and Layla out of their seats, screaming and clapping in excitement for Cal.

"Wow, this is amazing!" he starts his speech as the audience sits back in their seats. "I truly never expected this, and I am so very thankful to the Academy for this award." Tears stream down my face as he starts thanking everyone who was involved in this film. This film was not an easy film to make, demanding a lot out of him both physically and emotionally. It was also a test on our relationship, him being gone the majority of the time it took to shoot it. But we made it work and I couldn't be more proud and excited for him.

"To my daughter, Avery, who I know is still up watching, I love you and it's time to go to bed now." The audience laughs and then grows silent as his expression becomes somber.

"To my partner in life, Jenna." As he says my name, I feel everyone around me fade, as I stare intently at the man who has my heart. "I wouldn't be here accepting this if it wasn't for you. You make me a better actor, a better man and a better father to our daughter. Thank you for letting me be your forever. I love you!" He shouts and blows me a kiss as the music starts to play. I jump up and blow a kiss right back at him, not caring that my make-up is probably smeared all over my face from crying and that millions of people are watching.

Because they need to see that this is real.

This is genuine.

This is LOVE.

ACKNOWLEDGMENTS

It is a dream come true to finally be publishing this story after having it in my head for five years. Cal and Jenna will always have a special place in my heart with their story being my debut novel. I look forward to sharing more of their lives with you in Layla's story, Perfectly Lonely.

I don't even know where to begin with thanking people as I am beyond blessed to have so many generous, loving and supportive people in my life. My first thank you has to be to my husband. Without his support, I wouldn't be publishing this book today. To the rest of my family, thank you for your encouragement, love, support and always believing in my abilities to write my own book.

To all of my friends who cheered on my dream and gave me advice and encouraging words, thank you so very much for always believing in me and supporting me. I have to give some special shout outs to Erica, Crystal, Neil, Melissa, Sara, and Whitney for the extra advice and help with this book, especially when there were days when I wanted to give up.

To the bloggers and the readers for making it to this page, thank you for your time and most importantly, for your support!

ABOUT THE AUTHOR

Jessica Marin began her love affair with books at a young age from the encouragement of her Grandma Shirley. She has always dreamed of being an author and finally made her dreams of writing happily ever after stories a reality. She currently resides in Tennessee with her husband, children and fur babies. When she is not hanging out with her family, she loves watching a good movie, going dancing with the ladies, sniffing essential oils and daydreaming of warm beaches, winning the lotto and world peace.

Jessica would love for you to join her on all of her available social media outlets.

facebook.com/authorjessicamarin

twitter.com/authorjessmarin

instagram.com/authorjessicamarin

pinterest.com/authorjessicamarin

98689071R00183

Made in the USA
Lexington, KY
09 September 2018